A knock sounded lightly at her door and she moved on her bed to find Lord Wimborne filling the open doorway. "May I come in for a moment, Myriah?" he asked gently.

"Of course, my lord, do," said Myriah hopefully.

He came toward her, stopped himself short just a few feet away from the bed and clasped his hands together behind his back. "Myriah, is there something wrong?"

Yes, you big fool, she thought ruefully, yes there is something wrong. I want you to love me. She said instead, "Wrong? Why, no."

"Look, Myriah, I believe you are in some sort of trouble. You may need help and I wish to give it."

"I am afraid there is nothing you can do," she said with a heavy sigh.

He moved forward and took up her chin. "Tell me, my sweetings, what is it? Just confide in me and let me be the judge of whether or not I can help."

But Myriah knew she would never be able to tell him that he was the only person in the world who could help her now. . . .

Fawcett Crest Books
by Claudette Williams:

AFTER THE STORM

BLADES OF PASSION

MYRIAH

SASSY

SPRING GAMBIT

SUNDAY'S CHILD

Myriah

Claudette Williams

A FAWCETT CREST BOOK • NEW YORK

To my parents, Lawrence & Doris Nissan who have given me everything I have ever needed to have—love.

MYRIAH

Published by Fawcett Crest Books, a unit of CBS Publications, the Consumer Publishing Division of CBS Inc.

Copyright © 1978 by Claudette Williams
ALL RIGHTS RESERVED

ISBN: 0-449-23577-7

Printed in the United States of America

10 9 8 7 6 5 4 3 2 1

One

1813

Cascading ringlets of fire framed an elflike countenance of peaches and cream. Dark brows and curling lashes accentuated the almond shape of the blue-green eyes. Champagne organza fell alluringly about a form as delicate as it was provocative, yet the owner of these enviable attributes gazed at her reflection in the gilt-edged looking glass and sighed deeply.

A maid popped her linen-covered head into Lady Myriah's dressing room and clucked her tongue disapprovingly. "Tch, tch, m'lady, here you be, idling your time away with your papa that anxious for you down in the ballroom! Why, gracious, the music is sweet to hear, and the dancers looking fine as fivepence . . . and here you be, looking that sad! Why, it fair sets me in a huff, it does!" said the middle-aged woman, taking all the liberty that years of faithful service had won her.

Lady Myriah raised an eyebrow, and there was warning in her look though her tone was light. "Now, now, love, don't be hipped with me. 'Twould never do! I don't see why *I* must go down just yet, especially when I feel disinclined . . ." She stopped abruptly and noted the troubled look on her maid's face. "Oh, very well, don't worry yourself over me, I'll go," said Myriah with one of her spontaneous smiles.

"Good girl! 'Tis that much those fine bucks below be wanting a look at yer sweet face!" approved her maid.

"Nonsense, Nelly, love. They have seen it all this season and last! Allright, allright, don't get yourself all puckered up again. I'm going!"

She made her way down the red-carpeted, circular staircase, a slight frown between her eyes. She was troubled—even those who knew her but little could not help noticing. However, Lady Myriah was not of a confiding nature. She had for many years kept her own counsel, preferring to solve her own problems—only this time she found herself in a bind! The music floated up and enfolded her gently. Usually its mesmerizing effects lifted her spirits but now she only sighed.

Whatever is the matter? This one question haunted and irritated her—and left her burdened. She had no wish to hear the music she loved, no need to join the merry waltzing *ton* in the ballroom below.

Lady Myriah was about to embark upon the glorious age of one and twenty. She had already enjoyed two London Seasons and was about to take on her third. Yet —Lady Myriah was bored! Bored and totally disenchanted with the beau monde, London, and all its frivolous activities!

Ah, to be twenty-one and disillusioned with one's world—'tis a sorry state indeed! Myriah was too beautiful, too wealthy, too socially prominent, and still completely unattached and unspoken for! This last and somewhat astounding fact had not been achieved without some exertion on her part, to be sure, for Myriah had received no less than a dozen offers! Her papa and numerous interested relatives had spent much time and effort in their attempts to convince her that at least four of those offers were most exceptional. But Myriah had held out and refused them all!

Perhaps it was because of Mrs. Radcliffe's novels.

Myriah had often heard her aunts pompously deplore her father's leniency in allowing her to read such material. Perhaps it was Tom Moore's provocative poems—or Sir Walter Scott's gallants! Ah well, 'tis useless to speculate for by the time Myriah had reached her eighteenth year she had become most regrettably romantic! She had the very odd notion (during an age when people of her class married for many excellent reasons, none of them having anything to do with love), that *love* was *the* most important prerequisite to matrimony. But, strangely, Myriah had never been in love. Now, 'twould be most foolish to say that her heart, which was as passionate as it was gregarious, had not yet been stirred. Several fine young bucks had stirred it very well! However, it had not yet received its *coup de grace!* Thus, it was that Myriah's heart remained intact, albeit restless and seemingly fickle.

She was Lady Myriah, the only child of the Lord Whitney, and he was well able to indulge her many whims. At least he had always seen fit to do so in the past. Lately, however, her worthy father was beginning to lose patience with his headstrong darling!

She was desperately yearning for some unknown, and her yearning was finding expression in the most alarming ways. Only the other night, she had donned that frightful domino and gone off with those young scalawags to that dreadful masquerade at Vauxhall after he had expressly forbidden it! Good God! He shuddered violently whenever he thought of his sister Emily, calling down wrath on his head because Myriah had allowed herself to be seen by Emily's prattling son Herbert! Foolish girl! If that was not enough to try the soul of a patient father, there was her stubborn friendship with the rakish Lord Byron. Though the poet had a reputation with women, inwardly Lord Whitney knew his daughter was in no danger of losing her heart to the pretty boy. But he was heartily sick of hearing his sisters nag on and on about the doubtful friendship. The more they railed at Myriah, the more intimate she became with Lord Byron and, truth to tell, 'twas not seemly for a maid to be seen too often in his company. And, God only knows, thought he miserably, what next she would plunge herself into.

In spite of all these wayward activities, Myriah had lost no ground with the fawning *ton!* They seemed not at all disturbed over her mild indiscretions, calling her "naughty puss" and chuckling over her whimsies! Lady Myriah's weighty family name and its accompanying fortune allowed much! Though the dowagers frowned, though Lady Jersey chastised gently, though Myriah's relatives wagged their fingers, her charm and vitality gained her the *ton's* affection.

Myriah accepted their adoration as her due and, though she laughed at her aunt's admonishings, she was aware that her father would not tolerate her caprices much longer. The winter had been long, too long. Now Spring had come with its May flowers and May songs filling the air. This was the last rout of the London Season before the *ton* rushed posthaste with its Regent to Brighton. Myriah could only sigh.

The ballroom lay before her, wide, gleaming with hundreds of candles in wall sconces and chandeliers. The marble floor could scarcely be seen as the waltzing feet of fashionable dancers glided around in time to the music.

Small, delicate, and attractive, Myriah stood a moment at the entrance before she was surrounded and heralded into the room. Her name was on all their lips. Where had she been? Why hadn't she come sooner . . . promise a dance, Myriah . . . one for me, Myriah . . . God! Suddenly she felt suffocated! She broke loose with a laugh and caught her father's eye. He smiled warmly across at her, and she composed herself and blew him a gentle kiss.

"Sweet Myriah, have you one for me?" asked a quiet male voice.

She looked up into the face of Sir Roland Keyes, and a twinkle crept into her eyes. Now here was a diversion. "You, sir, have no need of such wispy things," she said coyly.

"You are never wrong, Myriah . . . for indeed . . . I have need of much more!" he said, taking her hand and leading her firmly onto the dance floor. They moved in rhythm to the music of the violins, and many eyes glanced curiously at them.

Sir Roland, a bachelor of nine and twenty, had many attractive qualities and more than one of Lady Myriah's suitors had noticed her apparent preference for the dratted fellow's company. Sir Roland's height was good and his frame was such as to catch any maid's eye. His thick curling locks were auburn with a hint of silver. He entertained Lady Myriah with an adroitness that kept her amused.

As the waltz ended, Myriah gazed quizzically up into his bright eyes. "Sweet Myriah, shall we continue our play on the dance floor—or shall we seek privacy?" he teased, kissing the wrist of her gloved hand.

"I think, Sir Roland, we had better remain here. I have already found that . . . that playing alone with you can be quite dangerous!" countered the lady.

"For whom, sweet beauty?"

She laughed amicably, for as always his forwardness excited her. He had skill, there was no denying this.

"You know very well for whom! Never say you fear for yourself?" she said.

"For myself, never! Ah, but for my heart, that is something altogether different! I have not attained my years and remained unshackled by toying with danger!" responded the gallant.

Her eyes flickered. "Well, there certainly is no danger of your becoming . . . how did you put it? . . . shackled? No, Sir Roland, you need have no fear that you shall become so with me for I have already told you that I cannot marry you." The teasing quality of her voice had begun to ebb.

Sir Roland smiled and took her hand. Without speaking, he led her into a country dance. He was aware that Myriah was attracted to him, and though he had not yet discovered the means to win her, he had no intention of giving the sport over! She was far too wealthy, and Sir Roland needed her money! His lands were heavily mortgaged, a state that had been achieved by his father's heavy gaming debts. He had tried everything else—even himself resorted to gaming with the little blunt he had left. Now, deeper in debt, he was desperate. Putting his estates in order had become all-important, and he needed an advantageous marriage to achieve this end. If this was not reason enough for wanting to marry Myriah, there was his desire for the chit. He wanted her! She teased him until he knew he must possess her, but she had made it clear that her virginity went only with marriage, and indeed a maid of her class could not be taken any other way. She dallied with him, taunted him, and flirted with him outrageously; he meant to have her and her money.

They had been presented to each other just two months ago, and Myriah found Sir Roland titillating, witty, and a stimulating companion. In turn he found her exquisite to behold, spoiled, wild, and irresistible, and yet . . . they were not in love! 'Twas a sad state of affairs, for when one sees two such creatures there is a tremendous desire to match them up—at least, so thought Lord Whitney and his many sisters.

As the young people met in the steps of the country dance, their eyes flirted, and it seemed to the onlookers that here was a match indeed.

Myriah's cheeks were flushed when the dance ended, and Sir Roland eyed her with concern. "You need air, love. Come, the night is too beautiful to ignore."

She hesitated and glanced doubtfully toward her father. Sir Roland tugged gently at her arm, and with a shrug she relented, allowing him to open the French door and lead her into the garden. It was a delicious night, smelling of roses and fresh grass. She looked up at the black sky and saw the half-moon shining down on her, its companions twinkling gloriously. It was the sort of night poets and minstrels sing about, and Myriah breathed it in with pleasure. They walked without speaking, without touching, and she pulled her light shawl about her arms.

"Cold, love?" he inquired quietly, and there was a subtle shading in his words that she chose to ignore.

"No," she replied and walked a bit away from him.

He reached out and held her back. "Don't run away from me, Myriah. There is no need. If you wish, I'll take you back inside."

"No, I don't wish to go back."

"Then come . . . walk with me," he said, linking her arm through his. He led her farther away from the house, down the path to a maze of neatly cut yews where a stone bench caught his eye. He coaxed her to sit down beside him. Suddenly, as if exasperated, he took the lady by the shoulders and turned her face to him. "You want to be alone with me, Myriah. Why do you pretend otherwise? You are no silly miss declaring no when she means yes. 'Tis not your way."

She laughed good-naturedly, "You *are* a rogue! Perhaps I *do* want to be alone with you . . . perhaps I do not. I really don't know. But that doesn't signify at the moment for apparently *I am alone* with you!"

His laugh was low and soft as he put his strong arms round her and drew her to him, marveling at the glorious firmness of her supple body. At moments like this, when she was inviting his caress, he felt that he might be happy with her as his wife. His mouth sought hers hungrily. She yielded to his lips, allowing him the kiss, hoping for thunder and lightning . . . for bells . . . for music . . . for something . . . She sighed at length and pulled away.

"I can't marry you, Roland."

He laughed and shook his head. "Who is the rogue now, my dear?"

She returned his look, an impish light creeping into her eyes. "Now there is no use telling me that I must not kiss a man unless I mean to marry him, for that is stuff and nonsense . . . and so you know!"

"So *I* do! But there are many who would not agree with such liberal thoughts!"

"That is because they are from another time and . . . and . . . I am different!" She moved farther away and frowned sadly.

"Myriah . . . what is it you want?" he asked suddenly.

"I . . . I don't know. Evidently something other than what I have. I want to *feel*. But all I can feel is this awful restlessness. Lord . . . when I was a child, I was never this way. 'Tis just this past year. Here I am flaunting myself for the London bucks . . . and Roland . . . I . . . I hate every minute of it!"

"Then end it . . . marry me!" said Roland, turning her to face him again, "We shall deal together, you know that we shall. Myriah, there is so much more . . ."

"Oh, Roland, you don't need me to tell you what wild fun you are. And there is no gainsaying the fact that I like you better than any other man of my acquaintance, but . . . I am not in love with you!"

"I could teach you to be," he said taking her into his arms and pressing her powerfully against him. She let him take her lips again, putting her arms about his neck, aroused by his hot kisses, aroused by her own needs. She returned his kiss, and her own was as urgent as his. She wanted this to be love . . . and knew it was not.

"Egad!" came a voice from behind.

Myriah jumped away from Roland's suddenly limp arms and looked at her father with dismay. The blood rushed quickly to her cheeks.

Sir Roland rose immediately and stood calmly facing Lord Whitney whose expression gave every promise of trouble. His lordship shook one irate finger at Sir Roland.

"What the devil do you mean seducing my daughter in my own home?"

"You mistake, my lord. I have just asked Myriah to be my wife," offered Sir Roland quickly.

Myriah's cheeks lost their heightened color, and she opened her eyes wide at her father's change of expression. The ominous cloud that had hung about him had totally disappeared and been replaced with an open grin. She felt the warmth drain from her body and a coldness clutched at her.

"Eh?" barked his lordship, opening his blue eyes. "She has accepted you. Excellent . . . excellent . . . knew she would. Told Emily, 'mark me now, 'tis Roland she wants.' Very pleased indeed . . ." her father rattled on.

"Papa . . . papa . . . I have *not* accepted Sir Roland's offer!"

"Nonsense! Saw you m'self," returned her father. Lady Myriah felt distinctly uncomfortable beneath his scrutiny. How could she explain?

"Nevertheless, papa, I did not accept his very flattering proposal."

"Well then, my girl, do so . . . now!" commanded her father, the smile leaving his lips. "No chit of mine is going to give away her favors freely!"

"Papa, do but listen . . ."

"Never mind trying to get round me! It won't fadge, girl! I saw you with my own eyes . . . giving Sir Roland that which should go only to your intended! It's clear I've let you run amuck! Well, I shan't let you ruin yourself. It's a husband you need, and Sir Roland here will fill the post nicely."

"Papa . . . please do not speak so to me. I am not going to marry Roland. You can scarcely expect me to marry a man simply because I have allowed him to *kiss* me?"

"What?" shouted her distraught parent quite on the verge of apoplexy!

"Well . . . really, papa . . ."

"Listen to me, young lady," interrupted her father, barely able to speak, "You are not only going to marry Sir Roland . . . *I* am going back into that ballroom with you both and make the announcement tonight! Good God! Next thing you'll be cradling a babe in your arms and telling me 'tis nothing at all! The very idea! Damnation, Myriah! I don't like admitting Emily was right, but you have proven her so! She warned me what you were heading for, and I refused to listen. Well, thank God, I have discovered the way of it before too late!"

Myriah's temper was as hot as her excitable father's. However, she had enough control left to contain her fire. She knew her father to be in the right of it . . . at least, his right of it. From where he stood things must look bad. When he was in a temper, there was no curbing his highhandedness. If she were to save the situation, she must act rationally. She calmed herself, knowing that to defy him now would not serve.

"Very well, papa . . . if you will but give me a moment to tidy myself . . . I shall be very happy to accompany you to the ballroom and hear my engagement to Sir Roland announced."

Sir Roland's eyes flickered and flew to her face. What was the chit about? 'Twas not like her to concede so easily. His lordship, on the other hand, thought too much of his authority over his daughter to question her sudden submission. He grunted and allowed her to pass.

Myriah raced up the back stairs, avoiding the servants as she made her way to her room. She would have to act quickly or be undone, for once such an announcement were made her father would never make a retraction. Indeed . . . she felt even she could not weather such a scandal. "Papa, oh dear papa," she thought sadly as she rushed about her room, flinging off her elegant gown and donning a smartly cut riding habit of dark blue velvet. Her father, beloved, doting, and kind, could be terribly steadfast in his decisions, especially when his sense of propriety had been ruffled. The only way to prevent doom was to absent herself! She flung two gowns into a small portmanteau, scurried about for her toiletries, pulled on her riding boots, and without another glance, made her way, bag in hand, to the back stairway!

The sounds of servants rushing about with food trays, wasping at each other in their haste, caused her to slow down cautiously. She must not be seen. Another movement brought her to the side door of the fashionable London town house, and a moment later she was breathing in the night air.

With a hurry born of need, she made the three blocks to the Whitney stables, for there was but one thing she could do and one place she could go; to her grandfather at Northiam!

The extensive Whitney stables loomed out of the darkness. It was late, well past ten, and she was certain most of the livery boys would be in bed. She pulled on the wide wooden latch, lifting it out of its catch and swinging the door gently open.

"Who's that?" came the gruff voice of a small man ambling toward her. The stables were dimly lit, and he pushed the candleholder in his hand toward the intruder's face.

"M'lady!" he cried out in surprise.

"Hush, Tabby," whispered Myriah, putting one gloved finger to her lips. "I need your help, old friend."

He squinted at her intently, his dark eyes noting her disheveled attire. He scratched his short gray hair, and his mouth moved dourly. "Eh, now, child . . . what ye got yeself into this time?"

"Oh, Tabby, there is no time to explain now. Just trust me and saddle my horse immediately . . . and Tab . . . I will ride astride!"

"Hold now, m'girl," said the groom authoritively. "You ain't thinking of riding out at this time of night?"

"Oh, Tabby, please . . . just saddle Silkie for me . . . at once . . . if you don't, I shall be undone!"

There was no denying the note of desperation in his lady's voice. He had mounted Myriah on her first pony. He had served her as he had served and adored her mother, but he was not beneath a-naying her orders. He hesitated. "First you best tell me what's got you running."

"Papa means to marry me to Sir Roland . . . he is in a temper, Tabby, and there is no gainsaying him. I must go to grandpapa."

"That won't serve, m'girl . . . it'll set up your father's bristles, it will."

"Get my horse, Tab . . . now!" commanded Myriah, out of patience.

Tabson grumbled but disappeared into the darkness while Myriah fidgeted, fearing her father's explosion on the scene. Perhaps he would not realize for a time, but then he would send up a maid . . . who would report not only Myriah's absence, but the topsy-turvy room she had left behind. In what seemed interminable but was actually a short time, Tabby returned with his lady's horse and a saddled roan for himself.

"Tabby . . . what do you think you're doing?"

"I be going wit ye! Not the devil 'imself could stop me!" announced her groom, as he watched her hoist herself nimbly onto her horse. She laughed.

"Now Tabby . . . I've been told my powers are far greater that those of his darkness . . . but I have a notion to let you come . . . so be it!" She flung him a purse containing a tidy sum and led the way, cooing to her glossy stallion as she urged him onto the cobbled street. His ears flicked at the sound of her voice. A breeze caressed her cheeks, and Myriah laughed a wild unbridled laugh as free as the moment and far more free than her mind.

Two

They picked their way through the narrow streets toward Charing Cross. Myriah's eyes were bright with excitement. Even the thought that London at this time of night was not safe for a well-armed man, let alone a young woman, could not disturb her spirits.

"Tis a wild ride we 'ave ahead of us, m'lady," said Tabson sourly.

"Ain't it grand, Tab? Imagine! Riding on the open road with not a soul to say us nay!"

"Humph . . . providing no bridle-cull spots us," returned the groom pessimistically.

"And if he does, we'll give him our trinkets and be on our way. 'Tis nothing!" said the lady, snapping her finger for emphasis and laughing at the thought of such an escapade.

A company of merry gentlemen stumbled out of a tavern singing quite loudly, out of tune and not at all concerned with this deficiency. They spotted Myriah and called out robustly for her to stop awhile. She chuckled but kept up her proud chin, urging her horse to move at a faster pace.

"Humph!" grumbled Tabby.

At last they reached the toll-gate and, after watching Tabby attend to the fee, Myriah gave her horse his head. They bounded forward in rhythm with one another, and Myriah's restlessness lost itself in speed. How she loved riding freely!

Tabby caught up after some effort and called to his mistress to slow her horse into a canter. "Don't be all Hell and fire, m'lady . . . leastways not in the dark! Ye'll be planting yerself in some rut or other and giving that stallion ye say ye love so much a strained fetlock!"

She laughed but did indeed ease her spirited horse into a slower gait. After the docile rides in Hyde Park, this carefree exercise created a certain euphoria, banishing Myriah's concern.

Tabson felt it incumbent upon himself to bring his mistress to a sense of reality and dispel the sweetness of fantasy with his gruff practicality. "T'won't serve, m'lady, and well ye know."

"Hush, Tab, I won't have you growling at me," laughed Myriah.

"Growl, is it?" said the man sticking out his lower lip, "and what will ye be calling it when yer papa bowls down upon us at Guildford House?"

Myriah sighed and a slight crease marred her brow. "Oh dear . . . he will do so, I suppose."

"Hang me if he doesn't! Then what will ye say? Fine set-to there will be!"

"Oh, Tabby, I never thought of that. Papa will be angry to be sure . . . but he and grandpapa are good friends . . ."

"Humph! Lord Guildford will take your side in the matter, and it's plain as pikestaff yer papa is bound to take umbrage. A rare set-to there will be!" grumbled the elderly man.

Myriah's frown deepened. "Oh, Tab, you are taking too doleful a look at the whole thing. I shall fix things up right and tight. See if I don't!"

To this her groom had little to say. However, he continued to mumble incoherently and Myriah, losing patience, moved her horse forward and left Tab some distance behind her.

Tunbridge Wells was reached, the horses watered, rested, and then once again they set south on the main pike. The adventure had lost its initial thrill for Myriah, and her mind was now busy with the problems facing her. There was Sir Roland—surely she had done him an injustice, by allowing him to think she had acquiesced to her father's plan. But then, she had not missed his expression. No—Roland had not been fooled! But Papa— there was no telling what *he* might do, though she was fairly certain he would post down to her grandfather's in the morning . . . and then there would be a scene indeed!

The road meandered past rich green farms through meadowlands boasting of spring wildflowers whose scent was carried on the growing breeze. The aroma cast her troubles aside. What had she to do with worries? Myriah said aloud, "just look about at all this glory."

"Look at what, m'lady?" asked her astonished groom coming up alongside her. "What can ye see in the darkness? 'Tis half-daft to try!"

"Oh, Tabby, don't vex me so! I can see . . . with my mind's eye . . . oh, Tabby, I do so love Kent!"

"Aye!" agreed Tabson relenting, for it had been his home as well and he too was heartily sick of town life.

They maintained a steady pace for the next half-hour without speaking. In her haste Myriah had neglected to put on a riding hat, and her fiery ringlets had tumbled down upon her shoulders. The breeze was stronger now and whipped the long thick locks across her cheeks. With an exasperated sigh she reined in, pulled off a glove, and pinned back the wayward tresses.

Tabson looked up at the sky and mumbled a complaint that made Myriah raise her eyes heavenward. "Oh dear," said she, "I don't like that." Clouds were gathering and obscuring the moon's glow. The travelers had been on the road for some three hours and were nearing their destination. With a weary sigh, Myriah led the way again, more slowly now, for a gray collection of mischievous clouds had taken an excursion from the sky and were playing with one another on the road.

"This mist is dreadful," complained Myriah. "I can barely see ten feet in front of me, Tab."

"Humph," agreed her companion.

For the next hour they continued, the silence punctuated now and then by an unladylike exclamation when Myriah would find she was off the road and into a thicket. At last a fingerpost loomed up at the crossroad, and she rode up to the narrow white wood.

"Dymchurch . . . 3 miles . . . oh, no, Tab!" ejaculated Myriah, reading the sign, "We must have taken the wrong turnoff . . . we are heading in the wrong direction."

"Humph. Thought the air a bit too salty. Nothing for it, m'lady. We'll have to take the coast road. It cuts through the marshlands farther down, and we can follow the river a bit to Northiam."

"Oh, Tabby, I am so tired. We've been traveling for hours . . . how much longer do you think it's going to take?"

He scratched his head. "Two . . . maybe three hours if this mist holds up."

"Two or three hours! Why, it must be past two in the morning! Good lord!"

"Best be moving on, m'lady. Dymchurch be no place for lingering at night."

"Why?" asked Myriah surprised.

"Because it ain't!" She was too weary to press him further, and this time allowed him to lead the way.

As suddenly as it had appeared, the mist vanished, only the dewy grass and moist bushes retaining evidence of its earlier visitation! Low flat lands were dark and foreboding in the blackness. The road cut through narrow dikes by glistening rills, and the shadows teased Myriah's imagination. She spurred her horse forward, wanting to reach her destination, suddenly afraid and not knowing why. A chill seized her, a strange sensation swept through her, and then she stopped—sure that she had heard something. Tabby halted his horse directly behind her and leaned forward in his saddle.

"What be . . ."

"Hush," commanded his mistress, listening intently. Again the sound came to her ears, and this time she could identify it. A horse . . . the snort of a lone horse! She squinted through the darkness, zeroing in on a clump of evergreens and shaggy bushes. There! She saw it! The animal had shaken its head and she had caught the movement, following the line down the horse's nose to a dark clump at its hoofs!

"O my God, Tab!" said Myriah, her heart racing. She couldn't really see and yet instinct—a certain 'feeling' —told her that someone lay injured beside the horse. Without another word she closed the distance to the object of her interest, slid off Silkie, and went down on her knees beside a young man.

His face was half-hidden by his arm, his fair hair was free of the hat that had fallen beside his limp form. She pulled the heavy material of his riding coat away from his chest as she eased him onto his back. Tabby had by this time come over to her, and she exclaimed in distress that the man was unconscious.

"I see that, m'lady . . . must have had a bad fall."

However, in an attempt to give the man some air by loosening his garments, Myriah's hand had come in contact with something warm and sticky. Horrified, she pulled her hand away. "Oh . . . oh, no . . . Tab . . . he's wounded."

Her groom knelt beside the unconscious stranger and the wound through which the man seemed to be losing his life's blood was located in his left arm.

"Tabby . . . I'll have to make a tourniquet . . . fetch some water from the dike. "She tore off a length of her muslin underskirt and handed it to him. When the groom returned, he placed the cool wet cloth on the man's forehead, while Myriah tore another strip of cloth, saying fretfully, "Oh, I do hope I can remember the knack of it. I remember when Sir Thomas took a bullet last hunting season a tourniquet saved his life until the doctor was fetched. Do hold his head up, Tabby . . . that's it," she said, slipping the material round his biceps above the wound.

"Now, Tabby, we'll need some of that heathenish brew you call whisky . . ." (she saw that he was about to deny the possession of any such thing) ". . . 'tis not the time to tell me round tales. You have not been my dearest Tab all these years without my knowing you! Now do get it, Tab!"

The groom grumbled heartily but a moment later produced a bottle of the questionable libation and he put it to the young man's pale lips. The fiery liquid proved to be potent indeed, for the lad coughed fitfully and his eyes fluttered open. His lips parted but he said nothing as he stared up into Myriah's face. Again the whisky was sent down his throat; again he coughed and attempted to focus.

His vision came slowly and indistinctly. He thought he saw flames dancing wildly about an exquisite though elf-like countenance. A feminine yet commanding voice seemed to be ordering him into obedience and a burning brew was being forced down his throat. He remembered falling off his horse; and it suddenly occurred to him that *he had died* and *was now* probably in hell! He was hazy and the loss of blood had left him cold and somewhat delirious. His voice was faint and gravely troubled.

"If . . . if . . . I'm in Hell . . . why . . . is it . . . so . . . cold?" he asked the creature leaning above him.

This produced a gurgle of mirth from Myriah, and even in his pain, the sound of her laughter brought a slight grin to his lips.

"That, sir, is no compliment! I have always thought men were supposed to declare themselves in Heaven after being brought round by *the* attending heroine!"

"Heaven? You . . . you don't . . . look like an angel," said the young man feebly.

Myriah laughed and arched a friendly brow. "Indeed . . . 'tis a lamentable truth, I must say, but 'tis most shabby of you to remark it!" She sighed mockingly, "Ah, but there is yet time to alter your hasty opinion once I put you into the hands of your local doctor."

"NO!" objected the young man cutting her off and attempting to raise his head.

"But, sir . . ." returned Myriah, firmly prohibiting such action. "You have sustained a nasty wound, and it must be attended to at once by someone far more experienced than I."

"Please, ma'am . . . if you . . . would be so good . . . help me to my feet . . ."

"On no account," returned Myriah authoritatively.

"She-devil!" muttered the young man.

"Have a care, my friend . . ." teased Myriah, rallying him, for he looked suddenly pale and helpless. "I may end by sending for that doctor after all." She sighed and put a hand over his mouth, preventing any further speech. "Evidently you have some aversion to the physician in question for reasons not known to me. Very well then. Where shall we take you? You cannot continue to lie here in my lap! I am getting most frightfully stiff, you know."

He grinned beneath her palm and she lifted it, allowing him speech.

"Wimborne Towers . . . just up the pike to River Road."

"Very well. Wimborne Towers it is." She turned and called sweetly to her horse. The dark animal snorted and shook its head but could not resist the sound of his mistress's voice. He walked over and nudged her with his nose.

"Down darlin' . . . that's my love . . ." urged Myriah to the handsome animal, watching him as he went down on all fours, proud of him and herself for having taught him the useful trick. With Tabby's assistance she got the wounded man to his feet and positioned him on the horse. Myriah then cooed softly to the stallion, bringing him back up.

Her thighs ached from the night's riding, the small of her back felt pinched, and her head was throbbing unmercifully. This was no longer an adventure, but a grueling, uncomfortable, mind-racking evening. She steadied herself before mounting the man's horse and allowed Tabby to lead Silkie while she followed in the rear. Before long they had reached the fingerpost which turned them onto the River Road. This led through a stretch of flatland, broken only by a scattering of low budding trees. It sloped gently upwards, passing a wooded cluster of birch and evergreens which opened into what had once been a magnificent park. Even in the darkness of night, Myriah was impressed with the estate's layout and with the huge Tudor home that beckoned. Concern for the young man lest he fall off her horse kept Myriah busy watching him, yet even so she felt that the house and the grounds had been quite regal . . . and not so very long ago!

After what seemed an interminable time they had reached the covered portico. There was nothing for it but to leave the horses standing as they assisted the young man off Silkie and brought him to the front double doors. He leaned heavily on Tabby who had little to say throughout these proceedings, and Myriah banged hard with the knocker.

The young man coughed convulsively and Myriah, worried lest the bleeding begin again, tried to hush him, but he pulled at a chain at his waist and produced a large brass key. "No . . . no servants . . ."

She exclaimed impatiently and worked the key in its housing, pushing the heavy doors open, then closing them after they had entered. He motioned the way to the second floor, and after some exertion they deposited him on his bed. He closed his eyes and lay back. Myriah winced for she could read the pain in his face. The three tiered candelabra she had found and lit in the central hall, was placed on his nightstand. With Tabby's help the man's greatcoat was removed, and Myriah gasped at the blood-soaked shirt beneath. "Good God, sir . . . you may be pluck to the backbone or a simpleton . . . I don't care which, for *I* shan't let you go on without medical assistance any longer."

"No doctor . . . please . . . get me Fletcher."

"Confound it, who is Fletcher?"

"My brother's groom."

"A groom . . . my dear sir . . ."

"They . . . fought together in . . . Spain . . . he'll be able to . . ."

"Damnation, man . . . where is he then?" asked Myriah, beside herself and fearful for the stubborn man's life.

"His room . . . above . . . our stables."

"Tabby," said Myriah turning round at once, "get this man called Fletcher. Have him come up at once. But you find some clean water and bring it up with you . . . and Tab . . . thank you."

"Yes, m'lady," said Tabson.

Myriah sank down upon a nearby chair and allowed herself a moment to study the stranger, noting for the first time that he was quite young, in all probability not much older than herself.

His cheeks were ashen and his brow furrowed with the etchings of pain. His face was angular, his nose straight, his lips thin and well defined. He was, even with his mouth distorted by quiet suffering, very attractive. His hair was spread upon the pillow, in the candlelight

Myriah noted that its golden streaks served to foster his youthful good looks.

"Faith, Myriah," thought she ruefully, "now you've gone and done it. Here it is no less than five in the morning . . . and where are you? At your grandpapa's . . . safe and warm, cosily tucked into your bed? Oh, no . . . not you, Myriah! Here you sit on a hard chair without the benefit of a fire, attending a man whose fame has bought him a bullet . . . and you don't even know his name!"

Three

A few moments later Myriah was poking about at the fireplace grate in an attempt to kindle a blaze. At last she was rewarded with a spark of light, and putting a weary hand over her head, silently gave thanks. The hard heavy strides of a man's boots taking the stairs came to her ears, and she waited, staring at the open doorway.

An elderly man, of average height and substantial girth, dressed in disheveled woolens, appeared on the scene. He shook his head and a long straight lock of silky white hair fell across his eyes. He glanced darkly at Myriah, strode heavily into the room, and stopped beside the young man's bed.

"Wisht, wisht, m'lad . . . Whet they doon ta yah, m'bonnie?" asked the newcomer, bending low over the wound and examining it carefully. "Ah . . . the divils . . . the divils! But ye would goa . . . ye wouldna listen to nobbut yeself! Ah Maister William . . . we be in for it now!"

"Can you help him, sir?" asked Myriah hopefully.

He didn't bother to glance at her but continued studying the bullet hole. Tabson returned, an iron pot filled with water in his hand. Myriah motioned for him to set it on the fire and turned to find Fletcher pouring brandy over the open wound. His master groaned and gripped his sheets. "Aye lad . . . 'tis gonna get worse . . . though thank the saints . . . it ain't too deep. 'Ere now, m'bonnie . . . drink up," he said, pouring some brandy down his master's throat.

Fletcher then sidled to the fire and began heating the sharp thin blade and pinchers he had produced from his pocket. This done, he returned to Master William and motioned for Tabson to hold him steady. Once again the fiery alcohol was poured over the wound, and then knife met with flesh. Master William stiffened with pain and Myriah silently prayed that he would pass out. However, it was not until the pinchers were inserted that the lad was given a reprieve. The mind has a way of doing its own battle with the brave. It detached itself from the proceedings, as though enough was enough—and the young man was spared a few moments of torture.

Myriah was beginning to feel queasy, but she continued to watch. Within a moment the offending bullet was produced and removed. The torn skin was cleaned and cauterized, then the bandages were wrapped round the battered arm. Myriah felt as though a vise had been squeezing her insides. Her back was tense, and her hands were white with clinching.

Fletcher covered his master with a clean sheet and blanket. He rolled up the bloodied linen and threw it onto the fire. He turned to Myriah and his features were inscrutable. "He'll wake soon . . . 'n'more'n likely he'll fever up. You best get some sleep . . ."

"Will he be all right?" asked Myriah anxiously.

"Thank'ee ma'am . . . that he will wit' God's 'elp. Yer man can bed doon in m'quarters . . . and ye might find 'is lordship's room to yer liking. It be jest across the hall."

"Thank you, Fletcher . . . I shall relieve you in a few hours." Myriah took one candle and went out into the hall. She bade Tabson good-night and opened the door almost directly opposite. She crossed the dark room, removed her jacket and boots, and dropped across the bed. A moment later she was asleep.

With a start Myriah brought up her head. The room was still clothed in darkness, yet a slit between the drapes allowed the morning's gray light to filter through. The strangeness of her surroundings puzzled her a moment, then as she felt the dawning of memory, she groaned. She raised herself to a sitting position and became aware of the fact that her body was making its own form of objection to the previous night's escapade! She felt as though she had been brutally beaten, and a longing to shirk her promise and return to sleep did private battle with her conscience. Alas, a conscience is a troublesome thing. Berating herself for a fool, Myriah rose from the bed and attempted to stretch!

With a groan she pulled on her boots and jacket and then encountered yet another problem. When she attempted to take her first step, she found her legs objects unto themselves. HOLD! they cried. Did you, Myriah Whitney, not subject us to cruel and flagrant misuse? The verdict came in guilty, and Myriah's hands went supportatively to her thighs as she crossed the hall to William Wimborne's room.

This feat accomplished, (Myriah felt it deserved applause), she took a moment's respite and leaned against the open door. Bolstering her courage, she walked stiffly toward Fletcher who offended her sense of justice by looking wondrously comfortable and deeply asleep on the Queen Anne chair beside his master's bed!

She gave the groom a rather rough shake, and he grumbled into consciousness. "Fletcher . . . you are relieved! How did he sleep?"

"Restless he was . . . gave him a bit of laudanum . . . he shood sleep now."

"Thank you," said Myriah, wishing she had stayed in bed.

The man shuffled out of the room, turning to advise her that he would have cook send up breakfast and warning her not to mention the cause of his master's indisposition to the servant.

"Cook?" asked Myriah. "Then there are some servants here after all?"

"Jest be cook and her two lads. They comes days, fix tha meals and cleans. That's all," said Fletcher, leaving her abruptly.

With a sigh Myriah poured some water into the wash basin and began setting herself to rights. She would have to ask Tabby to bring her overnight portmanteau up to her, for Mr. Wimborne's comb was nowhere to be found.

"Oh, well," said she aloud as she sank into the Queen Anne chair. She gazed at the patient. His hair was light brown, streaked with gold, much lighter than she had thought the night before, and again she thought he must be quite young.

There was a knock on the door, and a young, round, freckled face appeared with a tray. "I brung your vittles," said the wide-eyed boy as he placed the tray on a nearby table. "Fletcher . . . he said . . . young master took sick and you be tending him."

"Thank you," said Myriah dismissing the curious boy with a look.

She swallowed the tea and the buns in a trice, suddenly aware that some of her aches were due to hunger. Afterwards, she moved toward the long diamond-paned window overlooking the estate grounds. They were obviously suffering from neglect. The lawns were overgrown, the flowerbeds needed weeding . . . bushes sadly wanted pruning, and the stables were in dismal need of paint. It would appear the Wimbornes had fallen upon hard times. Surely this had once been an elegant home, for the furniture was exquisite, though the material could stand a good cleaning.

A sound from the bed made her look round—the patient was tossing beneath the covers. Myriah quickly soaked some cloth and began pressing it to his head. For the next two hours he tossed, fretted, and called for 'Kit.' It was all she could do to keep him from tearing off the bandages. At last Tabson came in.

"I've put your bag in the room you took last night, m'lady—thought ye might be needing it."

"Oh, Tab, thank you. But do stay here with him awhile. He is in a terrible fever, and I want to go to the kitchen and prepare a tisane to ease the fever."

"Yes, m'lady."

She went downstairs and cautiously made her way to the kitchen. Here she found a pleasant, round-faced woman scurrying about with pots and pans and giving orders to her sons.

"Excuse me?" Myriah said to call attention to herself.

The woman started, then waited, not sure what to make of the young woman before her.

"I am so sorry to interrupt your work. I am Miss . . . White. I was on my way to my family . . . in . . . Dover . . . when we lost the way. I remembered that my cousin's home was nearby, and so we stopped here for a night's shelter. Apparently Cousin William has a fever, and so my groom and I will remain until he is feeling more the thing. I do hope you will not be put out too unduly by our sudden descent upon you."

Cook liked the girl's manners. She smiled readily and replied that she was happy her master had someone to look after him. Myriah then asked to be given the herbs she needed for the tisane. The brew was prepared, and Myriah went back to Mr. Wimborne's room.

Tabby held him up while Myriah attempted to get the potion into him. This accomplished, Tab was dismissed, and Myriah continued applying cloth soaked in rosewater to his head. At last he slept.

A light lunch was sent up to Myriah, and Fletcher attempted to relieve her, but she would have none of him. For some odd reason she felt *she* had to care for her 'new charge'. At length his sleep seemed more relaxed; and then suddenly she saw him open his eyes. She was beside him instantly. He scanned her face and smiled feebly as his memory returned. His lids closed and he seemed asleep again.

For an hour Myriah watched the changes on his expression while he slept, sure now that the fever had broken, when all at once he was tossing again, fretfully calling for Kit.

Who the devil was Kit, she wondered as she soothed his agitation. His forehead was on fire, and Myriah had a sudden urge to cry. He couldn't die, she couldn't let him die, but he had lost so much blood! Again she wiped away the sweat from his face, neck, and chest. Again she cooled his forehead with rosewater. Again she prayed, and then he was sleeping peacefully.

Myriah sank down upon a chair, herself weary with physical discomfort and mental stress. She closed her eyes and laid her head back. For the next hour she tried to compose her faculties. Suddenly the sound of his voice broke in on her thoughts like a triumph to her ears!

"I may be in Hell . . . but *you* are an angel!"

"Mr. Wimborne!" exclaimed Myriah going to him immediately. "Oh, oh, you do look better—not well, but ever so much better."

"Thanks to you," said her patient.

"Oh, no. Thanks to your good man, Fletcher. He has a wondrous skill with a knife. But you lie still now . . . I shall be back in a moment. What you need now is some gruel."

"No," said the man, horrified.

"Well, not perhaps right away. First I will bring you some tea and toast," she said, taking pity and disappearing.

Four

Having plied her patient with buttered toast and hot tea, Myriah watched him fall off to sleep, feeling extraordinarily pleased with herself. A few minutes later Tabby knocked and requested to be allowed to relieve her. She smiled and acquiesced, for she was tremendously fatigued.

Moments later she lay beneath the satin coverlet in the room across the hall, peacefully asleep. Her dreams were muddled, lost in time, sending images to taunt her and toss her about in her bed. Then all at once her mother's face glowed before her . . . it was her own, a gentleness came over her, and Myriah relaxed.

The afternoon drifted away into evening and then suddenly Myriah was dreaming again. Without knowing why she woke, her eyes fluttered open. She looked about the dark room and sat up. She rose from the four-poster and made her way to the window, bumping into a desk with a thud before reaching her destination. She drew the heavy red brocade drapes and tied them back with their black tasseled ropes.

It was still a few minutes to seven, but what was left of the day's gray sky did little to brighten the evening.

A shiver tickled her bare back, and she returned to the nightstand and lit the candles. She washed with the warm water provided for her in a pitcher, threw off her nightdress, and donned one of the gowns she had so hastily thrown into her bag. It was a pretty peacock blue silk, high-waisted and tight-fitting with a matching blue-and-white velvet band edging the scooped bodice and repeated about the high waist. Hastily she slipped on her silk stockings and blue satin slippers, then viewed herself in the looking glass. She brushed her flaming locks vigorously until her hair shown and her head ached. Then she pulled her long tresses to the top of her head and tied them with a blue ribbon, allowing the long curls to fall about her head and shoulders. She looked and felt refreshed. She crossed the hall and found Tabby nodding off in his chair. Myriah roused him gently, "Tabby . . . there . . . I hope I didn't startle you."

"No, m'lady," said the groom rubbing his wrinkle-framed eyes.

"You had better go get a bite to eat and have one of cook's sons bring up something light for me and a bowl of gruel for Mr. Wimborne."

"Yes, m'lady . . . but . . . hadn't we better prepare to leave?" asked Tabby.

"As to that Tab . . . I am beginning to have other notions. But we'll speak about that tomorrow."

"Humph!" he said, leaving the room.

Myriah was about to take a chair when William Wimborne opened his eyes and grinned. "She-devil," he said, a term he continued to use when she was forcing tea down his throat.

"Ah! I see you are much more the thing and ready to pick up the cudgels again, Mr. Wimborne."

"How . . . how long have I been asleep? You . . . you look different."

"You have been asleep for hours and hours. And I

look different because, my odious friend, I have changed clothing and brushed my hair."

"Well, it's about time," said her patient.

Her blue-green eyes glared. "Just what I was thinking. That is why I have asked for the gruel to be sent up!"

"You wouldn't?" said her patient.

"Ah, but I would and I did. 'Tis just what you need to make you feel more the thing."

"Damnation, girl!" said the young man with as much authority as he could muster under the circumstances. " 'Tis food I need—not gruel!"

"And food is what you shall get—once you have shown me you can hold the gruel down!"

"I *am* in Hell . . . and you *are* a she-devil!"

"Really, Mr. Wimborne, this morning you declared me an angel!"

"This morning I was delirious, for you ain't an angel but a wicked she-devil bent on having her own way. Knew it the moment I laid my eyes on your hair!" retorted Mr. Wimborne.

"Aha! Not only are you an adventurer . . . you are an ingrate as well!" teased Myriah, pleased to see him in such spirits.

He smiled feebly but fatigue prevented him from further repartee. Myriah observed this and refrained from teasing him. She rose and put another log on the fire, then turned to find Tabby in the doorway.

"Cook left these trays warming on the fire in the kitchen, for she left awhile ago, m'lady. Here is the gruel for the young master and a platter for you."

"Thank you, Tabby." She watched him deposit the tray on a near-by table before he turned and left the room.

She picked up the bowl of gruel and sat down beside Mr. Wimborne. He opened his eyes and groaned. "Go away!"

She put the bowl down, propped up his pillows, and

helped him sit up. He stared hard at her as she brought
the first spoonful to his mouth. He took it and swallowed
hard, grimacing distastefully.

"Now, now Mr. Wimborne . . ."

"Billy to you!" replied her patient.

"I am afraid I cannot . . ."

"You cannot shove that slovenly mush into m'mouth
and call me *Mr. Wimborne!* 'Tis ridiculous! I'll not call
you anything but she-devil, and you had best call me
Billy!"

She wedged another spoonful into the poor man's
mouth and grinned, "My name, sir, is Myriah . . . er . . .
White!"

"Myriah . . . Myriah . . . hmmm . . . it suits you. You
look like a Myriah . . . 'tis but another name for she-
devil after all!"

She laughed and shoved another spoonful into his
mouth. However, that was the last he would take. She
sighed and went to her own platter of sirloin and roast
potatoes. He watched her pick at her meal and muttered
something incoherent. Myriah laughed and brought her
platter to the bed, whereupon the two shared the single
meal. Each seemed quite pleased with the other, and
Myriah left him resting peacefully, promising to return
with tea and biscuits.

She took up a candle and made her way downstairs.
This time curiosity drew her to an open door just off the
central hall. She entered the large room to find it a well-
stocked library, but what captured her attention was the
far wall which was covered with portraits. She lit a few
wall sconces with her candle and stood examining a
portrait of two young men. Why . . . here was William
Wimborne . . . and another man!

The portrait must have been done some years ago for
William was no more than fifteen or sixteen in the por-
trait, and the man beside him was about five years older.
There was a definite similarity . . . but the older man's

jaw was squarer . . . his hair was honey-colored, and his build more powerful. She wondered who he was as she made her way to the kitchen and prepared the tea.

A few minutes later she entered Mr. Wimborne's room again and merrily presented him with tea and biscuits.

"You look more than half-pleased with yourself," said he.

"And should I not be? Look what I have brought you."

"Egad! What are you trying to do to me? What I need is a bit of firewater, m'girl!"

"Drink!" commanded Myriah.

"Damn if I will! Take yourself off," countered her patient.

"Ungrateful puppy!" replied his warden.

"Puppy!" responded Mr. Wimborne, taking umbrage. "Now . . . that is really too much. From a child . . . a slip of a girl . . ."

"I'll have you know I am one and twenty!" said Myriah proudly.

"No!" said Mr. Wimborne in disbelief. "Wouldn't have credited it. I am myself going to be one and twenty this month."

"Oh! Well, as to that, I am not really one and twenty yet . . . but I will be shortly."

"Ha! I'll have you show some respect to your elders, child!" responded Mr. Wimborne.

"Drink your tea, Billy, before I pour it down your throat!"

He grinned and told her to sit beside him. She did and they proceeded happily to dunk their biscuits. "Billy, there is a portrait of you downstairs . . . with another man."

"Oh, the one done by Lawrence awhile back," said Mr. Wimborne.

"Well, I suppose. But who is he?"

"Who?"

"Oh, for gracious' sake! The other man in the portrait."

"Oh," said Mr. Wimborne, beaming. "That's m'brother . . . Kit!"

"Kit!" exclaimed Myriah. "Oh . . . he's your brother? You called out his name a few times. Oh, yes, that's right, you mentioned that Fletcher was your brother's groom. I had forgotten! Well . . . where is he?"

"Who?" said Billy.

"Good lord! Your brother Kit . . . where is he?"

"Oh . . . had some business in London. Don't expect him for another week."

"I see."

"Damned lucky as it turns out, for he'd be mad as Ajax if he came back and found I'd bought a bullet."

"Hmmm . . . I can imagine," said Myriah thoughtfully, wondering for the hundredth time how Mr. Wimborne had *bought* a bullet and why. However, this was something she felt she had no right to pry into and therefore refrained from asking.

"What about you, Myriah? What were you doing about here that late at night."

"Good thing I *was*, puppy!" retorted Myriah, evading the issue.

"Have a care, girl! I still have one good arm quite able to administer the spanking *you* might buy!"

She laughed. "Very well . . . if you can keep a secret. I was running away from home. My father . . . Mr. White . . . wishes me to marry a man I am not in love with and so I loped off. I was heading for my . . . aunt who lives in Dover when we got lost and came across you. A few days here will serve me very well. So if you don't mind, I think I shall continue in my post as nurse to you, Mr. Wimborne," said Myriah, telling a half truth. It would not do to reveal her real identity, for although she had no cause to mistrust him, it might not be a wise thing in the end.

"Well, I do mind!" replied Mr. Wimborne teasingly, "I don't want any she-devil attending me. Lucky fellow . . . the one you've run away from."

She tweaked his nose and advised him to go to sleep, for he was again looking weary. She watched him sink back into his pillows, then said good-night.

"Good-night, Myriah . . . she-devil . . . thank you."

She smiled, "You are most welcome, puppy. I shall leave both our doors open, and if you need me, just call."

"Good God, girl! My intellect is still in order, you know! Don't think I'd willingly call you down upon me!"

"Abominable ingrate!" laughed Myriah as she left his room.

Five

Lord Christopher Wimborne of Wimborne Towers rode slowly up to his weathered stables. It was past midnight, he was stiff from a long ride, and the wind had not been friendly that evening. The sound of his horse's hoofs clopped echoingly on the deserted path as he reined to a halt and slipped off.

Fletcher had come to a sudden stop in his lively conversation with his new mate, Tabson. He had heard the approaching rider, and it dawned on him with a sinking heart that his lordship had returned much earlier than was expected. "Gawd . . . but Aw be in fer it naw!" he said, scurrying down the wooden steps to the stable doors.

Even in the dim light, fatigue was clear on his master's face, and he decided to postpone any mention of young Master William's scrape until the morrow. Lord and groom exchanged warm greetings, for time and mutual experiences had made them more than servant and master. They shared a bond created over a period of six years—and such six years—fighting in the Peninsula side by side.

"What are you doing awake, you old geezer?" grinned Lord Wimborne.

"I be waiting fer yah," responded Fletcher sheepishly, for he could not mention Tabson's presence without disclosing the whole of it.

His lordship turned a quizzical eye on him. "Waiting for me . . . when you didn't expect me until next week?"

"Had . . . had one of me notions, aw did."

His lordship was too tired to carry this further, so he simply placed his horse's reins in the groom's hands. "See to him, Fletcher."

"Aye, sir," replied Fletcher, hoping his master would go straight off to bed without looking in on Master William.

Lord Wimborne knew the route to his chambers so well that he needed no light on the way. He mounted the oak stairs and entered his quarters through his dressing room door. He found the room in total darkness and stayed only long enough to drop off his greatcoat, hat, and gloves. From there he opened the door to his bedroom and, finding the room dimly lighted by the starry night, he crossed to his large chair. He pulled off his blue superfine cutaway and allowed it to fall onto the floor. Off went his neckcloth, and so too would have followed his white linen shirt when the sound of a rustling movement from his satin-covered bed halted him.

The moon's pale glow filtered through the terrace doors across his bed, and Lord Wimborne watched warily. He was a cautious man by nature, made more so by recent circumstances. Another movement from the bed produced a mass of flame-colored hair, and the contrast of its hue against the white pillowed background sent his lordship's thick dark brows up inquiringly. A few silent, steady strides brought him to the bedside, and a slow, amused curve began to form on his sensuous lips. The thought struck his Lordship that his young brother had managed to amuse himself rather well during his short absence from home!

"Allright my bird . . . let's have a look at you," he said

softly, his blue eyes twinkling as he sat beside the vision in his bed. His hands worked gently and deftly pulling away the thick fiery tresses from their owner's face and shoulders. The object of these ministrations sighed contentedly and fell from her side position onto her back giving the curious intruder a full view of her exquisite face.

This was not without its unintentional effect. Kit Wimborne, sixth Viscount of Wimborne Towers, released a soft whistle which would have conveyed to his intimates (had they been witness) his obvious admiration for the figure presently occupying his bed.

Lord Wimborne's lips pressed together, and he gave a rueful sigh as the thought came to him that his scampish young brother had certainly won himself a piece of muslin worthy of a full-grown man!

All youthful shyness had taken leave of Lord Wimborne some years and many women ago. Therefore, the decision to have a better and more detailed look at the creature lying unsuspectingly before him was as natural as it was inevitable. Again, his hands worked dexterously as he removed the quilted covering from Myriah's tantalizing form. His eyes wandered slowly and appreciatively over her lush curves beneath her soft white nightdress. She shivered suddenly, and his lordship sought to remove her discomfort by covering her—with his own body. He put his arm across her and leaned over her lithe form, a sudden spark reviving his blood and chasing away all thought of sleep.

"Now what to do with the lady . . ." he said aloud, grinning as he thought, one shouldn't infringe on one's brother's property—but really, Billy . . . why the devil did you put her in *my* bed? This question repeated itself and with a grin his lordship decided the only thing to do in such a situation was to wake her—*his way!*

His fingers moved sensuously as they stroked her soft bare arms, and he shifted position so that he was stretched alongside Myriah. He nibbled at her delicate ears and placed a warm kiss on her throat. Myriah groaned pleasurably. The sound stimulated him and one booted masculine calf straddled her outstretched legs as he leaned over her and took her mouth.

Myriah felt the sweet pressure and her dream took on a new force, one that sent a firebolt racing through her veins. Her arms went round the large virile body, the source of her dream's acute burning—and then suddenly her eyes flew open!

All at once Myriah was awake! Unable to speak in spite of the fact that her lips were now quite free, she lay staring in utter disbelief at the man she was still holding in her arms. She lay for a moment in quiet astonishment trying to collect her thoughts as she stared at the stranger's face. He was grinning provocatively and she noted the ruggedness of his face and somehow found it familiar. But he was a stranger nonetheless. It occurred to Myriah to drop her arms and pull out of range which she did quite speedily, wondering all the while how the deuce this had come to pass.

Her eyes glittered angrily as she sought words; a scream seeded itself in her throat and surely would have been emitted had not Lord Wimborne had the foresight to put his powerful hand over the lady's cherry lips. This quite naturally did little to alleviate the lady's fears, yet his friendly grin seemed to suggest he meant no harm. "Hush there, sweetings . . . I don't mean to take any more than you are willing to give," said the handsome man above her.

Outrage surged through Myriah's fiery soul, and she managed to work the skin between his thumb and forefinger into her dainty mouth, whereupon she latched her teeth into her target and bit down hard. This produced the required result and he jumped away. With an oath, Kit Wimborne withdrew his offensive and now somewhat damaged hand, rubbing it yet smiling at the lady.

"Well now . . . that is certainly a poor way to treat your host!"

"My . . . my host?" ejaculated Myriah, finding her voice at last. She sat up and gazed at him intently, her brows moving with sudden recognition. "You . . . you are Lord Wimborne! Well . . . of all the horrid . . . LIBERTINE . . ." She spluttered in her attempt to find him a proper description. He shifted his position once again, and his boots touched the carpet. He sat up on the side of the bed and faced her quizzically. "Easy now, love . . . shall we kiss and get off to another start . . . ?"

Myriah put out her hand to keep him at bay. "How dare you! My lord . . . I cannot believe you realize what you are about."

"All the more reason to humor me . . ." returned his lordship sliding closer to her.

"I think, my lord, that you should leave my room at once!" said the lady austerely.

"I . . . leave? My dear young woman . . . may I point out to you that this is *my* room!"

"That is most unhandsome of you!" retorted the lady. "Your brother needs me . . . and this room is most convenient, for if he should call for me, I would be able to go to him. And besides . . . *you* were supposed to be in London!"

"Ah, yes, my brother. I rather thought he had something to do with your being here . . . but never say the young scalawag . . . er . . . expects you to come running to him at all hours of the night," said his lordship, much struck by such a fancy.

"Well, he is the most darling thing and expects nothing. I doubt he will call . . . but you see I have left our doors open. In that way . . . if I hear him moving about restlessly, I can attend him," said Myriah innocently.

"You . . . could . . . attend him?" repeated his lordship, his eyes twinkling. "Why the devil didn't you just stay in *his* room?"

" 'Twould be most uncomfortable. I mean, really my lord!" snapped the lady much annoyed with his rudeness.

"Never say Billy snores?" asked his lordship, trying to get at the meat of the matter.

"Snores?" returned Myriah, beginning to think Lord Wimborne's head needed clearing. "No-o-o . . . at least I have never heard him do so . . . however . . . that would not have kept me from his side. You see . . . the danger is past now, m'lord, and there is no need for me to keep up the vigil."

At this juncture of the conversation, Lord Wimborne straightened and his face took on a troubled expression.

"Whatever do you mean? What danger?"

"But then . . . didn't you know? How odd . . . I rather thought at first you could not . . . but then when you asked me why I was not in his room . . . I just assumed you did know . . ."

"Never mind that now . . . know what? Speak up, girl!" he demanded.

Myriah had no liking for the manner in which he spoke to her, yet she was well able to read the concern in his bright blue eyes and decided this was no time to take umbrage. "Briefly, my lord . . . your brother was wounded by a bullet in his left arm. My groom and I found him on the main pike last evening . . . actually in the hours just before dawn. At his insistence we brought him home instead of to the doctor's. Your man Fletcher attended the wound . . . and quite expertly, I might add. Your brother was feverish all day, but at last the fever broke, and he is now recovering quite well." She had been watching his lordship's features and noted that his cheeks had lost their natural color during her recital.

"I see," said his lordship, "but that does not explain . . . who *you* are."

Instinct cautioned her—what Billy Wimborne took quite easily would not go unquestioned by his brother.

"My name is Myriah . . . White. My groom and I were

on our way to Dover when we came across your brother."

"I thank you for your help and will see to it that you spend the balance of the night undisturbed, for you have a long ride to Dover and need your rest," said his lordship beginning to rise from the bed.

Myriah's heart sank for she had quite decided to stay the week at Wimborne Towers, before exposing herself to her father's wrath. "Oh . . . my lord . . . if you would not mind . . . I would like to remain here for a few days."

He eyed her penetratingly. "Miss White . . . you must know already that our home lacks feminine supervision. You are in fact totally unchaperoned and beneath the roof of two bachelors! I am afraid it would not do!"

She scrambled from the bed, pulling the quilt around her only as an afterthought, a thing not lost to his lordship's keen observation.

"Oh, please, my lord . . . I would be so grateful for I am myself in a bit of a scrape. My father wishes me to marry a man I am not in love with . . . and it has occurred to me that if I go directly to my aunt in Dover . . . he will find me far sooner than his determination diminishes. As I have already set it about that I am a relative of yours, do you not think that would serve to spare my reputation . . . just for a few days . . . ?" Her blue-green eyes pleaded appealingly.

He studied her a moment. "You may remain a few days . . . but you are far too attractive for your stay to go on without the tattlemongers remarking upon it; therefore, I must ask you to limit it as much as possible."

"Thank you, my lord." said she sweetly.

"Don't thank me, sweetings. It would be a paltry thing indeed for me to turn you away after your assistance to my brother. Now . . . I think I'll go in and have a look at that brother of mine . . . good-night Miss White . . . and . . ." with a slow grin, "I shall be in my dressing room adjacent to this . . . and shall be available *if you . . . need me.*"

* * *

Lord Wimborne stood for a moment over his brother's still form. William looked absurdly youthful, dangerously pale, and helpless. His lordship decided not to wake him but instead brushed a stray lock of hair from his brother's forehead. Billy's eyes flashed open.

"Kit!" whispered young Wimborne as though he were looking at a god.

"Young fool . . . they tell me you caught a bullet," said Lord Wimborne gravely.

"Devil is in it that I did . . . but there was nothing for it, Kit . . . had to go out . . . for I got word . . ."

"Never mind that now . . . we'll talk about it later. I would like to know something about the chit in my bed . . . if you feel up to talking."

"Ah . . . you've seen my she-devil, have you?"

Lord Wimborne laughed, "If you mean Miss White . . . yes, I have." His voice sobered. "I am a bit concerned with her part in all this. What does she know?"

"Lord, Kit . . . she is a right'un. She hasn't asked me once how I come to have a bullet in m'arm! I hope you don't mind her taking your room."

"Of course not, scamp! I'll have another fixed up for myself tomorrow."

"Thank you, Kit. It was the least I could do . . . and you weren't supposed to be back until next week. What has brought you?"

"We'll talk about that tomorrow too," replied Kit Wimborne.

When he left his young brother a few moments later, it was with a troubled mind. It was time for a change . . . and soon . . . very soon it would have to be brought about!

Myriah dove under the quilt and heard him cross the

hall to Billy's room. She heard the quiet mumble of conversation, and the sudden explosion of laughter, and then his lordship crossed the hall again and opened another door. She heard his movements in the dressing room next door and the creaking of the daybed as he stretched his weary body onto its limited confines.

The vagaries of the mind are many. When both the body and the mind need sleep, it does not always come. Myriah found this to be so. Her mental capacity had been tapped, she could no longer sustain logical thought. Her limbs groaned and her eyes were blurred . . . yet she could not sleep! The feel of Lord Wimborne's strong masculine body still burned against her own, the memory of a kiss more tempting than she had ever believed possible nagged at her mind . . . and the movements of an uncomfortable man in the next room came to her ears.

Six

Myriah met the early morning sun with a smile, in spite of her inability to get back to sleep for some hours the previous night. She felt in spirits without any apparent reason and donned the day dress of peacock blue that she had worn yesterday. She washed her face and brushed her hair into a semblance of red silk before making her way to the kitchen.

The cook greeted her warmly and asked how the young master was. Myriah smiled, "I am sure he will be calling for a man's breakfast this morning. I thought I'd save your boys the trouble by taking it up to him myself."

"How kind of you, Miss," said cook beaming.

"Oh . . . and his lordship has returned, so perhaps one of your lads can fix up the spare room near Master William's quarters."

"His lordship be back, you say?" asked the cook curiously, putting a stack of sweet tarts on a tray.

"Yes . . . hmmm . . . they look good," said Myriah, eying a strawberry tart.

"They be young Wimborne's favorite."

"Have you been here long?" asked Myriah.

"M'mother was cook at Wimborne before me . . . 'tis a

49

shame what hard times will do to a place."

"And they have fallen onto hard times?" asked Myriah.

"That they 'ave . . . we used to have quite a staff running about . . . then something went wrong . . . jest this past year . . . just after his lordship come home from fighting the Frenchies in Spain. All but me and my boys were let go."

"How dreadful . . . those poor people . . . did they find work?" asked Myriah.

The cook cast her eyes away from Myriah's face and suddenly busied herself again, "Oh, as to that . . . they make out allright. There now, that should make Master William feel more himself."

Odd, thought Myriah, why had the woman become suddenly secretive. She shrugged her shoulders and took up the tray, marveling at its weight, and made her way to young Wimborne's room.

Without knocking on the open door, she sauntered in, placed the heavily laden tray on a stainwood table, and pulled it to the bed. Exclaiming disapprovingly, she made her way to the long hangings and opened them. "There, that's better!" said Myriah, hands on hips as the sun beamed its path to Billy's eyes.

"O God . . . she's back!" groaned young Wimborne.

Myriah said nothing to this but went to his water pitcher, poured some of the cool water into the basin and brought it to the bed. Dipping a washcloth in the water she moved it over her patient's face and neck, then left it in his free hand while she brought him a towel.

"There," she exclaimed with approval after these ministrations had been completed, and he was properly propped up. "Now don't you feel better?"

"She-devil . . . move aside and let me eat!" retorted her patient.

She laughed, drew up a chair for herself, and placed a tray of delectables on his knees. "Eat, puppy, and then you shall have a strawberry tart!"

"I shall have one now," he replied.

"After," she said, placing them out of his reach.

"Fiend!" he snorted as he put some egg and sirloin into his mouth.

She sipped her coffee and watched him eat. When he had finished, she poured him a cup and handed it over, spilling a bit as she did so.

"Careful, chit!" admonished Mr. Wimborne grinning.

"Ungrateful puppy! Be satisfied it was not dropped on your head!"

"Good morning," said a male voice from the doorway.

"What's good about it, Kit? 'Tis but eight o'clock and this she-devil is already at it!"

"Would you like some coffee my lord . . . I've brought an extra cup," said Myriah feeling for no apparent reason a sensation very much like shyness.

"Thank you, Miss White," said his lordship quite formally, and Myriah peered at him wondering if this tall, honey-haired man was indeed the same one who had leaned over her last evening. This morning he was cool and distant . . . but last night . . . .

His imposing figure loomed above them as he came over for the coffee cup. Myriah could not help noticing that his riding jacket fit his broad shoulders superbly, as did the breeches covering his powerful legs. His Hessians showed no sign of travel as the sun glinted against their blackness. He sat in a wooden chair across from the table Myriah had set up and sipped his coffee leisurely.

"Eat!" ordered Myriah returning her attention to Billy who had not yet started his tart.

"Fire-breather . . . no need for you to order me about. Was just about to," returned Mr. Wimborne grinning.

Lord Wimborne laughed, sat back, and relaxed as he watched the lively exchange between the two. He wondered about Miss White as she called herself. She looked and behaved every bit the spoiled lady . . . certainly her clothes had come from none other than Madame Bertin's

Salon. Then, too, there was something in her self-assurance . . . something that spoke of breeding and exposure to a London Season . . . yet he had never heard of the White family name. Then there was her story . . . it seemed odd and, though he believed it, there had been something in her eyes that hinted of falsehoods. It annoyed him and hovered about his thoughts like a fretful child. He watched her get up, and unconsciously his eyes meandered slowly over her body, but his eyelids quickly veiled his appreciation of her form. This was one pretty his instincts cautioned him to pass!

"If you will excuse me gentlemen . . . I am sure you two have matters to discuss, and *I* would dearly love a stroll outdoors," said Myriah, brushing a few crumbs into a napkin and leaving it on the table.

With her departure Kit Wimborne relaxed and chuckled as he watched his brother devour the strawberry tart. "Billy, you and Miss White seem to have progressed into an extremely comfortable relationship," he said, eying his brother speculatively.

"Hmmm . . . she is a top sawyer! Don't let her bossiness fool you, Kit. She really is grand, you know!"

"And how came you to this profound conclusion about a young lady you hardly know?" asked his lordship drily.

"Kit!" expostulated Billy Wimborne. "She saved my life! If Myriah had not found me and brought me home, I could have bled to death on the grass . . . or worse . . ."

"Very well, we will allow her that much. She did indeed deliver you into Fletcher's hands instead of hauling you off to the doctor's establishment as most might do. But really . . ."

"Kit!" objected Billy once again. "She did far more than that! Lord . . . ain't Fletcher told you . . . he did me! Seems she fastened some sort of a thing . . . a tourniquet that slowed my blood from spilling out altogether. And what's more, she never asked *how* I come by my bullet! Not once! Nor does she talk around it like some females

do when they daren't ask. I'd be itching with curiosity
. . . and Myriah must be . . . but she don't plague me."

Kit Wimborne laughed and put up his hands, "That,
of course, makes her a right 'un!"

"Yes, it does," said Billy defensively, "She is plucky
. . . for you must know her father has tried to bully her
into marrying some chap she didn't take to. Up she gets
and runs away! How many females do you know got the
backbone to take such a step?"

"And that step meets with your approbation, Billy?"
asked his lordship gravely.

"Now, Kit come down a leg! Lord, it ain't you to get
some preachy look over your face. 'Tis humbug you be
pitching at me and I want to know why!"

"Frankly, I don't wish for you to become involved
with a girl of her stamp . . ." started his lordship.

A gusty laugh drowned out Kit's words, "Involved?
Egad, Kit . . . Myriah is a dazzler! Lord don't know when
I've clapped eyes on a brighter flower. But she no more
wants *my* name than she wants that fellow's she is running
away from!"

"But . . . what do *you* want, my bucko?" asked Kit.

"I want a fairy queen with china blue eyes, corn silk
hair blowing soft in the breeze . . . and I want her *ten
years from now!*" grinned Billy.

Kit Wimborne smiled and stood up. "Allright, lad . . .
I'll plague you no more—for the time being. Get some
rest."

"The devil I will!" retorted his brother, " 'Tis your
turn, my lord."

"My turn, brat?" asked Kit, his brow going up.

"I want to know what is toward . . . why are you back?"

"Very well . . . and then *you* will give me the whole of
it . . . *I want* . . . unlike Myriah . . . all the details of
your escapade!"

Myriah meandered slowly down the front drive, marveling how different land looks in daytime. The lawns, though overgrown, were a lush green and with but a little mending would once again be something pure and soft to look upon. The road followed a winding, deeply etched, sea-green dyke. An apple orchard's rich blossoms filled the blue sky. Myriah felt strangely happy.

She liked Billy Wimborne. He was open, honest, unflirtatious . . . all these traits she found quite refreshing after her two seasons amongst the sophisticated London beaux! Lord Wimborne was a different thing altogether. He was an experienced man—in many ways. Of this she was certain—yet his merry blue eyes balked at sophistication! He had shown himself a dangerous flirt last night—from what she could remember—yet this morning he was the cool gentleman, totally disinterested in her. This circumstance in itself irritated Myriah. What had she done to cool his interest? And why did she care? There was a mystery here she would enjoy unraveling. Why had Billy been shot? Why had the Wimbornes fallen on bad times? And if they had, how did his lordship manage to acquire such superbly cut garments?

Just as these thoughts flitted about her mind, Myriah's feet felt the reverberation of horse's hoofs. Without knowing why, her heart skipped nervously, and she turned and made a dash for the house, cutting across the lawns and reaching the front doors just as a group of riders in military uniform appeared on the front drive.

She rushed into the house, went to a mirror, and tidied herself—and something deep in the pit of her stomach told her she would have to keep her wits about her.

A moment later the heavy knocker sounded. Myriah smoothed her blue silk skirt, took a long breath, and moved slowly toward the door fixing a becoming smile on her face as she did so.

Myriah opened the door wide and allowed her charm to play about her eyes and mouth, dazzling the young man standing on the portico. He whipped off his tricorne and tucked it under his arm. Myriah smiled shyly, apparently dazzled by his red and blue uniform. The officer cleared his throat and bellowed in an official tone, "Is this the home of Mr. William Wimborne?"

Myriah smiled prettily, and it would be a hard man indeed who could doubt her innocence. "Why yes, sir . . . it is . . . but pray, who may you be?"

Once again he cleared his throat and continued in the same tone looking straight ahead, "I am Corporal John Stone. Is Mr. Wimborne at home, madam?"

"Why, yes, sir, he is—but let us not stand *here!* Do come in," said Myriah disarmingly.

Before accepting her invitation, the corporal turned to the handsome collection of military minions astride their horses and ordered them to await his return. Myriah closed the door behind him, and turned once again to face him.

The corporal was not proof against her wiles, and with his men out of sight, he allowed himself the luxury of enjoying her friendly smile. "I regret, madam, that I must ask you to have Mr. Wimborne called," he said, beginning to open a small ballast bag that swung from his wrist.

She regarded this with interest, and as the corporal produced a somewhat damaged man's dark top hat, clapped her hands with a superb show of grateful animation, "Oh! That is William's hat! I am so pleased you found it. You can have no notion how disturbed I have been ever since I was so careless as to lose it."

The corporal looked taken aback and blinked at Myriah, "*You* . . . you say . . . *you* lost it?" He hesitated a moment and then looked at Myriah intently, "May I ask how it came to be in *your* possession . . . and *who you* . . . might be?"

She giggled and took the hat from him before he realized what she was about. With an admirable quickness of wit she discovered all that she needed to know and begged the Corporal to observe the line her finger traced: "There . . . do you not see how soiled the lining has become? I thought—this is a perfectly good hat—or at least it was until I was stupid enough to drop it . . . at any rate . . . I was conveying it to town to have a new lining installed. I did so want to have my cousin's name embroidered and then bring it back as a surprise. But how wonderful that you have found it, for perhaps *now* I can set it to rights!"

"I see . . . you said Mr. Wimborne is your cousin?"

"Why, yes . . . I am Miss Myriah White . . . I am staying just a few days before I leave for my aunt's in Dover. Do tell me . . . where *did* you find the hat?" continued Myriah sweetly.

"Not very far from the house, Miss White . . ." faltered the Corporal, his frown deepening, for his case had suddenly vanished, ". . . near a rather large area of stained grass."

"Stained grass?" asked Myriah surprised.

"Yes, Miss White . . . stained with blood," said the Corporal without caution.

"Oh . . . oh dear . . . blood, you say . . .? Oh . . . I do feel ill . . . was it an animal . . . poor thing?" cried Myriah putting a wavering hand to her eyes.

"Yes . . . do tell us . . ." said a deep authoritative voice from the stairs. "Was it *animal blood?*"

The young military man blushed profusely. "Well, no. Actually we are certain . . . we have reason to believe a man was shot."

"Why?" pursued his lordship, his face stony.

The corporal eyed Lord Wimborne, "Confound it, my lord, you know very well why! We shot at a *smuggler* and found on *your land* . . . a *pool of blood!*"

Lord Wimborne's hard blue eyes never flickered. His lips were set and his tone was dry, "Then . . . it appears to me that *you* should be seeking the desperate individual in earnest and *not* . . . delivering hats!"

The riding officer's cheeks flushed. His knowledge . . . the facts that he had in his possession were such that in his own mind Lord Wimborne and his young brother were convicted moonshiners. But he had not the power of evidence and was already on dangerous ground. "But . . . but my lord . . ."

"Shall I fetch Master William . . . perhaps if he were to confirm the ownership of the hat in question . . ." started Myriah soothingly, purposely round-eyed!

The young man turned and rubbed his hawklike nose and smiled at her. "No, that won't be necessary, ma'am. *Your* confirmation is adequate, thank you. I shall be getting back to my men . . . my lord . . . for, as you say . . . we should be about *trapping* our smuggler! Good-day," he nodded briskly and was gone.

Lord Christopher Wimborne stood looking at the closed door, and they waited—he and Myriah—for the retreating sound of the riding men. At length they sighed silently, and Myriah turned to find Lord Wimborne descending the remainder of the stairs. He approached her slowly, and his face was not alight with his usual pleasantness. "You make an excellent prevaricator, Miss White," said he.

"Thank you, my lord," said she, not sure she should be doing so, for his tone had the ring of something undefined and it needled her.

"Would you do me the honour of advising me *why* you felt it necessary in *this* circumstance."

She looked at him full, her delicate dark brows defined archly on her brow. Whatever was the matter with him? Didn't he realize she had playacted to protect Billy? Apparently not, for it was evident he was displeased with her! "My . . . my lord . . . I . . . I thought you overheard all . . . he wanted to *see* Billy."

". . . and you felt he should not?" asked his lordship.

"I . . . I . . . of course I felt he should not. My goodness . . . he was an exciseman, as you very well know.

Furthermore, they were looking for a man they had shot at and hit—and had they seen Billy with his wounded arm, naturally conclusions would have been drawn. I would not wish your brother harm, my lord."

"Then, Miss White, you believe my brother to be a smuggler?" asked his lordship, his expression and tone unfathomable.

"No! As a matter of fact . . . no . . . indeed, I do not! I believe that Billy became embroiled," she then muttered, "as *I* often have been, in . . . in an excursion that somehow got out of hand. I don't know what that . . . excursion was, nor do I care. What I do care about is your brother's well-being which means keeping his name off the tongues of the tattleprates!" said Myriah, chin well into the air.

In spite of himself a smile worked its way across his lordship's rather hard-set lips, but his voice was nonetheless cold. "I thank you, Miss White. Your intentions are founded on notions I am sure are quite . . . selfless."

"Then . . . then . . . you do not disapprove of . . ." began Myriah, her eyes fluttering uncertainly over his countenance.

"Disapprove? Why, no . . . you did just what *I* would have done . . . had I answered the door of *my home!*" returned his lordship drily.

"Oh!" said Myriah, the color rising to her lovely cheeks. "I . . . I am so . . . sorry . . . indeed the circumstances which threw your brother and me together . . . were such that all formalities were dropped. I . . . it . . . seems I have presumed . . ." she said, turning her face away. A painful hollow was created somewhere in the region of her chest . . . a hurt known as rejection! Myriah had never before been rejected, and it came as a facer from this handsome blade!

Kit studied the back of her head a moment. He could not allow himself to trust her. He sensed a lie about her . . . and yet when her magnificent eyes had met his own

so innocently searching for approbation, he had wanted
to reassure her . . . and couldn't! He was angry, far too
angry with her for having spoken to the exciseman, for
if she had not been suspicious before, she certainly would
be now! Yet guilty pinchings swept through him. It was
unlike him to be rude to anyone . . . least of all a lovely
woman, and there was no use denying his attraction for
Myriah. She would have to go . . . and soon!

"If you will excuse me, Miss White . . . it seems I have
been most rude. *While you are* at Wimborne Towers, do
consider it your own!"

Myriah was on the defensive, and she turned giving his
lordship the sight of a titian beauty.

"Consider Wimborne Towers *my own?* My lord, I
take leave to tell you that I would not . . . with the exception of your brother, associate myself with anything
that is *yours!*"

She turned on her pretty blue slipper and sped to the
second floor, leaving him gazing after her, a slow warm
grin covering his countenance. Had Myriah seen it,
she would have thought him far more charming than he
had hitherto given her reason to believe!

Lord Wimborne made for the stables, called Fletcher
to saddle his horse, and a few minutes later was on his
way to Rye. There were things he needed to arrange . . .
there were plans that needed thinking out . . . and there
was the titian-haired chit teasing his brain!

Seven

Myriah slammed the door to the bedroom and leaned back against its cool whiteness, arms folded and smooth cheeks flushed. The utter . . . want of civility of him! The . . . the inconsiderate . . . ill-breeding! thought Myriah heatedly. She crossed the room quickly, picked up a well-used deck of playing cards, and handled it agitatedly. Lord . . . if he but knew who she was—but she did not want that! She did not want Lord Wimborne to be civil to her because he was impressed by her name . . . her wealth. No—she wanted him to like her for herself! For some inexplicable reason he seemed bent on finding fault with her. 'Twas not only over the incident with the military men, but earlier that morning in Billy's room. She had felt his coldness—even his dislike—and was surprised by it.

She looked at the deck of cards in her hand for the first time and thought of Billy Wimborne, and a soft smile crept into her eyes. At any rate, here was someone who took her as she was! She turned and left the room, crossed the hall, and knocked on Mr. Wimborne's door.

"It's about time!" yelled the young man inside, and as Myriah entered he pulled a long face and complained,

"Thought you had all forgotten me, and I'm devilishly hungry!"

She laughed. "Well, 'tis not even noon yet so you shall have to wait, but how would you like a game of faro to help pass the time?"

"She-devil!" returned young Mr. Wimborne. "Here I am half-dead and you after m'blunt!"

For answer she laughed and drew up the stainwood table, sitting across from him and smiling amicably. "I shall deal."

"Then do so, but I warn you, m'girl . . . keep your hands above the table!"

They played a few hands before Billy asked casually who had been at the house. Myriah eyed him for a moment, "Why do you ask?"

"Because Kit left m'room to go greet our guests—we get so few these days—then he up and disappears. And you . . . you slam doors . . . well, it fair sets a chap to wondering," he said, raising his eyes to her face.

"Your odious brother does not like me—not that *I* care . . . but he need not be so rude. After all . . ."

"After all what? And my brother is not at all odious!" snapped Mr. Wimborne, quick to range himself on his brother's side.

"Well, of course, *you* would not think so. But then he was not uncivil to *you!*" retorted Myriah, flushing.

"Was Kit uncivil to you?" inquired Billy, much surprised.

"Somewhat. But in all fairness, I suppose I was presumptuous."

"Fiend seize it, girl! What *are* you talking about?" asked Billy, frowning.

"Oh . . . those men . . . landsmen . . . came here with *your hat*. It seems they found the blasted thing near your blood . . . on Wimborne lands. Well . . . I simply threw them off the track by saying that *I* had dropped your hat when I was on my way to town to have a new lining and embroidery job done on it. They wanted to see you . . . and I pretended to be willing enough which seems to have done the trick, for then they decided 'twouldn't be necessary to see you after all. But then your brother came upon us . . . and he was most disturbed that *I* had answered the door."

"Good Lord! Yes, I can imagine!" replied Billy, frowning darkly.

"Billy!" exclaimed Myriah.

"You don't understand Myriah! Bless you . . . for you did just as you ought. Always knew you were a right 'un. But Kit . . . he don't like the notion of you smelling out our business!"

Myriah took umbrage, "Billy Wimborne! I have not tried to *smell* out your business. I have already told your odi . . . your brother . . . that I am not interested in your business. Though, to be sure, I have developed a certain . . . absorption in your welfare."

"I know that, m'girl! Lord, I trusted you with m'life, didn't I? You never asked why I didn't want a doctor brought into it. 'Tis Kit . . . he doesn't trust so easily. I suppose it was the war . . . you know he only sold out a year ago . . . and . . . well, never mind that now. Don't fret it . . . he'll come round."

"Well, I don't care if he does or not . . . for I shall soon be going," announced Myriah haughtily.

Mr. Wimborne eyed her for a moment and said slowly, "You know Myriah . . . I have been thinking that you shouldn't leave for quite a spell . . . might end up with the knot neatly tied if you do . . . for your father is bound to be in a rage."

Myriah bit her lip and imagined what might lay in store for her if her father were to find her while he was still bent on marrying her off.

"I know Billy, but your brother really dislikes having me here . . . so I thought I would be off on the morrow!"

"My brother will allow you to stay as long as *I* wish you

to stay. And Myriah, *I'm not* about to allow you to be eaten alive after you have been friend enough to *save me!*"

"Billy, he will be so angry . . . I know."

"Kit? Funny you should think that. It ain't like him to lose his temper. Friendly sort . . . always has been. No . . . he'll come round."

"Very well. I thank you, sir," smiled Myriah.

"Good Lord! What have I done?" bantered Mr. Wimborne.

She tweaked his nose and told him to go to sleep. He eyed her defiantly. "The devil I will . . . where is my lunch?"

"Oh! I quite forgot about food. I shall go have cook send it up at once," said Myriah, moving away.

Myriah watched as a tray of food was carried out by one of cook's boys and turned once again to the woman, placing a coin in her hand and smiling warmly. "I do feel so distressed about asking this . . . for I can appreciate how difficult 'twill be when there are only your two boys . . . but I would so like a hot bath . . . ."

"Never you fret it, miss! I'll have those rascally brats of mine carry up the hot water right away." Cook was beaming at Myriah's generosity, "And, Miss . . . will you be wanting a luncheon tray?"

"Oh, no, thank you. I'm not really hungry today." Myriah went into the library and began fingering some of the leather-bound volumes. Her eyes strayed to the leaded, diamond-paned windows and saw a rider making his easy way up the front path.

Honey-colored hair, uncovered and lit by the full day's sun, billowed about a handsomely rugged countenance. Myriah's eyes lingered, discovering once again the broad shoulders encased in a well-cut dark brown riding jacket. She felt a tingling sensation, and on sudden impulse she dashed out of doors, blue silk rustling behind her. She would go see Tabby, she told herself. Of course . . . why shouldn't she go and see her groom?

* * *

Lord Wimborne's visit to Rye had proved fruitful. A meeting for the following night had been agreed upon. He rode his dark roan into the stable and found Tabby brushing down Myriah's black stallion. Lord Wimborne dismounted, put the reins of his horse into his groom's hands with a smile, and looked appraisingly at the black horse. He was an excellent judge of horseflesh, and the animal that stood so regally before him was certainly prime blood. So . . . it seemed that Miss White was well able to afford what was most certainly a very expensive piece of livestock. He turned his attention to Miss White's groom and smiled amicably, "Finest piece of blood I've clapped my eyes on in an age."

Tabby beamed, "That he be."

"Your mistress was certainly fortunate, for I have been looking for just such an animal these three months. But, of course, I don't get too many opportunities to go to Tattersall's in London," said his lordship, calculatingly.

Tabby was no fool, but he had no reason to suspicion he was being pumped, and he answered candidly. "They get the best, they do."

Kit put his finger to his lips, "Then . . . she did acquire him there . . . your mistress . . . now how could I have forgotten her name . . .?"

"White!" said Myriah from the doorway, thanking providence she had arrived in time to supply this information, for she had neglected to inform Tabby that she was keeping incognito!

Kit Wimborne turned and his habitually merry blue eyes glinted angrily. He had felt certain that he was about to hear a name other than White, and it struck him as an odd coincidence that Myriah should have entered at that precise moment!

Tabby glanced hastily from Lord Wimborne to his

lady and caught the look in her eyes and sent his own downwards. He had no notion what she was up to, but he would have no hand in her undoing. However, when he looked up again it was to meet the questioning eyes of Fletcher.

"Ah . . . Miss White . . ." said Kit, "We were just speaking about your magnificent black here . . . and where you purchased him."

"Oh? It was purchased for me . . . I believe at Tattersall's. Silkie was a gift from . . . my mother . . . five years ago," said Myriah, and a sadness hovered about her eyes. Kit Wimborne observed this and his curiosity received a nudge. "Would you enjoy a tour about Wimborne Park?"

Myriah brightened at once. "Oh, that would be lovely. Thank you."

He offered his arm and then stopped as if suddenly remembering, "Oh, do excuse me. I am taking you away . . . for apparently you came to the stables with . . . something in mind," said he, watching her face without a show of interest.

She blushed and he could not help but note it and thought: so . . . she does hide something . . . and is still youthful enough to feel shame!

"I . . . I had wanted to speak to my groom about a matter, but that can wait. It is so warm and lovely that . . . I should hate the chance of missing a guided tour." She cast her eyes up to his and allowed him a full look.

Fiend take her, thought Kit, she is too beautiful . . . and my blood will need cooling if I drink in those eyes. He led her for a time, down the main drive to the pike, turning off onto a narrow trail and pointing towards a body of sea-green water, "That's Rother River . . . it borders Romney Marsh."

"Oh, it is quite lovely here . . . as lovely as my own home," said Myriah, off guard.

"And where is that?" asked his lordship.

She looked away, "It doesn't matter."

"Ah . . . you don't trust me." he mocked.

Her eyes snapped at him fiercely. "And should I, my lord? *You* haven't trusted *me*."

"I don't have reason to, my girl." said his lordship, uncompromisingly.

"он!" ejaculated Myriah, "он! I mean . . . I don't expect gratitude . . . faith! As to that, one never thinks . . .'I will put myself out so that this one . . . or that one will be grateful' . . . at least *I don't* and *didn't* when Billy needed help. No, my lord . . . I don't want your gratitude . . . and perhaps have no right to expect instant faith in me. But really, my lord, however did your brother come to think that you were a friendly sort? For you must know that I find you nothing more than a . . . a . . . boor!" said Myriah, turning and very much on the point of abandoning her guided tour.

He laughed suddenly and there was a beguiling quality in his voice as his hand reached out and caught Myriah's bare arm. She turned her wild countenance upon him as a thrill taunted her flesh. The sudden memory of his lips flashed over her and she turned her eyes away.

"Miss White, I make thee my bows. A perfect flush hit and one that was well deserved. You have indeed done me a service . . . and I have treated you abominably. Let us call a truce."

She pulled her arm out of his hand and surveyed him coolly. Who did he think he was? She was no inexperienced girl to be bantered this way and that! "Five years ago I ceased to believe in miracles, my lord. It *would be* a miracle to keep a truce with *you!*"

Myriah left him standing there, looking after her as she made her exit. Her indignation made her unreasonable, and her fury carried her all the way to the house and to her waiting bath.

Lord Wimborne's deep blue eyes watched Myriah's body as she moved away. He had his doubts about her . . . and somehow could not shake them. Yet she had been instrumental in saving his brother's life, and Billy was his treasure. There too lay another source of his discomfort. He had no desire for his brother to develop an attachment to Myriah. Billy had said he wasn't interested, yet Lord Wimborne found this hard to believe. Indeed, he could not imagine how any *experienced* man would not fall prey to Myriah's charms . . . and certainly Billy was no sophisticate! In fact, his preoccupation with the flaming chit was beginning to disturb his *own* peace of mind. Again he thought, she would have to go . . . and soon!

Fletcher eyed Tabson who stood a good foot beneath him and waited for his new friend to return the look. "Weel now, Tabby, m'bonnie . . . whet sort of rahned tale ye be telling m'maister?"

"I don't know what ye got in that noodle of yers . . . so how's a man to answer ye straight?" replied Tabby, not wanting to lie to a man he had fast learned to respect.

"Aw heard yah meself, aw did! Called her *Lady* Myriah, yah did. It has me fairly stalled to know how that coom aboot!"

"Is that what's got ye fretting? Lord love ye . . . why I been calling her that since she was a babe! Jest somethin' between us . . . seeing how she likes to fancy herself titled . . . nothing in it," said Tabby, for if sides he was forced to take, 'twould be better dead and on his lady's side than alive and with another!

"Hmmm . . ." said Fletcher, scratching at his beard but saying nothing more on the subject.

Eight

Myriah sat haunched on the soft hearthrug in young Mr. Wimborne's bedchamber. A blazing fire crackled and sang cheerily as if pleased to be of service. Myriah's back was to Billy while her head was bent forward, her long red tresses thronging over her face as she toweled them dry. The fact that she was clothed in nothing more than Master Billy's long dark brocade dressing gown and that she was in a state of dishabille seemed insignificant to both parties as they bantered amically with each other.

Forgotten were conventionalities and pompous aunts . . . especially Emily who would have raised her eyes to heaven and declared Myriah quite lost to a sense of the proprieties. Here was a friend . . . the brother she had never had—and Myriah so needed him!

London had made her lonely. Odd . . . for she had been surrounded by gay society, but her dearest friends were married and away in the country. Others saw themselves competing with Myriah for beaux and had no wish to! Males too often felt it necessary to make of her an object they believed needed coddling, and Myriah discovered she was not formed for such a life! She felt estranged from mankind and needed someone to laugh with, be at ease with . . . to understand and be understood!

The headiness, the intimacy of the situation with Billy Wimborne had made them fast friends. Each was in need of companionship, and neither saw the other as anything but a friend. All reserves had somehow dissolved before such things had the chance to seed.

Myriah had come into Billy's room earlier in search of a dressing gown to wear after her bath as she had neglected to pack a wrapper in her portmanteau. She had been stormy, a state resulting from her disagreeable conversation with Lord Wimborne. Billy had laughed at her and called her a veritable titan, saying her face was the color of her hair and didn't it look odd against her blue-green eyes? This brought a giggle to her lips and having found that his dressing gown would serve, she made for her bath a bit more in spirits. The soothing hot water rinsed away her bad temper, for Myriah was one of those creatures who frenzies quickly but rarely sustains it.

When she was nearly finished with her bath, she heard Billy shouting her name. Drying herself quickly, she shrugged on his dressing gown and sped across the cold wooden floor to his room. He grinned at her boyishly.

"There now, m'girl . . . ain't I bright . . . had the fire lit for you!"

She pulled a comic face. "Puppy! Is that what you rushed me out of my bath for? Horrid boy! I would have stayed another hour soaking if you had not sounded as though the house were coming down round your ears!"

He laughed and looked her over and laughed again, "Lord . . . you look like a damp she-devil, don't you?"

She proceeded to take her place by the fire. "The very least you could have done was to have the fire lit in *my room.*"

"Would have been a waste, m'dear! We are thrifty here

. . . or haven't you noticed?" said he and the lack of gravity in his voice caused Myriah to glance at him sharply. "Thrifty, that's what we are. And since I was feeling a bit chilled, thought I'd . . ."

"Odious boy!" exclaimed Myriah from beneath her hair, blowing to keep it out of her mouth. "Trying to make me think you'd done it all for me!"

"Rather clever, ain't I?" he grinned.

It was at this moment that Lord Wimborne appeared in the doorway of Billy's room. He scanned the cozy scene and, though the proprieties had never really governed his lifestyle, it would be factual to describe his reaction of stiff surprise as definitely bordering on prudery . . . a thing most odd in a fellow whose social delights had little to do with priggish manners!

Lord Wimborne observed little of the natural ingenuousness of the scene, for what he saw was a wildly alluring female, obviously naked beneath his brother's dressing gown! If that was not enough to shock the soul, there was the disconcerting circumstance that he was unable to take his eyes away from the open neckline, too large to hide the tantalizing whiteness of Myriah's full womanhood. This bewitching creature seemed totally unembarrassed . . . indeed she appeared to taunt his young and innocent brother by flaunting her wild red hair. To further fuel his indignation, he could not help but notice that his brother—scamp that he was—seemed himself fully at ease with the minx! The thought occurred to him that perhaps Myriah was not the respectable maid she would have them believe but an adventuress . . . and his brother her *prey!*

"Indeed . . . do I intrude?" said his lordship, blue eyes hard on Myriah.

Billy looked surprised at his brother's tone, "Hold, Kit . . . what's towards?"

Kit turned angrily and for some inexplicable reason felt irritated with Billy. "*You* . . . ask *me* what is towards?

Indeed, Billy . . . in face of this . . . *delectable* scene, I find it a bit much!"

"Eh?" replied Billy, for he was genuinely all at sea.

Myriah understood Lord Wimborne's meaning all too well and the gingerness she had experienced when she first heard his voice was replaced with seething indignation! She brushed her flaming locks away from her face and her own eyes flashed uncompromisingly at his lordship. "Your disgusting insinuations do your brother little justice my lord. Or do you believe him as boorish as yourself!"

Billy's eyes lighted with sudden understanding, his face with openmouthed disbelief, for the notion struck him as insanely ludicrous. All at once the room exploded with his laughter, and he made an attempt to raise a pointing finger at Myriah. "You . . . think . . ." at which he burst out roaring once again.

In the face of such mirth Myriah regarded herself, glanced at Billy, advised him that she didn't see anything funny about it, and herself burst out laughing.

Lord Wimborne re-evaluated the situation, and finding that he had made a cake of himself, began chuckling. Soon all three were howling and shedding tears of laughter.

Dinner was served in Billy's room with Myriah and Kit seated across from one another beside Billy's bed.

"M'lord . . ." said Tabby knocking on the open door. "M'lord, Fletcher sent me to fetch ye real quick. There be a riding officer . . . a corporal at the stables, and he means to come 'ave a word with Master William."

"What?" shrieked Myriah.

"I was afraid of this. It seems he was able to think clearly once he got away from your pretty face, Miss White," said his lordship with a frown. "Very well, I'll handle him. Keep him below. I shall be down presently."

"My lord, Billy will have to show his face. If we hurry, perhaps we can pass through the thing creditably," said Myriah, an idea flashing through her head as she rushed back to her room to fetch the dressing gown she had discarded when she had once again donned her blue silk.

She returned to find both men staring at her speculatively. "We will put him in the brocade gown . . . over his nightdress . . . his legs, thank God, are in good working order and with any luck, the wound will not open."

"My dear girl, if Billy attempts to take those stairs, there is every good chance that the wound *will* open up and *that* is precisely what our hungry exciseman is looking for!" snapped his lordship.

"But Billy will not take the stairs. He will stand at its height and haughtily request to be told why he needs be disturbed from his bath!"

"Splendid!" declared Billy. " 'Tis just what I shall do! Stoopid fellows . . . did they think they had me boxed in!"

Lord Wimborne's eyes narrowed, but he had already picked up the robe and was assisting his young brother into its folds. Billy winced for his arm was stiff and bending it into the sleeve sent excruciating pains through the limb. Kit stopped and eyed him anxiously, "It was bad, eh, lad?"

"Stuff!" retorted Billy.

His lordship helped him to his feet and with a steadying hand left him to Myriah. She clucked her tongue for he was white with pain, and she looked worriedly at his arm. They waited at the doorway . . . listening to Lord Wimborne slashing at the exciseman below . . . waiting for the right moment to make their appearance.

"May I ask why my brother must be summoned . . . or do you landsmen make it a practice to deal with your betters in such a manner?" said his lordship cuttingly.

The young military man blushed the color of his red coat, for although everyone knew the Wimbornes were dished . . . without a sou to their name . . . they still had their name and in Sussex 'twas a weighty one.

"I am extremely sorry, my lord . . . but as the matter is of the gravest nature . . . and one of our men felt he recognized your brother as the man we were shooting at . . ."

"My cousin has already told you that Mr. Wimborne's hat was in her possession, and therefore he could not have dropped it the other night."

"Yes, my lord," interjected the landsman, "and I do not doubt her. However, your brother must show himself, if only to clear his good name, for the man we pursued *was* hit . . . and badly!"

"I, sir?" said a proud young man from the top of the stairs. "I have no need to *clear my name* . . . 'twas never in question! I find your statements to his lordship most insulting and have every intention of making a report to your superiors."

Kit's blue eyes twinkled as he watched Billy above him. Myriah caught the look, and her own danced in time.

"Oh, cousin Billy . . . I am sure the good officer meant you no harm." She cast the suffering man a look of gentle understanding. "He was after all only doing his duty."

Corporal Stone shot her a grateful look and, finding that Billy Wimborne was all in one piece, made a silent oath to have the heads of his men for this. They had sworn up and down that they had seen young Billy's face in the moonlight. Humph! Billy Wimborne in the company of smugglers! Indeed!

"I am very sorry to have troubled you and shall do so no longer," said the man, making his bows.

The double doors were closed behind him; three pair of eyes lit with triumph, and after a careful moment the halls of Wimborne Towers reverberated with the sound of laughter!

* * *

The excursion had tired Billy more than they had at first realized, and when he was at last returned to his bed, he closed his eyes, thoroughly exhausted. Myriah and Lord Wimborne left him sleeping and retired below-stairs to the library where a fire was still dimly burning. Lord Wimborne positioned another log on the fire, dusted his hands against one another, and turned a warm smile upon Myriah. They had scraped through a very sticky business, and he was disposed to feel a bit friendlier towards her.

She looked stunning in her peacock blue and in the firelight her curls glittered temptingly . . . urging him to touch . . . and it dawned on him that if she was but a maid, as she claimed she was, then 'twasn't right for them to be alone like this! He was not the sort that ruined innocent females . . . and she had done him a service—he must keep that in mind!

Myriah eyed him, feeling strangely missish. "You are suddenly very quiet."

He smiled ruefully. "Was I? I was thinking that . . . you shouldn't be here. I wouldn't want it said that . . ."

"No one knows I am here!" she said, hurriedly interrupting him, afraid he would send her away, and desperately wanting to stay.

He smiled sadly, "Is he so very perfidious . . . this man . . . the one you have run away from?"

"Sir Ro . . . I mean . . . well . . . never mind his name! To answer your question, no, he is not. In fact he is probably any maid's dream. He is handsome, strong, amusing . . ."

"A veritable god!" snapped his lordship, "It staggers the mind, my girl, why you have balked!"

"But my lord . . . I am not in love with him," answered Myriah wide-eyed.

"Ah! So it seems you don't give over without the questionable emotion," teased Kit, his eyes taking on merriment.

"Certainly not!" retorted Myriah. "Would you?"

He chuckled. "As you see . . . I am still a bachelor, my girl."

"So you have never fallen in love?"

"Luckily I have escaped the plaguey thing."

"But . . . but you must be . . . how old *are* you?" said Myriah.

"Seven and twenty this past March," responded Kit flicking her nose. "And you, sweetings?"

"I shall be one and twenty in a month's time."

"Ah! A veritable old maid!"

"Odious creature!"

"Tut, tut! Name calling, my dear, is not nice!" admonished her companion playfully.

"Then do not call me 'sweetings'! My name is Myriah."

"Myriah . . ." he said slowly, looking her over, "your name suits you well . . . for if memory serves me, it means *pernicious!*"

"Oh! Wretch! Pernicious indeed! Your memory does not serve you, my lord, for it means no such thing! It is a biblical name . . . though I do spell it differently, and it means spirited!" She sighed and moved away from him, but the sadness in her voice was not lost to him. "Mama had the naming of me . . . she nearly died giving me birth for I came early . . . she said I was just a slip of an infant, and my fighting for life at birth won me the name Myriah. But papa would have it that Myriah was what he always called mama . . . and because I was her image, he claimed he had the naming of me."

"And from that moment on, of course, you have tried to live up to your name?" teased his lordship.

"I have never had to try!" she sighed heavily. " 'Tis no pleasant thing to have the blood of a runner and be made to walk! I am forever being told, 'No, Myriah.' 'It would not do, Myriah.' 'Don't, Myriah.' Faith, you can have no notion what it is to be able to fly . . . and be forbidden the use of your wings!"

He read the pain in her face, and it brought a frown to Kit's dark eyebrows. "Your parents are no longer pleased with your spirit?"

"My parents? Oh, papa . . . well, he is a man, and to be fair, he is really good about most things. He says I am mama . . . all over again . . . and that pleases him. But he has sisters, many sisters—and they don't see it quite in the same light! He has to deal with them, and it isn't always easy. How could it not affect him?" She sighed again and played with her fingers. "It was different when I had mama! She always understood. She said it was like watching herself growing up. How we laughed together . . ." her voice trailed off, and her heart rediscovered a scene long ago.

Kit felt rough fingers work at his heart. "When did you lose her, Myriah?"

"Five years ago. I came home from school to find her with fever. She died shortly after. She had never before been low or ill. Papa was in shock for such a long time . . . but he and I are friends. Papa says I am mama in every way. But he is wrong. She was contented, so sweetly contented . . . and I no longer am!"

Myriah had never before spoken to anyone about this. She did not now understand why so much had flowed so freely. She only knew that she had let down her guard before this man—who was virtually a stranger.

"Poor Myriah . . . but it is not Myriah *White from Dover* . . . now is it?" asked Kit because he had an urging to hear the truth from *her* lips. He had a need to trust her completely . . . to have the lie dispelled.

Myriah's guard was up. Why did he harp on that single point? What was he after, confound him! She couldn't tell him who she was . . . she didn't want him to know she was an heiress . . . a lady—not when it was so obvious *he* was in need of money! She had begun a lie to spare her name from gossip; she was continuing it for altogether different reasons.

"I . . . I don't know what you mean," said Myriah.

He was at her side, pulling her up to him by her delicate shoulders. His blue eyes smouldered above her own. "Don't you know that you have not learned the knack of it, Myriah? Your eyes . . . your cheeks . . . they give you away! You shouldn't lie . . . unless you can!"

"Why . . . my lord," she said coyly, thrilling beneath his touch, "just this afternoon you declared I lied very well—when it served you!"

Suddenly she was tight in his arms and his kiss was burning her mouth with its intensity. Her body felt numb, helpless to extinguish the fire flashing through her limbs. Her response was as natural as it was spontaneous, for she had wanted this moment . . . wanted it with all her heart. Her arms wrapped round his neck as she returned his kiss, surprised by her own passion, pleased with his—and the thought tickled her mind that perhaps *here was love!*

Should she love him? How could she love him? He was a stranger . . . a handsome one, to be sure . . . but still a stranger! The wonder of her discovery made her pull away. She wanted to gaze into his eyes, she wanted to see there a reflection of her own emotion.

His lordship had taken her in his arms because he burned, and burning, could not stop himself. He too was surprised by *her* response . . . so quick and as intense as his own. She played no teasing game . . . she gave openly, beautifully, and yet he knew she had lied. It dawned on him that she was no inexperienced miss, delicately bred; but perhaps the adventuress he had thought her—running, not from a would-be husband . . . no . . . *she was running from a lover!* For some obscure and detached irrationality, this notion had a stinging effect. The hard, sardonic veil it brought to his eyes, was not belied by his husky voice and seductive arms. Myriah saw and seeing made her tremble with the frost. He drew her to him again, "No, sweetings . . . you are no *maiden miss.* I have never come across one who could *kiss as you do!* There now, my pretty bird," he said, tightening his hold and looking at her delectable mouth, "your body craves more . . . as mine does." His lips sought hers again but his kiss was hard, and its force was almost bitter.

If he had felt stung by *his* flight of mind, she felt betrayed by the masque of harsh reality. Pain comes in many forms, and the sort that leaves no mark can be just as agonizing as those that do! How does one describe the invisible? That which cannot be seen, but is felt in all its intangible powers upon the frail human flesh. Myriah did indeed feel the dull knife, slowly, laboriously cutting a circle round her heart! It left her nerves damaged and bleeding, but also it left them so that the heart was able to communicate its pain to her brain, and her brain . . . it came to her defense!

She yanked away from his embrace, acutely aware that her openness of feeling had put her in such a position. *Faith . . . he thinks me a doxy! Foolish Myriah . . . he offers you passion and you take it for love!* But . . . his kiss . . . was it not more? Her mind berated her once again, taunting with its logic . . . *his kiss was a lie,* Myriah.

Tears glistened in her eyes, for not all the London bucks and not all the London sophistication could erase the sensitivity of her heart. She paled and her hand shook as she raised it to hide the emotion on her face, and she was turning to run!

He frowned, surprised by the childlike hurt on her countenance and his hand reached out and took hold of her arm. She was trembling and Lord Wimborne was obliged to wonder at it. "Lord, child, it matters not to me. We shall forget your past . . . you have left your lover and I am most willing to . . . protect you against him . . . and others! Come, sweetings, come . . ." he said soothingly, running his left hand round her waist.

Myriah choked on the sob she had been trying to smother, and one delicate white hand slammed hard across his cheek, bringing him out of his heat, before she sped from the room.

For the second time that day, Lord Wimborne's blue eyes followed Myriah's retreating form, but this time he no longer wanted to be rid of her!

Nine

Myriah's hot-tempered head was lost in the blackness of uncertainty and the heretofore untraveled valley of ironic despair! She found herself totally, irrevocably, and most painfully in love. Love—it promises much and certainly should give it—and yet very often throws its victims into the whirlwind of conflicting sensations!

Myriah arrived at her room and slammed the door hard behind her. She cast her eyes desperately around as if searching for an escape from her acutely uncomfortable condition. The uncovered terrace doors showed the stars twinkling in the smooth blackness of the night, and the tears on Myriah's cheeks glistened in sad response to their greeting.

Oh, Myriah, thought she miserably, now you've gone and tipped yourself a settler! You search about for a gallant with the magic to win your heart and when you find him, he turns out to be a penniless and secretive lord . . . who sees through your little disguise! Oh, yes, *Miss White*, you have not made the mark and are not to be believed. Ah . . . but *Miss Fancy Piece* . . . that he believes quite well! You pour your heart out to him and he throws it to the seas . . . and why? Because he smells a lie . . . and . . . and because he thought you a bit lax in your morals, my girl! After all, you *did* return his kiss, did you not? That is not how the thing is done, you know! Oh, no! You should have batted your lashes and cried, "Oh, no!" You should have fluttered . . . or anything rather than what you did, for clearly now it appears there is something to what Aunt Emily is forever croaking!

The more she dwelt on the absurdity of her dilemma, the more wretched she felt. To confess her identity now would most assuredly deliver him to a sense of what *she,* as Lady Myriah of the Whitney line, was due. But—she wanted his respect, admiration, and his love in blind faith. She wanted him to love her spirit . . . her soul . . . *not her name* . . . and never . . . NEVER *her money!*

A good while was spent in unhappy thoughts and self-pity. However, Myriah was made of staunch and steady stuff, and she soon addressed herself to the problem at hand. What she needed was a plan! Yes, a plan of action was all that was needed to bring his lordship to his heart. Ah, solutions come quickly to an active mind and several presented themselves to the lady. Much of the night was spent in laying out her strategy and sorting out any fancies that were not employable. At last satisfied, her heart ceased its palpitations, pleased with the mind for its cleverness, and both organs allowed the human to sleep— and to dream.

Lord Wimborne by nature was a merry, pleasant young man. Six years in service of his King and Prince Regent, fighting the Frogs in the Pyrenees, had taught him many things. One of the very first notions that settled in his ordered intellect was that the fair and lovely sex was to be prized; adored, and rarely trusted! He had his share of youthful romances with their accompanying pangs and inevitable flights and, in truth, enjoyed them all. Though he was still a bachelor and had not planned on changing his comfortable state in the foreseeable future, he had

always felt he would one day take a wife. A special creature she would be, with the honesty her sex lacked, with
the beauty of love and innocence in her soul as well as
in her form. He wanted no coquette, no fluttering, fainting
wench. No! His dream bride was perfect in every way—
as are most dreams!

His mother, who survived his father's death by many
years, had been all a mother could be, and her sons
had grown whole and healthy. They had lost her two
years ago, while Kit was in Spain in the midst of battle.
His brother Billy had still been at Oxford where he stayed
on until Kit returned home. That was just over a year
ago. Lord Wimborne, a major in his regiment, had sold
out and come home to take up the management of his
estates. He found them in miserable condition, simply
because there had been no one about to attend to them.

A heaviness hung about his lordship, for there would
be no picking up his regimentals and rejoining in the
near future. The Towers needed him. And then, shortly
thereafter, he found yet another activity to keep him
occupied.

Billy finished his term and joined Kit at the Towers,
and it was not long before the young man had embroiled
himself in his brother's strange activities!

The emergence of Miss Myriah White on his plane had
chained the dance in Kit's blue eyes and kept him wary.
He mounted the wide stairs to the second floor and moved
down the corridor, stopping briefly before the door he
had—until just yesterday—called his own.

A troubled expression ruled his countenance, and he
went to the doorknob, stopped, growled in frustration,
and continued down the hall to the chamber that had been
prepared for his use. Fiend seize the chit! he thought.
Lord, but she was a puzzle. *Miss White*, indeed! It didn't
ring true! Whenever she spoke about herself he had the
sensation that she was mentally expunging bits that would

prove contrary to the *facts* she would have him believe!
A bevy of subtle contradictions hung about Myriah. He
ran his hand through the honey-colored waves of his
hair; for one thing—her horse . . . that stallion was no
less than five hundred guineas . . . and this suggested that
Myriah was well provided for. Therefore, why would a
doting father—and he was such, both by her description
and her possession of such an animal—force her to marry
a man she had no liking for? Surely not for financial gain.
Oh, no. Her clothing, her confidence, all spoke of a
sophisticated London Season—she must have had her
pick! Then why? It just didn't make sense.

Then there was his unreasonable agitation regarding
her laxity over the proprieties. Now he considered himself
a rather broad-minded fellow . . . and indeed he was . . .
yet he had still the vision of Myriah on his brother's
hearthrug! Granted, Billy behaved as though she were
some sort of school friend . . . but *that* was no excuse
for *her* lapse in conduct! Where had she got such easy
manners? She seemed not to care for the world's opinion.
And then . . . he had taken her into his arms . . . and
what did she do? Good Lord! For a young, inexperienced
maid who had every reason to hold her host in disgust
for his purposely rude behavior until and including that
moment, Myriah's response was prodigiously friendly.
While as an aggressive male, he found this as enjoyable
as he did stimulating, he also found it somehow disconcerting. The immediate question arose: where did she
learn to kiss like that?

From this point, inevitably, a pinching fancy took him.
Perhaps the lady was no lady! Perhaps she was a fashionable London courtesan, escaping from an irate lover—and
this thought made him edgy!

Yet, everything that came to mind afterwards served
to convince him that this was a very good possibility.
Hadn't Harriette Wilson and her fashionable sisters left
their father's shop in Mayfair and set themselves up as

the most fashionable courtesans in all of London? Why—
'twas all the crack to be seen with them at the opera . . .
or in their lodgings. There they were . . . daughters of
a mere cit . . . a shopkeeper. Yet they put a high price on
their head, and even Wellington himself considered it
'the thing' to be seen in their company!

Well, Myriah's sauciness was very much like their own.
They too thought little of displaying open manners in
gentlemen's company! Following this trend of thought
confirmed his notion that Myriah might very well be
avoiding a discarded lover—and this answer, far from
satisfying his curiosity—frosted his heart!

Are you a fool? he asked of himself with asperity. Are
you falling in love with a fashionable courtesan? Oh, God!
Was the female of his heart one who had learned passion
from another?

The heart does strange things to its companion, the
mind. It sends it messages of need . . . needs the mind
cannot supply and lacking an answer, the mind retaliates
on its poor friend. The sad victim of such horrendous
goings-on is offered much violence and has but one outlet
—sleep. It comes even in the midst of such battles, and
it ends when the organs in question discover there is one
more thing that must be said to pay back the human that
cares for them with bitter nightmares!

Myriah awoke early. The sun was hiding its Spring
glory behind clouds of white foam and only an unrelenting
glare met Myriah's searching eyes. With a sigh, she
washed, and dressed in the ivory silk she had brought.
It was a beautiful creation, scooped at the neck with a
narrow flounce of ivory lace as its trim. The high waist
was banded with brown velvet as were the sleeves at her
elbows, from which layers of lace belled out. The pattern
of brown banding and lace was repeated at the knees and
the lace dropped in graceful layers to her ankles. She
brushed her long red hair into shining billows which she
caught at the top of her head with a ribbon. The curls

cascaded about her elflike countenance creating the mischievous mystery that was Myriah!

She pulled on her boots of brown kid and hurried downstairs. She had an errand to discharge and wanted to do so before Lord Wimborne was about. Myriah closed the library door behind her and rushed across to the writing desk. The quill was dipped into the ink and a hasty note composed and then sealed in a plain white envelope.

A moment later Myriah was crossing the drive and making for the stables. It was a marvelous Spring day, in spite of the fact that the sun had clothed itself in froth. The sweet morning breeze enveloped Myriah, greeting her as one of nature's treasures, and she was conscious of its soothing effect.

It was past eight and Myriah glanced back at the house worriedly. She did not want to be seen just yet! Tabby was walking his roan out of the stables, and Myriah put up her hand to call his attention. He awaited her approach, wondering what new fetch his mistress had dreamed up this time!

"Good-morning, Tabby," she said, coming up to face him and handing him the white envelope.

He looked down at it and then at her, "I dessay this be for yer grandfather," he said, his face expressionless.

"Yes, Tabby . . . for he will have had a visit from father by now, and I don't want him worrying about me. However, you will not give it to him in person, for you know as well as I that you would then be forced to give him my whereabouts—and I don't want to be found just yet!"

"Now, Lady Myriah, 'tis time ye went home and faced . . ."

"Tabby, you will hand this note to the gatekeeper and have him take it to grandpapa, and then you will come straight back here!" she said firmly.

"Yes, m'lady."

"Oh, Tabby, don't pull a face. It will all turn out just

fine . . . you'll see. Now . . . have you eaten?"

"Yes, m'lady." Clearly he was put out with her, for he was sure her father would be fretting by now.

"Very well. Then you had better leave at once if you are to be back by lunch," ordered Myriah, giving him her back and making for the house.

Kit Wimborne watched as Myriah returned hastily to his house, and his blue eyes were not smiling! He had seen her put an envelope into her servant's hand. He had watched them exchanging words . . . and he saw Tabson ride off on his roan. What was the chit up to? What had she given her groom . . . and where was he going?

It suddenly dawned on him that Miss Myriah White, innocent miss or seductive courtesan, might have a purpose all her own for being at Wimborne Towers. Was her presence here because of *his* activities in Romney Marsh? Was Myriah White . . . an *informer?*

Myriah followed the young serving boy upstairs and opened the door to Billy Wimborne's room allowing the lad to enter. The heavily laden tray was placed on the stainwood table beside Billy's bed, and the boy scurried off.

Myriah pulled open the drapes, and light flooded the room, causing Billy to shield his eyes with his good hand. His eyes fluttered open and discovered Myriah. "Oh God!" he groaned.

"Good morning, Mr. Wimborne. Never say you do not want your breakfast." said Myriah, lifting a silver cover off a plate filled with eggs and ham.

"Leave it and begone, she-devil! Faith, why must you blast at me early in the morning! Let there be light, sayeth Myriah, and there is light. Let there be food, continueth the she-devil, and there is food."

"Let there be silence . . . or thou shalt feel the rod!" said Myriah.

They laughed in unison and Myriah brought him the

basin of wash water, placing it on the bed and spraying it with her fingertips into his face. "Let there be cleanliness . . . and quick, before your food gets cold."

He washed, wincing with the movements, and Myriah looked at his bandaged arm. The circle of brownish dried blood looked as though it had crept into new areas, and Myriah bent over it, touching it gently.

"Billy, I think you must have bled a bit more last night," she said and the frown was in her eyes.

"No doubt, with all the prodding and pulling you and m'brother had at me," he agreed, grinning at her.

"Stop dazzling me with your teeth! Seriously, Billy, you had better stay in bed today . . . and try not to move."

"What I need is my shirtsleeve sewn back on!" retorted Mr. Wimborne, "Ain't proper for you to be continually gazing on my bare arm. Might give you evil notions . . ." He looked up to find his brother's twinkling eyes upon him. "The sort Kit here has," said Billy, enjoying Lord Wimborne's discomfiture.

"Careful, brat," warned his brother.

Billy chuckled and watched with interest as both Myriah and Kit went to an extraordinary amount of trouble to display to one another their total lack of interest . . . in each other!

"I trust you slept well, Miss White," said his lordship idly, taking the cup of coffee she handed him.

"As well as could be expected," she returned, sipping her coffee.

"It appears your groom has . . . errands . . . elsewhere this morning," said Lord Wimborne blandly, his eyes intent on her face.

"Does it? How . . . observant of you," replied Myriah.

"I am accounted such, thank you, Miss White," returned Kit.

"Oh, pray do not thank me. It was not meant as a compliment," responded the lady sweetly.

"Ho!" cried Billy much amused, "don't bandy words

with the she-devil, Kit . . . you don't stand a chance."

"No, it seems not, brat. Your she-devil is quite full of words."

"Touché!" declared Billy impressed, "that was very good, Kit!"

"I am surprised you doubted me, lad," said his brother glibly.

Myriah took a huge bite of Billy's strawberry tart, concealing the fact that another tart lay hidden beneath its silver cover.

"Hold there, titan!" shouted Billy, noting the pilferage.

"It would serve you right, odious boy that you are, if I ate the entire thing! And so I shall," threatened Myriah.

"You do and you'll put on five pounds, wench!" returned Billy, reaching out for the tart with his free hand and getting it . . . full in the hand! He proceeded to busy himself with licking his fingers and giving them a panegyric on the foibles of females. Myriah presented him with the remaining tart and sat back in her chair to enjoy herself.

Lord Wimborne having observed the raucous scene was hard put to keep from declaring the girl a magnificent woman worthy of his heart! Surely she really did care about Billy; and her innocent play with him was, in fact, innocence in play. Yet the contradictions were there . . . and the white envelope . . . and the disappearing groom!

He left them abruptly, saying there were matters that needed his attention, and Myriah and Billy looked at each other.

"Had a turn-up with m'brother, eh?" said Billy curiously.

"Hush, slug-a-bed, and eat," said Myriah.

"Slug-a-bed!" ejaculated the affronted Billy. "Devil you say . . . 'tis you that has made me so!"

Ten

Two men stood with their backs to an elegantly furnished drawing room and stared into an unlit fireplace. There was little to say . . . too much had already been said. The two pairs of blue eyes continued to stare unseeingly until a knock sounded on the double mahogany doors.

A serving boy carrying a luncheon tray entered and began setting the covered plates on a stainwood table situated in a bay window overlooking the lawns of Guildford House.

"Lawrence," said Lord Whitney gently, "come, they have sent in the collation you requested. Let us eat together." He had respected and loved his father-in-law for too many years to allow a few bitter words to fester between them.

Lord Guildford ran a hand through his white-and-yellow locks and sighed heavily. He said nothing, but his expression told his son-in-law he felt much the same. They sat down facing one another and began picking at their food.

"Don't understand Myriah all the time," said her father sadly. "Sometimes I think I've got her way of thinking, and then she is off surprising me. That's the way it was, Lawrence. Never really thought that she held Sir Roland in aversion. Lord . . . how could I? She was in his arms . . . kissing the fellow . . . as though she had her heart in it."

"Why wouldn't she marry him if she had her heart in it, Whitney?" grumbled Lord Guildford. "Never knew her not to take what she wanted."

"That's the thing that has me baffled. Thought at the moment she was just being perverse because I forced her hand. But she balked! . . . ran away. I was so certain she was on her way here . . . to you . . . that I didn't bother coming after her until the next morning." He shook his head sadly. "Thought we got along . . . thought she could come to me . . . and if not to me . . . then to you."

"Well, if that don't beat all!" said her grandfather, losing his temper again. "How the devil could she come to you? You told me yourself you were in a rage and determined to make the announcement right there and then."

"Now, now, Lawrence . . . I mean she did kiss Roland. I couldn't know she would kiss someone she didn't want to marry."

"Confound the dratted fellow. She can't be expected to make proper comparisons if she don't kiss a fellow now and then!" said Lord Guildford, defending his granddaughter.

The younger man opened his eyes wide but refrained from pointing out to his father-in-law that as a grandfather he seemed to hold far different opinions from those he had had as a father! "Well . . . the point is . . . why, then, didn't she come here to you? Always did whenever she was in a pucker."

"It's clear to me . . . ain't it clear to you?" grumbled Lord Guildford.

"No, it ain't! Very little of what Myriah does these days is clear to me."

"Well, she didn't want this confounded scalawag, Roland. Can't say as I blame her, for he should not have allowed you to bully her into such a position. But that don't signify. Since Myriah can take care of herself, she don't need defending by the likes of him."

"Lawrence . . ." said the other man.

"Hold! I'm coming to the thing. Now, there she is, on her way to me with Tabby right behind . . . and 'whoops!' she thinks. 'If I go to my grandfather, papa will follow and there'll be a row over me. Can't have that,' says Myriah to herself. She changes her plan . . . goes somewhere else!" said his lordship, solving the problem.

"Thank God, Tabby is with her, for he'll see no harm comes to her. But even if what you say is true, and she decided to descend upon someone else . . . *where* is what I want to know."

Lord Guildford threw down his fork and put his hands into each other leaning heavily upon his elbows. His mind sought other times . . . happier times. He had survived the death of a wife he had adored, only to be struck a few years later with the death of his only child, Myriah's mother. His losses had made him a recluse, for he preferred to remain at Guildford House where he could be comfortable, away from society. There was only one who had been able to coax him out of his quiet, protective shell, forcing him to go riding . . . forcing him to Brighton . . . even to London—Myriah! She was the image of her mother and her grandmother before her. She was his sole interest, his joy, his only grandchild! How often he had smiled with pleasure to see her riding up his drive! His heart full with the knowledge that she adored him. How she would tease him, "Do let us go out, grandpapa, best of my beaux. Come, grandpapa, the London bucks are nought to you . . . come with me to London."

As he remembered her last visit, a guilty pang swept

over him. He had noticed she was listless, he had seen the sadness in her eyes, and had somehow felt unable to help her quiet desperation. She always confided everything to him . . . and he could not remember her mentioning anyone with whom she had grown close in the last two years. Indeed, hadn't she said that she had lost all her best friends to marriage?

"There is no one to whom she could have gone. I know of no one," said Myriah's grandfather in a low voice.

"There must be *someone* . . . and Tabby is with her." supplied Myriah's papa.

Rother River wound its gentle path through the meadowlands, and as Tabby cut along the river road past sheep munching contentedly on the sweet grass, his eyes glimmered with the savory memory of scenes long past. Northiam lay just ten or so miles northwest of Rye village, and he was nearly there. The road, the staggered trees, and patchwork fields were a part of everything he loved.

He had been fifteen and half-starved when he came to Guildford House so long ago. Lord Guildford hadn't asked for papers, he hadn't asked what he could do. He simply led him to the kitchens and had him fed and gave instructions to place him in the hands of the head groom.

He eyed the countryside. How many times had he ridden over it trying to keep up with Myriah's mother! Lord! In those days she was every bit as wild and lovely as her daughter. He had first laid eyes on her when he went into the training field looking for the head groom. All at once he heard a young woman shout at him to run, and he turned and saw her . . . red hair flying . . . running across the field in breeches and yelling for him to jump the fence. But there wasn't time . . . that big black snorting wild thing had beat at the ground, furious at the intruder, and he could see the devil in the red glint of the animal's eyes. Then all at once *she* was there, calming the beast so that it fondled her, transformed from blood and fire into the gentlest of nature's creatures. 'Twas at that moment he lost his heart!

Well—that was long, long ago, and *she* was gone. Yet . . . there she was in Myriah! He would always serve the daughter just as he had her mother. 'Twasn't right to allow Lord Guildford and her father to fret. But, he'd not disobey her. 'Twas her will, and 'twas his to obey!

He approached the hamlet of Northiam, turning off the narrow road onto another just before he reached the edge of town. He steadied his horse and stood in the stirrups to stretch his short legs. He could see the rolling green lawns and the rows of rhododendron trees with their huge buds just beginning to hint at the deep purple beauties they would become. He loved the Guildford estates, he always would. Longing to ride up its front drive, he put his desires aside and stopped at the thatched-covered white gatehouse. He slipped off his roan. "Heigh-ho . . . be you a-sleeping, you old dog!" cried Tabby, excited at the prospect of visiting with an old friend.

An elderly gray-haired man with rounded shoulders and wearing woolens came hobbling out of the door. His face lit up with pleasure: "Tab . . . Tab . . . yah devil! Rogue that you are . . . I disremember being more pleased to see yah. Jest let me look at yah!"

Tabby laughed and they held each other by the shoulders a moment, for much of their youth had been spent in each other's company.

"Come . . . come . . . I've got coffee on . . ." said the gatekeeper, leading the way into his two-roomed cottage. "Lord Whitney . . . he be here . . . heard tell there be strange things afoot . . . and they had words, they did! Heard tell 'twas over our lady!" said the gatekeeper, frowning.

Tabby frowned and squinted his small eyes. "Afraid

that would happen. Well, I dessay it'll mend. Got a note you needs be taking to his lordship . . . but I can't wait for no answer . . . and as it happens, I best be going now afore I gets seen."

"Eh . . . so that's the lay of it. Got herself into deep doings," said the elderly man wisely.

"That she has and she don't listen no better now than she ever did," grumbled Tabby.

"Have a bit of coffee before ye leaves . . . I'll put a ball of fire in it fer ye, Tab . . . jest the way ye likes it."

Tabby glanced out the window before consenting. It was another ten minutes before he was outside and mounting his horse, and so occupied was he in his leave-taking of the gatekeeper, that neither one noticed the lone rider keeping his horse just a short distance down the road.

Sir Roland had agreed with Lord Whitney that under the circumstances no announcement of his engagement to Myriah could be made at the ball, since she was not to be found. In deep thought and somewhat put out, he returned to his own lodgings wondering where she had gone off to at that time of night.

Her father set out the next morning for Lord Guildford, for he was certain his daughter had run to her grandfather. But before he left he had a visit from Sir Roland.

"Why, my lord, do you believe she would undertake such a journey at that time of night? Why not assume she has simply gone to a friend here in London?" asked Sir Roland, eying him speculatively.

"Because she ain't overfond of scandal, my boy! It would be all over town in a trice if she were so unwise as to do so foolish a thing. Myriah may be headstrong . . . but she ain't cotton-headed!"

Sir Roland was in accord regarding this, and it was

agreed that he would follow him to Lord Guildford's family estate in Northiam on the morrow. Sir Roland was out of temper, for he was being dunned daily. Myriah would have to be his—and soon! He fully intended to use any means that presented itself in order to achieve this end and gave Whitney reason to believe that his daughter would come round in the end.

As Sir Roland approached the Guildford grounds, he spied Tabson deep in conversation with the gatekeeper who held an envelope in his weathered hand. Roland's sharp eyes flickered for he recognized Myriah's groom, and a sixth sense urged him to halt his horse and watch. Tabby moved his horse south, and Sir Roland waited until he was out of sight before approaching the gate-keeper.

"You, there!" commanded Sir Roland imperiously. "Open the gates. I am Sir Roland and believe I am expected."

"Yes, sir. That you are . . . their lordships been waiting on you," said the man unlocking the gate.

Again Sir Roland's extra sense worked, "Of course, but tell me is Lady Myriah here?"

"No, no, she ain't here . . . nor has she been," frowned the gatekeeper. "Now come along . . . sir . . . for I've got to go up to the house and . . ." said the gatekeeper catching himself short and watching round-eyed as Sir Roland urged his horse into a canter in pursuit of Myriah's groom.

He paced his horse carefully, keeping the curves of the road between him and his quarry. He was certain the groom would lead him to Myriah. Perhaps then his goal would be achieved. It was beginning to be an obsession with him. Sir Roland's brow went up as he followed Tabby onto the river road . . . for it led to Rye. What would she be doing in Rye? Why, 'twas nothing but a small harbor town, and he knew of no one she could be visiting in

Rye. "Good Lord, Myriah . . . what would you want in Rye?" he said to himself with no little exasperation.

A strange sensation tickled the nape of Tabby's neck as he moved his horse along the river road. He couldn't shake the uneasy feeling that he was being followed. "Whist, who would be at your back, you old fool?" he asked himself looking round uncertainly. However, as time progressed, Tabby found himself sure, without the least bit of fact to sustain his suspicion, that someone was indeed following him. "Hang me if I can't lose the devil!" spat Tabby at the air. The river was now hidden by a deep wooded patch on one side, while grasslands stretched out on the other. He walked his horse close to the trees, stopping him and then suddenly breaking out into a spanking pace. 'Twas to no avail, for the tickle at his neck remained—yet he could see no one at his back.

A narrow path from the roadway into the heart of the woods caught Tabby's squinting eyes, and with sudden determination he sent his horse careening into the woods. Before long they were lost to sight, and breathlessly Tabby backtracked parallel to the road some two hundred yards and waited. At last he was rewarded for the sound of a horse's snort met his ears!

Cautiously Tabby wound his horse through the pathless thicket until he caught sight of a man astride a bay, and Tabby whistled low to himself. "So that be the way of it . . . the flashcove be after m'lady!" Tabby put on a superior sneer, "Follow *me* will ye! Humph! Allright then, covey . . . so be it!" As quickly as he could, he headed south once again, cutting through the thick of the woods and re-appearing on the road just in time to give Sir Roland the sight of his back.

Sir Roland slowed his pace and wondered what the deuce the groom had to do in the bushes . . . and then thought perhaps 'twas nature's call and continued his steady tracking.

Soon the woods and the grazing sheep were left behind and the dark green bay was visible. Tabby grinned to himself as he led his hunter into Rye Village! The conical towers of the Land Gate arched above the road was passed through and then suddenly Tabby was no more.

Sir Roland stopped some feet away from the Land Gate and pondered the problem of which street to take. Deciding to make for the center of town he headed for High Street. For the next twenty minutes Sir Roland attempted to catch sight of Myriah's groom and met with failure. Tabby had totally disappeared, swallowed whole, horse and all, by the air.

With a resigned sigh, Sir Roland looked up to find himself before the stableyard of the Mermaid Inn, and with a distempered oath called an ostler to care for his horse.

Tabby had slid off his horse and turned down a narrow walkway, leading his horse by the reins. At last they reached Fisherman's Wharf from where he backtracked once again. He cut through the marshes gingerly, before remounting his steed, sure in the knowledge that Sir Roland was no longer with him. With a grunt of satisfaction he hurried to Wimborne Towers, his chest puffed out with pride, and his mind eager to relay his deed to his mistress.

Wimborne loomed up before him and he hurried his weary horse to the stables. Slipping off the animal's back, he handed the reins to Fletcher who had come out to greet him.

" 'Ere Fletcher . . . I'd be that obliged if ye would take care of the love for me . . . I've got to go see m'la . . . m'mistress," said Tabby, out of breath.

"Aye, that aw will, but it queers me what ye be aboot," said Fletcher, pulling at his beard thoughtfully.

Tabby didn't stay to explain but hobbled as fast as his

weathered limbs would take him and pulled at the
knocker. A moment later Lord Wimborne appeared,
opened the door wide, and raised a brow inquiringly.

Tabby fidgeted with his woolen hat and looked uncomfortable. " 'Tis Mistress . . . I be needing a word
with her if ye please, m'lord."

"Of course, Tabson," said Lord Wimborne, noting the
man's state of excitement. "I will go and . . ."

"No need," said Myriah from the top of the stairs.
"Tabby . . . I am coming right down." Myriah skipped
lightly down the stairs, her skirt in her hand. She dismissed his lordship with a look, but he had the poor
manners to ignore her meaning and remained standing
interestedly by.

Myriah pulled a haughty face and turned to Tabby
who was still trying to catch his breath. "Come, Tabby,
we can be *private* outdoors . . . and I need the walk," she
said, leading the way.

They walked towards the rear of the house, making a
wide circle round the overgrown bushes that lined its
stone walls. "Whatever has you frenzied, Tab?" asked
Myriah, surprised.

"I gave the note to Old Tim . . . like you wanted me to
. . . though it be just like I told ye it would. Yer papa
and grandpa had a set-to."

"Oh, dear . . ."

"But that not be what 'as me worked up, m'lady . . .
'tis that man . . . the one you be so set on jilting . . ."

"I am not jilting him, Tabby!" objected Myriah. "How
could I be when I have not accepted him?"

"As to that I ain't one to know . . . not being in the
petticoat line meself . . . but the cull tried following me,
he did!" said Tabby portentously.

"What?" shrieked Myriah.

"Never you fret none, m'lady . . . I twigged the covey's
rig, I did!" said Tabby, dropping into street vernacular,
"Lost him in Rye!" The glow in his leathery cheeks told

Myriah how proud Tabson was of himself for such a feat and, though she was worried by Sir Roland's proximity, she did not at the moment show it. Instead she gave the elderly man a squeeze, causing a warm color to rise in his cheeks. "Oh, you are a dear! Thank you, Tabby. I shall have to be very careful to stay out of sight, for it seems Sir Roland is a determined man!" said Myriah thoughtfully. Then looking at her groom she smiled, "Now . . . *you,* sir, must go and have something to eat! Cook tells me she has made something special . . . in *your* honor. Imagine that, Tabby . . . she has fixed up a dish . . . just for you! I didn't realize you and cook . . . had become so . . . friendly," teased Myriah.

Tabby's eyes dropped and discovered the grass beneath his feet was looking particularly green, so green, in fact, that he was unable to take his gaze from its rich color! Myriah chuckled and gave her retainer a push towards the back door . . . herself returning by way of the front entrance. Myriah reached the double doors and pulled a face for they were locked. She was obliged to give the knocker a heavy clang and await an answer. Once again Lord Wimborne opened the door, but no smile lit his blue eyes as he bowed her in. She picked up her skirts and lifted her chin. She tried to pass him when his hand reached out and took hold of her arm.

"Miss White . . ."

"Release my arm, my lord," demanded Myriah harshly.

"Not until you have heard my . . . apology . . ." said Kit attempting one of his more charming smiles, but unable to banish the coldness from his hard eyes. He knew if he was to discover her purpose, her real purpose for being at Wimborne Towers, he would have to make peace with her.

She saw the ice in his eyes, and his smile stung with insincerity, "Apologize? Why, whatever are you sorry for, my lord? Ah, yes, for kissing me." She snapped her fingers in the air. "*That* for a kiss . . . I gave it willingly enough! For your stupid accusation?" Once again her fingers worked the air, "Your opinion has no more meaning for me . . . than your kiss!" She stared hard at him, all her well-laid plans to bewitch him lost somewhere in the black recesses of her dying hopes. His disrespect, his mistrust, and even his disgust of her were too apparent to be ignored, and this made her angry. She was in a rage, furious and bitter.

He threw down her arm. "Very well . . . we understand one another. I wonder at your persistence in wishing to remain under my roof . . . Miss White!" sneered his lordship derisively.

"Do you? And *I* wonder how such a man as William Wimborne can be brother . . . to *you!*"

He laughed without mirth. "You will be out there, sweetings . . . *he* don't find your beauty . . . to his particular taste!"

Myriah's eyes snapped. "My lord . . . if *I* wanted him to . . . make no mistake . . . *he would!* As it happens, I don't wish to be a part of *your* family!"

"Tart!" hissed his lordship, enraged beyond reason. "How dare you speak so to me? Who the devil do you think you are?"

The word slapped her like ice water in the face. Myriah fought the tears starting in her eyes. She fought the urge to advise him just *who* she really was. She controlled her trembling hands and something in her eyes caught Lord Wimborne's heart and tugged reproachfully.

"I shall not tell you what you obviously must realize you are. You are not *worth* the effort! However, you have referred to me in a term normally reserved for women more deserving it. As I have done nothing to call down such shame upon me, I object most heartily and were I a man . . . I would meet you for the insult! However I am not." She hesitated. "Did you know that in spite of your boorish manners, your cavalier treatment, your . . . inhospitality . . . somehow I found something in you to like. Last night, and then again now, I have proven myself a fool," said Myriah on a final sob, rushing up the stairs and making for her room.

Kit Wimborne watched her go and felt as though he were being eaten alive by parasitic insects. He was everything she said. For the first time in his life, he was not behaving rationally . . . and he felt himself the lowest of cads! His heart berated his mind and his mind . . . found excuses!

Eleven

Myriah sobbed into the bedcovers and stopped on a sniff as she heard the front doors crash. This served to renew her anguish, and it would have lasted a considerable time had not Billy Wimborne laid a hand upon her shoulder. She jumped, startled by the touch, and ashamed to be caught in such a state, and stared into Billy's face. He stood frowning in his nightdress, his gold-streaked hair falling wildly about his head and his face pale.

"Myriah . . ."

"Oh, Billy!" she said wiping the tears away with her hand, searching for her handkerchief which *he* found and gave to her. His injured arm was slung across his chest, held with a shawl Myriah had earlier folded round his neck. "You . . . you should not be up."

"Never mind me, Myriah. Look, you and Kit had a row. I couldn't hear all of it, but . . . but I did hear what he . . . well . . . he shouldn't have, Myriah! I don't know what has got into him . . . or why he would call *you* . . . well . . . he didn't mean it, Myriah . . . really."

"Don't make excuses for him, Billy. He is a big boy . . . well able to care for himself!" said Myriah bitterly.

He sat beside her on the bed. "You don't understand.

Look . . . it must be plain as pikestaff . . . that something havey-cavey is afoot at Wimborne. You ain't daft, Myriah, so don't be pitching any gammon at me."

"Well, yes, of course. You didn't get a bullet playing with dolls, silly. Everyone knows the Romney Marsh area is buzzing with smugglers. I expect you were out on a lark and . . ."

" 'Twas no lark. Look . . . maybe I'm wrong to trust you like this . . . maybe 'tis Kit that's right. But I mustn't let you go on thinking of him as you do! He has reason to worry over what may seem nought to you."

"Oh, well, that doesn't explain . . ."

"No . . . it don't . . . and it don't excuse him . . . but he can't take chances . . . too many people . . . too many things depend on his . . . meeting with success. You pose a threat to . . . our . . . operations because you are an unknown, and he don't quite swallow your story. Don't know why—but there it is; he's oddly suspicious about you." He hesitated and a frown quivered above his light eyes. "Though in truth that don't explain his calling you a . . . well, Myriah, *you* must have said something devilishly biting for him to have uttered such a thing. But never mind that now," he said suddenly grinning. But his breath was coming in hard gasps. "He'll come round and make it up to you . . . see if he don't."

Myriah eyed him intently for his color had gone pink and now white. Beads of perspiration were forming beneath the fringe of gold across his forehead. She put her hand out and touched his cheek. Kit Wimborne was for the moment forgotten in her concern for Billy. "Forget it, puppy. As you say, we will make it up! What does matter is that your head feels frightfully hot. Oh, Billy!" She gasped as her eyes went to his bandages, "you've bled again! Now come along with me. You must get back into bed."

She led him protestingly to his room, saw him settled against his pillows, but try as she might he would not lie down. Then she was off to the kitchens, promising to return speedily with chicken broth. "Oh God!" exclaimed the patient to her retreating form, "couldn't you find something better to do? Why must you forever be pumping disgusting liquids into me?"

She laughed and disappeared, but true to her word, she returned and plied him with the wholesome brew before bidding him good-afternoon.

"She-devil!" muttered the ingrate as she left him to rest.

Myriah went to her room and crossed to the terrace doors. A longing to be outdoors, astride Silkie, and riding at a hard gallop swept over her . . . but there was danger in going abroad. Roland was lurking about!

She settled for what she had and opened the big glass door with its diamond-pane design and stood on the small rectangular balcony. She leaned against the stone balustrade and breathed in the cool freshness of Spring. It is a season whose fragrance stands alone, for it is the scent of life at its start, it is the aroma of innocence, the aura of gentle awakening.

There was much Myriah had to think about, and her mind pressed her to do it now. Gladly would she put away all concerns, all doubts, and concentrate on her goals, but Billy had dropped his words and those words were disobedient to her command. They haunted and teased, and Myriah could not banish them!

What had he done to her peace with his fragmentary secrets? He had told her too much and yet had said so little! What had he said? Some obscure revelation about the *'success of their operation'*. There was really only *one* thing that such a statement could mean when considered with all that had happened. Faith, Myriah! thought she morosely, what a tangle you have spun for yourself!

'Twas ridiculous, absurd, but there it was with no hope for it. She was for some unfathomable reason (though reason had little to do with it) in love with Lord

Christopher Wimborne! He, on the other hand, for some unfathomable reason, seemed determined to dislike her. This thought brought her brows together, and as if that was not enough, it further occurred to her that Kit Wimborne thought her a woman of questionable morals! This was enough to dampen any maiden's hopes, but Myriah was not of a brooding nature. Her spirits revived and spurred her to action. She spotted a red-breasted robin perched on the branch of a near-by dogwood tree. Its pretty white blooms were just beginning to burst from the buds. "How . . . how could he?" asked Myriah, and the robin tilted his head, finding the question reasonable but quite beyond him. "After all . . . who is *he* to judge *my* behavior when in all probability he is nothing more than a . . . a . . . smuggler!"

This rather clever conclusion to her train of thoughts did very little to assuage her troubles. Indeed, it nibbled hungrily at her mind, causing a buzzing sensation to filter to her ears. 'Twas one thing for Billy, young and sporting for a lark, to embroil himself in an escapade of that sort . . . he was but a lad with his oats still to be sown. The sixth Viscount of Wimborne Towers should never . . . oh, dear! It was frightful to think about!

The most dreadful of all was that it fit. It made sense, for the Wimbornes were obviously in financial difficulty —*and Romney Marsh was at their back!*

French brandy, French silks, and the like had always been dear because of the duties imposed upon them. With the French coast just twenty-five miles or so across the Channel, smuggling had for centuries flourished in both Kent and Sussex.

Then came the Napoleonic Wars, and new efforts were being made to deter and eliminate the wide-scale smuggling along the English coast. It was no easy task, for an official coastguard had not yet been set up, and the Riding Officers and excisemen found the villagers to be close-mouthed. Farmers left their gates open at night for the land smugglers to pass with their cargo, taverns housed and secreted the Gentlemen's goods. Even the affectionate term *Gentlemen*, which was given to the smugglers, showed the open friendship the residents felt for these men. However, the aristocracy began to raise an eye, and what was once winked at was fast growing unpopular. For in addition to the crime of escaping customs, the smugglers were trading with an enemy of the Crown and in so doing were actually aiding the French. They were buying French brandy with English guineas! Napoleon, hungry for British gold, looked the other way, while his 'citizens' carried on their questionable activities with the English tidesmen crossing the Channel.

There too were the bloodthirsty gangs who had terrorized the countryside, killing those who stood in their way. Such was the Hawkhurst Gang, and the nobleman who once had called the romantic smuggler 'a courageous thief' was now referring to the pack of them as a traitorous lot! Myriah had often heard her father call down such a term upon their heads, and she sighed in perplexity, "Oh, faith! Whatever shall I do?" This time the robin felt himself to be in too deep and decided there was but one thing to do—take to the air!

Sir Roland dropped his portmanteau onto a wooden stool in the corner of his room at the Mermaid Inn. The roof of his surprisingly large bedchamber was pitched at an angle over the bed. A small leaded window overlooked the rear stableyard. He eyed his surroundings and sighed heavily, for though the room was bright, clean, and well kept, the furniture was sparse, old, and in need of refinishing. 'Twas not his idea of luxury, and Sir Roland preferred luxurious surroundings. It would have to do, however, for his purse could ill afford better.

A quick wash, a freshly starched neckcloth, and a comb through his auburn curls made him feel much more the thing. He gazed at himself in the looking glass and a slow smile worked his mouth. 'Handsome devil!' he thought and moved to the door. His greatcoat, hat, and gloves were picked up and then after a second thought dropped onto the large quilt-covered bed. He could always fetch them after he had eaten. He made his way slowly to the stairs and in his high-collared brown velvet cutaway, his cream silk waistcoat, buff-colored breeches, and shining hessians, he looked very much the gentleman of leisure. At the foot of the stairs, he found several options of direction. A fire was crackling in the room immediately ahead. A short, narrow hall led to a small ale room on his left, and to his right was a long corridor. He took this and noted that another sitting room opened off this hall, while windows and a door made up the walls on his other side. These gave onto an enclosed outdoor courtyard. It was some fifteen-by-fifteen feet square with a fountain in the center. At the end of the long corridor was an open, arched doorway to the large rectangular tavern room within.

Before entering the tavern room, he peeked into the sitting room and found there a wall made up entirely of books, for the Inn whose construction dated back some two hundred years had once belonged to a gentleman of letters. However, he had no fancy to read, and the aroma of good plain food was too tempting.

Sir Roland gazed languidly at the many oak tables of various sizes and shapes before deciding which would best suit his needs. The Inn was doing a booming business, and nearly all the large tables were filled to capacity. At length he spotted a small table nicked into a corner of the room and made his way there. This was precisely what he wanted.

Sir Roland's hazel eyes found a pert-looking potmaid carrying a tray of food and ale, and a slow smile curved his lips. He watched her serve a bunch of rowdy fishermen nearby, noting that her buxom form and pretty face were to his liking. She glanced at him as she passed, and

he caught her round the waist, pulling her into his lap
with one movement. She allowed the empty tray to dangle
from her hand and eyed him saucily, "Eh, now, m'fine
swell . . . what be it ye want?"

He kissed her behind the ear and whispered something
that made her whoop and give him a jab with her hand.
"But food, my buck . . . ye'll be needing food . . . so
what be yer pleasure?"

"A plate of your best, my pretty, and a bumper of ale.
That will do for now . . . later we shall see about *dessert!*"

She gave the handsome rake an appreciative eye and
rose to do his bidding, saying over her shoulder, "If that
is your pleasure, sir, 'tis mine . . . to give it!"

He smiled, amused with the wench and watched her
saunter away before casting his eyes round, scanning the
room for a familiar face. He would have to be patient.
He would have to hope that he might meet a chance
acquaintance here . . . someone who knew Myriah,
perhaps had seen her about. After all, Myriah could not
show her face in such a small town and not be remembered! If something did not present itself soon to foster
this plan, he would have to try yet another solution . . .
for he had little time, and he realized all too well that
the only way he would get Myriah for bride would be to
force her unwilling hand.

Twelve

The sun, its full strong rays earthbound, made a pattern through the terrace doors. It stroked Myriah's face gently as a mother does her babe. Her lids fluttered, her almond-shaped eyes opened to the ceiling above, and Myriah stretched.

"Oh, my! I have slept away the afternoon," said she softly to herself as she scrambled off the large bed and shook out the wrinkles from her ivory gown. She stretched again and stumbled sleepily towards her wash basin.

Ah, that's better, she thought splashing cool water over her fresh complexion. Now, to see about Master William . . . She crossed the hall, knocked on Billy's door, more for warning than permission, and getting none, walked briskly into the room.

"Billy . . .?" she called softly, standing over him. Her heart beat faster and her brows drew together at the sound of his labored breathing. He was in a fitful sleep, his face moist with perspiration, and his forehead was burning.

"Good God!" said Myriah, much upset. She rushed about the room, found the bottle of rosewater and the wash cloth, and put them to young Wimborne's head. He opened his eyes and smiled at her.

"At it again?" he asked weakly.

"Billy, why didn't you call me, you horrid boy? You're in a dreadful state!"

"Hush!" managed the patient.

"Hush indeed!" she snapped, throwing the wash cloth down on the nightstand and giving him her back. "I shall return in a moment, Billy Wimborne!" threatened Myriah, disappearing from his hazy view.

The kitchen was reached in less time than even Myriah would have thought possible and cook, wide-eyed, stood aside for the determined young woman.

"I am so sorry to take over like this, cook, but Master William is feeling poorly, and this tisane helped break the fever before. Let us hope it answers now!"

"Yes, Miss," said cook, handing Myriah a cast iron pot. " 'Tis that lucky his lordship has ye to look after the young master!"

"Hmmm," said Myriah busy with her herbs. At last the hot formula was prepared and poured into a pewter mug, and Myriah was mounting the stairs.

Lord Wimborne entered the house to find her back to him and, having come to a decision earlier, he called out her name. Myriah turned to face him, forgetting at the moment to be more than mildly put out with him for his previous behavior. "Yes, my lord?"

"Miss White, do put down whatever you are carrying. I should like the opportunity of private speech with you," said his lordship, a smile lighting up his face. He wanted to make it up with her. He was displeased with himself, unused to acting the cad, and he meant to put an end to it.

"I am very sorry, my lord, but your brother is in a fever, and I want him to have this while 'tis still hot," said Myriah, not very graciously.

Lord Wimborne took the steps in a trice, reaching her side and glancing down hastily at the libation on the tray she carried. She put up her chin before he could say a word, and her mouth curved into a derisive sneer, "Don't worry, my lord, 'tis not poison!" said she, moving down the corridor.

He stopped her gently, "Don't be a fool! You say he is in a fever? Why? What brought it on?"

"Really, my lord . . . I am not a doctor. I don't know, except that he *has* bled again . . . and perhaps you should bring in a doctor—from Hastings where it might go unnoticed?"

"Come!" he said, making for Billy's room.

She followed him, and between them they managed to pour the tisane down poor Billy's throat. "You mean to kill me, the two of you," accused Billy.

"If you get up from that bed again, William . . . I just may do so!" threatened Kit, his eyes softening the words.

Lord Wimborne withdrew and allowed Myriah to continue her ministrations with the wash cloth and rosewater, and it occurred to him, how very much he owed her . . . in spite of all her contradictions . . . and his suspicions!

"Now you rest, Billy . . . and since I can not trust you to call me, I shall remain in your room for the time being," said Myriah, smiling down at him.

"Miss White . . ." called Kit softly.

She turned her blue-green eyes upon him, and he felt her beauty strike him a blow. "Yes?"

"Earlier . . . I behaved most heathenishly. I believe I insulted you . . ."

"You *believe?*" interrupted Myriah in wide-eyed astonishment at the mildness of his confession, "you *believe?* Why, my lord, really . . . however came you to such a conclusion?" she asked sweetly.

"Please, Miss White. Don't make this any more difficult than it already is. There is no excuse for the manner in which I spoke to you, and I am heartily sorry for it. There now . . . are you satisfied?"

She put up her chin and looked away from him, "Are *you*, my lord?"

"Damnation, Myriah! What would you have from me?"

"Nothing, my lord! I want nothing I must ask for!" said the lady, giving him her back and sitting down on the chair beside his sleeping brother.

Lord Wimborne felt very much like shouting. His usual good humor had disappeared, it seemed, on the day of his meeting Myriah. He bowed stiffly to her back. "Very well, madam, if you will excuse me, I have business in town and shall not be home for dinner!" said Kit, making for the door.

"*Just* a moment my lord!" said Myriah, indignantly standing up, and her tone made him turn to face her. "*Your* brother lies here . . . ill with fever . . . and *you are going out?*"

Kit's eyes troubled over. "It cannot be helped, madam, and I know Billy is in good hands. If I know *nothing else* about you, that much I do know!"

"And . . . and a doctor . . . shall I send Fletcher for a doctor?" inquired Myriah, wishing he would stay.

"Fletcher will be with me. However, if you feel a doctor must be called, do so! I am sure your groom will be most discreet. And I will see that he is well paid!" replied Lord Wimborne, his brows knit above his shielded eyes.

"I see. Very well, then . . . good-night, my lord," said Myriah, and she watched him go before resuming her seat beside her patient.

Cook sent up Myriah's dinner and a broth for Billy some forty minutes later, but both recipients left their meal untouched. Billy tossed and turned in delirium, and then suddenly the wound was bleeding profusely!

Tabby appeared like a gift from Heaven, and Myriah nearly fell on him with her worries. "Tab, the bandages will need to be changed . . . and I need basilicum. You must ride into Hastings at once."

No further word was needed. Tabby was on his way immediately, and Myriah was once again beside Billy, pressing white linens against the flow of blood. "Oh, Billy, do stop moving so," she said, but he was in the heat of fever, tossing wildly—until at length he tired himself into sleep.

Myriah tied a tourniquet above the wound and, satisfied that she had checked the flow, sank down onto the wooden chair. Time seemed to play with her pitilessly, the seconds dragging by, and she covered her eyes, wanting suddenly to cry.

"Never say . . . the she-devil don't feel the thing," said a weak Billy Wimborne.

She looked up into his silly grin, and a sudden fulfilling warmth swept over her. "Oh, Billy, you dreadful, odious boy. You have tossed yourself out of your bandages . . . and I have had such a time with you!" She touched his forehead and sighed, for the fever seemed to have subsided. "Oh, Billy, I have been so worried! I sent Tabby to Hastings for basilicum . . . because your bandages will need changing . . ."

"Hastings? Damnation, Myriah, that ain't far enough. I'm too well known . . ."

"Hush, silly boy. *You* may be . . . but Tabby is *not!*"

He smiled stupidly. "Got a bit of a point there."

"Certainly I . . . whatever is all that clanging?" said she, turning with surprise. "Well, cook and her boys have gone some time ago, so I suppose *I* shall have to play butler," said Myriah, making for the doorway and turning round for a moment to cast her lovely smile upon her frowning patient. "Don't fret it, Billy. Whoever it is, I shall handle it!"

"I don't doubt it, girl!" he agreed.

However, as Myriah descended the stairs to the central hall she was far from feeling so confident. What if it were Sir Roland? She pulled one of the double doors open and stood in the dimly lit hallway facing a small wiry man clothed in dark superfine and an old-fashioned low three-cornered hat.

"Yes, sir, may I help you?" inquired Myriah curiously.

"No, ma'am, my business is with Lord Wimborne," said the gentleman.

She frowned for the man spoke with a note of authority, and his voice held a hint of London in its inflection. "I am sorry, but his lordship is not at home at the moment."

"And who might you be?" inquired the gentleman.

"I? Oh . . . I am Miss White, a cousin of his lordship's," said Myriah uncertainly.

"Are you now? Well then, where might he be? Can he be sent for?"

"I . . . I don't really know. Perhaps if you tell me what this is all about . . ." said Myriah.

"Perhaps I shall. But do you think I might step inside before we start exchanging information?" returned the stranger.

Myriah moved aside and allowed the man to enter the hallway. He faced her squarely and purposefully. She could see that he had just come from a long hard ride, for his clothes were covered with dust and in spite of his determination, he seemed weary. "Well, now, Miss, I haven't time to dawdle. Can you tell me if he can be fetched home?"

"Well, perhaps his brother may know."

"Ah, now . . . then William is at home. Take me to him . . . for I haven't any time to lose."

"You haven't told me your name, sir," said Myriah suspiciously.

"I am sorry . . . but I can't at the moment do that. No matter . . . take me to William."

"Without your name . . . I don't know that I can do that!" said Myriah haughtily.

"The devil you say! Then *fetch him here!*"

"I can't do that either. If you will but give me your . . ."

"Lord, Miss . . . very well . . . tell him . . . Mr. Dibbs is here."

Myriah eyed him with misgiving. What the deuce was all this mystery about? However, she did take the name to Billy, and a moment later was showing the strange Mr. Dibbs to Billy's room.

Myriah hovered in the background like a watchful mother while Mr. Dibbs made his greetings. "Confound it, young William . . . sorry I am to see you laid so!" offered the small man with a shake of his head, "but ain't no time to mull over it now! Need to see his lordship . . . must make my way back . . . hold now . . . best *she* . . ." he jerked his head in the direction of Myriah, "be leaving us a spell."

"Never mind, what you can say to me can be heard by Myriah," said Billy, staunchly loyal and making Myriah feel a queen.

"Eh? Very well, there you have it at any rate . . . now where is he?"

"He has a meeting at the Mermaid tonight. You can find him there," said Billy frowning.

"No, I can't! Don't want to be seen in public . . . with him . . . wouldn't do!"

Myriah's brows went up. What sort of individual was he that he mustn't be seen with Kit in public? This was becoming interesting, and she studied the man carefully.

"Must send someone for him," decided Dibbs.

"Can't . . . there is no one here, and I am afraid she-devil here won't let me budge out of bed. Nothing for it, Dibbs . . . you'd best risk it and go there . . ."

"Just a moment! I can fetch Lord Wimborne home if you like," offered Myriah.

"No, you can't, stoopid!" replied Billy disdainfully. "You are a female, can't go into the Mermaid at this time of night . . . wouldn't do . . . and wouldn't be safe."

"As to its not being safe . . . Kit will be there, so it couldn't be safer," stated Myriah.

"No, Miss, the lad is right. And besides, 'twould draw too much attention to his lordship . . . don't want to create a stir," said Dibbs.

"Look, if my being a female is the problem . . . well then, I'll just change into a male!" said Myriah, crossing the room to a wardrobe closet.

"Ha! Listen to her . . . she-devil that she is . . . change into a man . . . ha!" tittered Billy, falling limply against the pillows.

"Hush, Billy, or you shall start bleeding all over again! Never you mind. Just wait!" With that she disappeared into the dressing room armed with an assortment of Billy's clothing.

When she reappeared some ten minutes later, she was wearing a brown riding jacket that hung loosely about her shoulders, a linen shirt, brown baggy breeches, and her own knee-high riding boots. She dove once again into his closet and produced an old brown hat of sorts and stuffed her hair into its crown before turning to face them.

Billy roared and ended in a fit of coughing, bringing down Myriah's rebukes upon his head. However, Mr. Dibbs rubbed his chin thoughtfully.

"Tell you what, Miss. Sling a cloak of the lad's about your shoulders, hide the fit of the jacket, and you might pull it off if no one looks too close. Yes, you just might."

'Twas done and Myriah bade them farewell. Her heart beating high, Myriah crossed the driveway to the stables.

Thirteen

Clouds made an eerie frame about the moon and their jagged lengths formed a dimming mist, allowing only a hazy glow to soften the blackness of the night. The streets of the village known as Rye seemed strangely quiet, and Myriah could hear the sound of the sea lapping against the shore. The wild sound of two cats crying to each other in an ecstasy of feline song tore into Myriah's ears, and she grimaced and shook her head in protest. In spite of her earlier bravado, Myriah was frightened, tense, and already beginning to regret her impulsive action. What would her father say? Good Lord! What *wouldn't* he say?

She slipped off her horse and spoke to him gently, soothing herself as well as him, "Now then, love . . . easy, sweet darling . . . come then . . . that's it . . . come with Myriah . . ." She tugged at his leading string, and he objected to the pull by bobbing his handsome black head powerfully in an up-and-down motion that caused her to giggle and reprimand him, "No, Silkie, no. 'Tis no time to balk . . . be my good darling . . ." she said urging him up the cobbled slope towards the Land Gate entrance to East Cliff street. They passed through the

ancient archway and she eyed the stone-pillared towers
that flanked both sides of the street. Land Gate dated
back centuries, and there were many tales in its moss-
covered stones—a wealth of them—but this was not the
time for such musings, she told herself. Now she had to
get through the next few moments—she had her own
tale to tell.

Silkie's hoofs clopped along the deserted street and
echoed loudly in the stillness. Myriah watched warily as
they passed stores and narrow darkened alleyways on
their path down to High Street. They turned the corner
onto High, and Myriah pulled out the crude map Billy
had had Dibbs draw for her. Yes this was the way, and
she continued down High Street towards the center of
the village. The sound of life—life at its pleasure began
teasing her ears, echoing mockingly in the stillness of the
night, demanding of all that chance to hear, to give over,
and join in. Myriah reached the landmark for which she
looked and turned into the narrow alleyway that led to
the Inn's rear entrance and stableyard. The alley was
just wide enough for her and Silkie to pass. It was lined
with two-story buildings, and but a few windows gave off
light. The sounds of revelry, fuller now in its proximity,
made her tense with fear, for she had never before gone
into such a place—and had never before even thought of
going alone down such a path. A man popped his head
out of an open window just above her, and Myriah
jumped, startled by the unexpectedness of the action. He
laughed coarsely, "Fidgety lad, ain't ye?"

She ignored both the man and his taunt and continued
to lead her horse up the sloped alleyway to where a large
square stableyard formed, then surrounded her. Ostlers
came scurrying out of everywhere anxious to be of service,
hoping to receive a sizable gratuity for their service. She
gave Silkie's reins into the hands of one of the boys and
dropped a coin in his palm.

"Water him, and hold him ready for me, I shall return

shortly," she said in a voice she felt was credibly masculine.

However, he was far more interested in the coin she gave him than in the huskiness of her voice. She stalked into the Inn, passing through a rear, small tavern room where several old men sent an interested glance her way before she entered the door to the long hallway. She had not seen Kit in the small room, nor did she find him in the sitting room to her right. A quick glance out the hall window into the enclosed courtyard told her that he was not lurking about outside, and a turn at the end of the hall round its corner brought her into the belly of a substantially sized Innkeeper.

"Eh, now, laddie . . . what be yer hurry? Ye look a bit young to go sauntering free as ye please into my ken," said the man, wiping his hands on his white apron and looking friendly enough.

"Oh, if you please . . . I am looking for Lord Wimborne," said Myriah, hoping her voice would pass.

He eyed her a moment thinking her a sickly looking lad. "Got business with 'is lordship, 'ave ye? Well now, why don't ye give me yer name, and I'll go inform 'im you be 'ere wanting a word with 'im."

"Very well . . . tell him Master White needs him immediately."

The innkeeper went off in the direction of the main tavern room at the end of the corridor and left "Master" White to pace the hall in what may have seemed to any interested observer a most frenzied fashion!

Sir Roland rounded the corner of Westminster Street and walked up High Street, making for the same alley Myriah had passed through only moments ago. As it turned out, his dessert was taken at the potmaid's quarters just a short distance from the Inn and, having found the wench learned in many respects, he had whiled away several enjoyable hours in her company. When he reached the rear entrance of the stableyard, Sir Roland's observant eye found a very interesting object—Silkie! He was well acquainted with Myriah's handsome stallion. Indeed, there were very few London Corinthians who did not have the ability to recognize an animal of such a stamp. His step quickened and brought him up along the horse's side, and he ran a practiced, gloved hand over the animal's lines. The ostler eyed him curiously. "Prime blood he is!" said the boy.

"That is certainly so. And the owner of this prime blood?"

"Oh, he just went inside . . . a slip of a boy," said the ostler, not much more himself.

"I see," said Sir Roland, "a lad, you say?"

"Aye," replied the ostler.

Odd, he thought, making his way into the Inn. He couldn't be wrong. That horse was most certainly Silkie. He must be Myriah's stallion. He had seen her astride him often enough to be sure. Yet the ostler had said the owner was a boy. Could there be two such stallions? And wasn't it a bit more than coincidence that he should discover such a thing in Rye, the very town he was certain hid Myriah.

The innkeeper did not return, but Myriah looked up as the door opened to disgorge more of the tavern room's revelers along with Kit Wimborne and Fletcher at his back. Kit took long hard strides, and his face was cross with the flurry of consternation. He was worried . . . of course, she thought, he was worried about Billy . . . she must set his mind at rest. But then suddenly he was upon her and heedless of the proprieties, he caught her shoulders in his large, strong hands. "Billy?" he asked, and his voice was strained with emotion.

"No, no, 'tis not Billy," she hastened to reassure him. "He is well . . . the bleeding has subsided . . . but there is a man . . . a Mr. Dibbs . . . he . . ." She had no time for more, as he took her arm firmly, and with Fletcher still making up the rear in silent faithfulness, swept her out of the Inn. 'Twas done with such speed that she nearly collided with the fashionable gentleman passing them in the hallway. Even in the dim candlelight, Myriah's eyes had no trouble recognizing Sir Roland. Her mouth dropped and with it her chin in an attempt to hide her features. He did not catch her face, but she felt his eyes on her back, and as she mounted her horse and waited for Kit and Fletcher to have their animals readied, she kept her cloaked back to the Inn door. Sir Roland followed them curiously. There was something about them . . . though to save his life, he could not say what. He watched the three ride off single file down the alleyway, sighed, and returned to find the innkeeper smiling obsequiously at him.

"Tell me," ventured Sir Roland, "the gentlemen who just left . . ."

"The one with the boy?" said the innkeeper, smiling more broadly as he found a coin placed in his hand.

"Yes, the one with the boy," returned Sir Roland, smiling condescendingly.

"Aye, now . . . that be Lord Wimborne. The lad . . . he's new about. And t'other is Fletcher . . . Wimborne's man!"

"And his lordship . . . his estates are in the vicinity?"

"Estates . . . aye, such as they are now. Just three or so miles up the river road," answered the innkeeper. It wasn't his business, but he'd keep it in mind to advise his lordship that this gentleman had paid for information about him . . . information he fully intended to keep to a minimum.

"Thank you," said Sir Roland, well pleased with himself and making his way to the tavern. He felt well disposed to having a pint of ale and mulling over what he had learned.

Kit Wimborne's mind was busy. What was Dibbs

doing here? He thought everything had been settled on his last trip to London. What had gone wrong—if anything—but if nothing had, then why *was* Dibbs here? Kit had asked his men to wait on him . . . for the last details of their next crossing . . . the night after this when the moon would be at its peak. They needed enough men ready to unload when they returned . . . the timing would have to be perfect. And, good God! Hadn't he enough on his weary mind without having to see Myriah's face at every turn! Then, there she was and his heart beat at a rate which spoke of unmistakable truths . . . and again she was helping him! Who *was* Myriah?

Myriah's thoughts were a jumble as she rode Silkie hard in an effort to keep alongside Kit's dark roan. So, Sir Roland had put up at the Mermaid Inn. Thank the Lord, he had not seen through her disguise, for he would be upon her in a flash. And then . . . oh, faith, t'would take a miracle to keep the knot from being tied.

If such was not enough to worry a girl, there was the other—the mystery surrounding Kit Wimborne! Who was this odd man, Dibbs, and what had he to do with Kit? What was Kit doing at the Mermaid Inn? Who had been with him in the Tavern? Why had Fletcher been with him? Absolutely no answers presented themselves to Myriah before they were turning onto the drive that led to Wimborne's front double doors. Kit had not said a word to Myriah since his first questions, and except for a sideways glance every now and then, she had not been sure he cared whether or not she and Fletcher kept up the pace. However, he was off his horse and scooping her down from hers before she realized what he was about. Surprised by his sudden solicitousness, she eyed him shyly, unsure of herself. He smiled and took her hand. "You look a veritable child," he whispered softly before turning to Fletcher. "See to the horses. I'll be down to the stables momentarily."

"Aye, that I will, though yah best be nobbut a moment,

fer thars no tellin' how long thay'll wait on us," said
Fletcher.

"Don't be such a woman, Fletcher!" laughed his lordship, taking Myriah's arm and leading her into the house.

"Wisht, wisht, that won't hold!" returned his groom,
leading the horses away.

Kit rushed up the stairs, pulling Myriah with him, and
very much in spirits he seemed to her. She had no notion
what had occurred to send him soaring, but was heartily
thankful that he was at least at peace with her.

They reached Billy's room when Myriah stopped sud-
denly and looked inquiringly into his face, "My lord, I
believe you will want to be private with Mr. Dibbs, and
I am sure Billy will want to be in on the conversation.
Therefore, I shall retire to my room until such time as
I am needed."

He looked down into her piquant face and smiled, and
the glow in his eye set Myriah's heart racing. "Will you
never cease to surprise me, sweetings?"

She had no answer to this question and thought that
the moment to retreat, which she did. Now Myriah was
as curious as any female, and the questions that taunted
her needed answers, yet she was often governed by instinct and 'twas instinct that made her retreat suddenly.
Sitting in the darkness, waiting for a knock on her door,
Myriah smiled to herself. Finally, yes, finally, the high
and mighty Viscount of Wimborne Towers was beginning
to find her not so very hard to like! She had done him
a service . . . she asked nothing in return . . . not even
the chance of listening to their secrets. Well, apparently
'twas the right road to take to her goal.

The knock on her door came some ten minutes later,
much to Myriah's surprise, for she had not expected it
so soon. She rushed across the blackness and pulled open
her door to find Kit Wimborne standing before her. He
raised one brow, and Myriah was struck with the look
of him. He was powerful—so ruggedly powerful—and

when his voice came, she felt herself tremble. "In the darkness, Myriah?"

"What? Oh, it helps me to think . . . at times," said Myriah, and her voice was barely audible.

"And you have so much to think about?" inquired Kit, standing too close, and looking at her in a way that made it difficult for her to think at all.

"Faith! Can *you* ask such a thing? Here you are . . . each of you a mystery . . . the Towers itself a mystery . . . and I am human, thus I must admit to my curiosity . . . in fact, 'tis threatening to overcome me . . . and you want to know what I have to think about!"

He laughed good-naturedly and flicked her nose, "Thank you, Myriah . . . for everything . . . for the questions you don't ask . . . and for what you did tonight . . . though, in truth, I never want you to try such a thing again. 'Tis too dangerous, and I don't like you going about at night alone . . . but . . . I do thank you . . . it was more than anyone else would do under the circumstances."

"You have this lamentable habit of exaggerating, my lord! Really, I don't know what to make of you. One moment you think me some sort of monstrous female seducing young lads with bullet holes in their arms . . . and then, Lord . . . suddenly, I am a heroine of stupendous qualities!" She chuckled, "My dear sir . . . I am quite certain I did what anyone would do . . . given no other choice . . . and I *had* no other choice! Tabby is off in Hastings procuring bandages and basilicum for poor Billy. Needless to say, Billy could not go. And that very odd Mr. Dibbs had the fancy that 'twould do his reputation no good to be seen in public with *you!*"

He laughed uproariously. "I see you must have a very peculiar notion of me indeed. But let it go for the present . . . as it must. However, I must reiterate that there are very few who would have involved themselves in what must appear at best a most havey-cavey affair!"

"At best!" agreed Myriah, smiling.

He took her hand and a sudden tingling sensation swept them both. A slow smile spread across his face and into his eyes. Its warmth filled her, and the moment held them fast with its simplicity. "Come, Myriah," he said softly, leading her across the hall.

They entered Billy's room and were greeted with a sunny smile. "Never say you've brought *her* back in here Kit! Hang it man . . . why would you want to do that to me . . . didn't I tell you she's a devil! Even let my broth get cold . . . she did!" accused Billy Wimborne.

"Odious brat! If you don't have a care, I shall not make it up to you by bringing you another bowl!"

"She-devil . . . that is precisely what I have hoped for. If you don't bring me some meat, Kit, she'll be pushing that mush at me. What sort of a brother leaves his own flesh and blood to the dealings of such a female!" protested Master William.

"Hold, hold, Billy. If I brought you meat, how the deuce would you slice it with your one bad arm?" offered his lordship grinning.

"Bring me the meat . . . I'll find a way."

"Oh, very well. If *you will eat that* . . . perhaps I shall fetch it, and if you are very, very good . . . perhaps I shall even slice it for you," offered Myriah sweetly.

Myriah suddenly remembered Mr. Dibbs and looked about, asking in a tone of surprise, "Wherever is Mr. Dibbs?"

Kit Wimborne cast his brother a look of warning and hastened to respond, "He was due back at his destination and thought it best to ride off at once."

"Oh . . . but you make it sound so very mysterious. I know very well he is from London and no doubt plans on returning there—though how he is to manage the trip tonight on the same steed is beyond me!"

"Damnation, Kit . . . I told you." laughed Billy Wimborne, not at all displeased. "She is a knowing one. Up to every trick!"

"What?" asked Myriah haughtily, "because I knew he was from London? He spoke like one born and bred."

"And being from London yourself . . . of course, you recognized that?" asked Kit, putting up a brow in a manner she could not mistake.

"Yes, I've spent time in London. Picking up some knowledge of the great city's dialect is not difficult and does *not* take much time, my lord."

"I see," said his lordship quietly.

"Well, so he is returning to London tonight. How will he manage . . . his poor horse must be ready to fall!"

"Dunce!" declared Billy laughing, "He is using posting house horses, changes 'em at the posting house at Tunbridge Wells."

"Oh!" said Myriah. "Of course, I had forgotten about that."

"Well, my Billy, I leave you in the best of capable hands," said his lordship suddenly. Myriah turned wide-open eyes upon him, thinking, so that was what Fletcher was mumbling about.

"Can't mean to leave me with the she-devil?" cried Billy desperately. "Kit . . . Kit . . . you call yourself brother . . ."

"Hush up, puppy, or I shall bleed you!" threatened Myriah before turning towards Kit. "You . . . you are going out again?"

"I must. I left some rather unfinished business at the Inn. There is no hope for it . . . I must go back. I shouldn't be too long and will relieve you here when I return." He touched her hand and a prickling sensation shot through her arm. He watched the color flow and ebb from her cheeks, and he laughed suddenly, a youthful joyous sound, and its music thrilled her heart. Billy's eyes went from his brother to his nurse, and a slow smile curved his lips, and then suddenly Myriah's light

was gone. She sighed and turned to find Billy grinning at
her.

"What's so funny?" she demanded.

"You and m'brother!" he answered, unashamed.

"Horrid puppy!"

"Me horrid? Lord, just think—if it takes—a she-devil
for a sister! Ain't right, Myriah . . . said you might stay
awhile . . . not a life-time!"

"Oh! Oh! If you weren't so ill, Billy Wimborne, I'd
make certain you would be! As to being your sister, I
don't know how that could come about, so don't talk
nonsense at me!"

"Stuff!" he retorted, unabashed.

Fourteen

Sir Roland folded his greatcoat over the extra wooden chair beside the small corner table he had occupied earlier that day. His curly-brimmed top hat and white gloves followed before he took up his seat. He glanced around the half-empty tavern, idly stroking his chin which was just beginning to shadow. Strange, thought he, still immersed with his problem, very strange indeed. What would that boy be doing with Myriah's steed? He had never before known her to allow anyone the use of Silkie! And that horse *was* Silkie, of this he had no doubt.

This and many other questions occupied his busy mind, proposing several fascinating possibilities, and it was not until the uniformed young man standing before him had coughed deprecatingly several times, that Sir Roland looked up into the shallow eyes of Corporal Stone.

"Pardon?" said Sir Roland, frowning up at the young man.

"So sorry to trouble you, sir, but may I sit with you a moment?" His voice was urgent.

Sir Roland's brow went up and a haughty look commanded his features.

"I am certain you have your reasons for wanting to

128

do so, but I do assure you that while I have no objection
to company ordinarily, I must decline your offer as I
chose this table for the privacy it affords," said Sir
Roland depressingly.

Corporal Stone looked a bit harried, "To be sure, sir,
I understand. However, if you would but allow me . . .
there is an urgent reason I must convey to you why I
needs must intrude upon you." He took the liberty at
this point of pulling up a near-by chair and looking
anxiously at Sir Roland for his approbation.

"Very well." He had no liking for excisemen, however,
his curiosity was beginning to nibble at him.

Stone breathed a sigh of relief and straddled the chair
he had appropriated, leaning forward over the chair back
and peering intently at Sir Roland's countenance across
the table. " 'Tis this, sir. I'm on government business
tonight. If you will but cast your eyes in the direction
of your left shoulder, you will see a table full of coveys."

Sir Roland sighed heavily and turned his head slightly
in the direction indicated. He shrugged a shoulder and returned a bored countenance to Stone. "Evidently a rough
lot . . . but they appear no more so than any other
fishermen I have seen. Really, sir, I fail to see what all
this has to do with me."

"Fishermen? Lord love ya . . . 'tain't so . . . though
they would have us think so! Look, it's not anything to
do with you at all. Fact is . . . you be new in Rye! Made
it my business to know that. That's how I come to trust
you with this much. You've got no call *not* to cooperate
with me. You see, sir," explained Stone, lowering his
voice and yet managing to convey the portentousness of
the information he was about to impart, "those coveys
are held to be *smugglers!*"

Sir Roland's brow shot up and his head went round
involuntarily for another look at the alleged tidesmen.
Stone, satisfied that he had impressed the nobleman,

grunted in a tone meant to convey his momentary gratification.

Intrigued, Sir Roland's eyes brightened and he sat up, ready now to continue the conversation. "Upon my word . . . never say you are about to make an arrest tonight?"

"Arrest?" said young Stone opening his eyes wide. "Bless me, no!" His voice took on an inflection of disgust. "Haven't the proof, you see . . ."

Sir Roland stifled a yawn and as he observed the innkeeper crossing their way, he put up a hand for service. The tavernkeeper caught Roland's motion and sidled over, sniffing affably. "What be yer needs, gents?"

"A bumper of ale," said Sir Roland.

"Make it two, Thomas," added the landsman.

"Aye," agreed the innkeeper, going off.

Sir Roland turned back to Stone, and the look of boredom had descended over him again; he had some serious thinking to do, and what did he care about smugglers and such? "I am certain you will think me a dunce, but it is still not clear what all this . . ."—he languidly waved his hand in the air—"has to do with me."

"Eh, sorry, thought I had explained, sir. You see, I need to keep m'eyes on 'em! Best vantage point be this table. That way I can observe all their comings and goings. Traitorous lot, the pack of 'em!"

Sir Roland resigned himself, "Yes, I suppose, but . . ."

Stone's eyes flew suddenly to the narrow doorway, and Roland followed the man's glance. There stood Kit Wimborne, his uncovered honey-colored hair falling in waves around his ruggedly handsome face. His tall figure held a three-tiered cloak, slung back across one shoulder, exposing a superbly cut riding jacket and tight-fitting breeches of the same material. His Hessians were covered with dust from his recent hard riding, and his eyes were alight with merriment and more—the quality of command.

"Back are ye, m'lord?" cried the innkeeper loudly as

he spied Kit in the entranceway and hurried over to stand before him. He dropped his voice to a whisper and his words tripped out quickly, his eyes darting sideways as he spoke. "Thought ye ought to know. That flash sitting wit the bloody revenuer . . . he was asking after ye jest when ye brushed off before."

Lord Wimborne's blue eyes found Sir Roland, though his glance in that worthy's direction was perceptible to no one. "Thank you, Thomas. I'll be taking the blue room. See to it that we are not disturbed."

"Aye," said Thomas, moving off.

Kit's eyes found those of his men, sitting patiently round the oak table, beneath the observation of the excisemen. They were to all outward signs every bit what they appeared to be—big, hard-working, hard-living fishermen. Not a word passed between them and Lord Wimborne. Then Kit, with Fletcher silently at his back, turned and took the corridor to the stairs.

The table beneath Stone's view suddenly emptied and, open-mouthed, Stone watched them file out of the tavern-room. He got to his feet and rushed after them, noting with a grunt of annoyance that any hope of discovering anything of use was put to the stake. There would be no getting near enough to overhear anything they said, for any room they occupied would be well guarded against eavesdroppers.

He gave a chair in his path a vicious kick which sent it hurling and brought some attention upon him, before he returned to Sir Roland's table. Thomas, the innkeeper, gave him a long speculative look as he slammed the two pints of ale down on the table and waited for his money. This produced, the exciseman suddenly reached out and held the innkeeper by the arm. "Thomas . . . you know what is afoot tonight. Spill it out man—'tis your duty as an Englishman!"

"You be daft, man! Ain't got a notion what ye be blabbering about!" snapped Thomas, pulling away his heavy arm and rushing out of reach.

"No notion . . . no notion at all!" said Stone contemptuously. "You'd all sell your souls if there were a profit in it. They are all closed-mouthed about the *Gentlemen*—ha!—such a name for smugglers!"

"Lookee 'ere!" shouted the innkeeper from across the room. "There ain't no call for the likes of ye to talk to me that way! 'Tis none of m'affair what me customers do! That's a fact! Onct they pay their due, makes no ha'-porth o'difference to me where they go . . . or what they do!"

The exciseman, barely twenty-five, eager, ambitious, and drastically impaired by the close-mouthed community of a smugglers' village, was continuously put out by such attitudes. He was stifled by a job with little reward and little chance of success. What he needed was a royal coastguard to aid him. What they had now—the few revenue cutters were at sea—and these were simply not enough!

He sat down heavily and began downing his ale, sniffing, and cursing the fates, for what he needed was a break . . . just one break and then he'd have 'em! Sir Roland's interest had revived with Lord Wimborne's emergence on the scene. He sat watching the young exciseman, for now, here was something!

He had not noticed Kit glance his way; however, he had been quick enough to note that the so-called fishermen—alias Rye smugglers—or Gentlemen, as they preferred—had indeed picked themselves up and followed in Lord Wimborne's wake! This now—especially in view of the fact that Myriah was most probably connected in some way with the dashing lord—might prove useful!

"Tell me, was that not Lord Wimborne who nearly descended upon us, but saw fit to do otherwise?"

"Aye—the devil!" answered Stone sourly.

"Oh? Why do you say so?" asked Sir Roland, raising an inquiring eyebrow.

"You saw. 'Tis plain as pikestaff . . . he has thrown his lot in with the scurvy lot of 'em!"

"I am not quite certain I catch your meaning," said Sir Roland, fishing.

"Don't you?" replied the young exciseman, allowing his pleasant features to be distorted with a sneer. He brushed at his hat resting on the small oak table and let go a wild breath. "Confound it all! Must I spell it out for you! Very well then, Sir Roland, so I shall!"

"Yes, indeed, but I believe you have the better of me, sir. You are acquainted with my name, and although we have been sharing the same table for the better part of an hour, I am still ignorant of yours!"

"Corporal John Stone, sir, at your service," said the young man inclining his head and taking the card Sir Roland had produced from a leather wallet in his inner pocket. He scanned the gold print and read out loud, "Aye, Sir Roland Keyes, there is much I could tell you."

"I am quite certain you could, and I couldn't be more interested to hear what you have to say."

"But there would be the devil to pay if m'superiors got wind of it! Wimborne is an old name in Sussex—carries quite a bit of weight."

"Then it is surprising the present lord would mingle with a pack of . . . fishermen," said Roland, luring the exciseman on.

"That ain't the heart of it, man! Why a fellow would have to have his upper works out of order not to realize 'tis Wimborne himself that leads 'em across the Channel on their dirty business!"

"That, my good man, is a very serious and dangerous accusation," cautioned Roland, still baiting.

"Aye, that it is, and *that* is why I ain't made it— officially. Already told you I ain't daft. I ain't the brightest fellow ever wore the uniform . . . but I'd have to be a dunce to go off half-cocked aiming a finger without the proof. I knows what he's up to . . . got all the reason in the world, he does . . . why, he is up to his head in debt . . . has been dished this past year . . . maybe more! How else would he get the blunt to stave off the dunning?"

Sir Roland, no stranger to debt, was struck with a momentary feeling of pity for Wimborne. However, it passed. "I see . . ."

"Do you? No . . . you only think you do! We nearly had him the other night. Red-handed, we almost had him . . . damnation! We were so close!"

"Do you mean that you actually observed Lord Wimborne in the act of landing a cargo?" ejaculated Roland in a startled whisper.

"Dash it, man . . . not *him* . . . his snip of a brother. Young pesky fellow with the face and years of a mere boy and already deep into the business! The scalawag is in league with the devil himself, he is, for I am certain we put a hole in him! Knew it . . . saw him slump over . . . but then . . . there he stood . . . as hale and uppity as ever!"

"Hang it, Stone! Either you shot him or you didn't!" exclaimed Roland, losing patience and beginning to think all this would prove useless to him.

"That's the point . . . the tear in the tale . . . can't be sure anymore, for while my men could have sworn 'twas his face we saw against that lantern he held—and there was the blood on Wimborne land—and his hat . . ."

"Devil you say! Proof—that seems proof enough to me!" said Roland raising a brow.

"Aye, so it did to me . . . but then came the lovely. Claimed she was the one who lost the hat . . . something about taking it into town for a new lining . . ."

"Lovely . . . do you refer to Lady Wimborne?" said Sir Roland, sitting up.

"No. Neither of 'em married . . . though when I first clapped eyes on her, she looking every bit the lady of the house, I thought perhaps his lordship must have up and tied the knot when he was in London last."

"Well then, Stone, who the deuce was she?" questioned Roland intently.

"Some cousin . . ." he lowered his voice and his eye took on a different glow, "and if she didn't have a grace about her, would have thought maybe they had up and got themselves a fancy piece. But anyone can see she ain't that! Sweetest, loveliest creature ever I clapped m'eyes on!"

"And you trust this lady's word . . . about the hat?" asked Sir Roland, frowning.

"Don't signify whether I do or don't. She gave her word on it and I don't have proof otherwise. And besides, there he stood, not a speck of blood on him, not a scratch. The man that lost that blood must have had a good sized hole in him . . . to bleed the pool we found. Good Lord, man . . . was still wet, it was, when we found it the next day!"

"Hmmm . . . and she . . . a fine figure of a woman I suppose. Do you remember what she looked like?" asked Roland, barely able to disguise his interest.

Stone eyed him a moment. "Won't do you no good . . . talked to the Wimborne cook. She tells me the girl is on her way to her relatives in Dover."

"Too bad. But you said you found her lovely. And she being a cousin, I suppose she is fair-haired like Lord Wimborne?" asked Roland blandly.

"Fair-haired? Faith, no! That's the first thing that struck me . . . her hair . . . 'tis the color of firelight. It strikes you and warms you and then you are lit upon with those almond eyes . . . blue-green they are . . . and a body formed for loving . . ." He sighed. "Ah, well, 'tis another thing this job will never get me—a creature like that!"

Roland smiled to himself. "It will take quite a man to catch Myriah," said he in a low voice and looking at the oak beams of the tavern wall without really seeing them. He gritted his teeth and his eyes took on a steely look as he thought of Myriah situated at Lord Wimborne's.

"What did you say?" asked Stone.

"Nothing, really, only that it would take quite a fellow to capture the dream you just spoke of."

" 'Twas no dream, Sir Roland. She was real, she was."

"I am very certain of that! Come, then, have another bumper of ale with me. I find this conversation of ours fascinating and would know more!"

Pleased with his audience, Stone consented, and the innkeeper was hailed.

Fletcher, staunch as ever, peaked wool cap pulled low over his forehead, leaned up against the wooden door of the room his master now occupied. He watched the end of the corridor for signs of an intruder. He was quite ready to handle the situation should anyone be so unwise as to attempt to disturb the meeting being held behind the closed door.

"Well, there you have it, lads," said Kit Wimborne, putting a hand through his hair and setting a foot on the chair in front of him. "We cross tomorrow night for the last time . . . hopefully! Dibbs has come with the last of it . . . I hope!"

A heavy-set man, clothed in a dark wool shirt and a worn dark jacket, pushed his chair back and eyed Kit with the only eye left to him, having lost the other in service of His Majesty some years ago. "Begging your pardon, m'lord—yah seen us through a fetch or two— and you've got *me* through more than I can count . . . I'm thinking ye'll see us through a good sight more without us getting twigged! The blunt is too good to brush off in the wink of an eye," said Fry, leaning back on the wooden chair and waiting for his master's reaction.

"Damnation, Fry! Do you question my judgment?" snapped Kit.

"Hold, m'lord . . ." this from a young man similarly

dressed, "Fry here be in the right of it. We trust ye with
our lives we do . . . and coz 'tis so is why we vote to
famble as we 'ave! I got four young brats wit their
mouths open all the time . . . and another one cooking.
'Taint any way I can feed 'em without the ready . . .
and this way be as good as any other."

Kit shook his head and pulled a contemptuous mouth
with just enough precision to put his men to the blush.
"Is that the way of it? After all these years . . . you
don't trust me? Even you, Fry?" He waited just long
enough to allow Fry to expostulate before slamming his
fist down hard. "Damnation! Yes, I saw you through a
time or two! Pulled you out of hell, Fry . . . in the Pyrenees . . . think I'd throw you into it this side of Freedom?
Hang me before I do! What do you all think . . . that
I'd leave you to fend for yourselves? What sort of paltry
covey do you take me for? You Bilkes with your brats . . .
you'll take care of Wimborne grounds . . . just as you did
before we started this heathenish business . . . just as
your father did before you . . . and you, Fry . . . you've
worked Wimborne stables as far back as I can remember
. . . you will do so again! All you damn fools will work
Wimborne . . . just as you have always done! Stupid lot
of brutes I've got for myself . . ." said Kit grinning at
them.

The man called Fry had the grace to take on the look
of a sheep, "What of the Winchelsea Boys? They won't
like us pulling out."

"Those lads are a hard lot . . . they have always been
smugglers . . . they always will be smugglers. Don't think
they were living on the thirty or forty kegs *we* passed
from time to time! They went in with us for the money,
but they got their own ken . . . their own galleys and
you needn't give them another thought!" He scanned the
faces and, satisfied with the results, he resumed his seat
and drew up paper and quill. "So then, mates, let's get

on with it. We'll have to plan it to the minute for our
landing crew gets fidgety when we're not on time."

Tabby, out of breath and mumbling to himself about
his mistress, the lateness of the hour, the scrapes she
got herself into, and the work she sometimes put him to,
finally reached Billy Wimborne's room to find the lad up
and playing faro with Myriah.

"Oh, Tabby! You wonderful man," cried Myriah,
spying him in the doorway. She turned to Billy, "Do you
not see . . . thank him, Billy Wimborne."

"Was just about to when you opened your mummer,"
grumbled Billy, turning and thanking the groom properly.

Myriah fetched the warm wash water she had procured
earlier and began removing the blood soaked bandages.
The wound, which did not appear as bad as she had
feared, was soaked and cleaned in spite of Billy's painful
protests. The basilicum powder was produced, applied,
and once again young Wimborne's wound was properly
dressed. "Sadistic wench!" he complained ungratefully.

"Yes . . . you have no idea how much pleasure it gives
me to have you at my mercy. 'Tis what I have been
wishing for all these years . . . a wounded young man at
my disposal to torture!" giggled Myriah.

Tabby shuffled out of the room, once more grumbling,
and Myriah and Billy watched him go before breaking
up into uproarious mirth. Myriah scrutinized her charge
and noted the fatigue about his eyes. She mixed a bit
of laudanum for him and bade him drink, which he did
without argument. However, when the glass was reset on
the nightstand and his pillows adjusted for sleep, he gave
Myriah a long look and pulled a grimace. "Don't you
think a fellow is entitled to privacy when he sleeps? Go
to your own bed, woman. 'Tis most improper for you to
stay alone with me . . . *beside mine!*"

"You are sweet, Billy . . . but I won't feel right until
I have assured myself you won't fever up again. Don't

mind me . . . get some rest . . . your brother will relieve me soon."

"Don't want either of you fussing over me. If you're not careful, you shall both fall ill and then . . . good God! I might have to tend you." He smiled comically. "Do you know the thought is exciting? Might actually get the opportunity to poke and prod at *you!* I shall dream about it."

"Odious boy!" said she.

Fifteen

The clock over the fireplace said but a few minutes past twelve when Fletcher bade his master good-night at the stable doors. Kit produced the brass key and opened the front door, letting himself in and taking the stairs, feeling strangely exhilarated. He dropped his caped cloak and kid gloves on the empty wooden chair beside his brother's bed, then touched Billy's forehead and smiled at the coolness of his brother's flesh. He turned and found Myriah slumped over in the cushioned Queen Anne near the low-burning fire.

The flame from the hearth suffused Myriah's features with a warm glow. Her red hair lay tousled over her shoulders, and her legs were curled up beneath her skirt. She looked like a woman-child, and Lord Christopher Wimborne felt his heart swell. He strode quietly to her side and knelt beside the chair, one finger traveling over her small upturned nose, then tracing the outline of her well-shaped lips, and placing a gentle kiss upon them.

Myriah's eyes flew open and he looked directly into those blue-green pools. He drew in his breath in admiration. "Oh, Myriah!" he whispered, "you have no idea how wonderful you are!"

She blinked and sat upright with a start. "My lord," she said, attempting to pull herself together, "Billy . . ."

"There is no fever, and his breath is even. Come . . . 'tis time you went to your room and allowed yourself the comfort of a bed." She permitted him to take hold of her shoulders and leaned up against his tall hard body for support . . . for she was not quite steady. However, by the time they reached her door she had drawn away from his strangely comfortable arms and given him her hand. He kissed it lightly and his eyes were full of emotion she could not help but see. She wanted to fall into his strong arms . . . to declare herself, for it was her way to be open about her feelings . . . to hold back was unnatural to her. Yet—hadn't she done just that once before . . . to have it end in his calling her a *tart* the following day? Myriah held back, and Kit, overawed by his own feelings, unsure how to handle himself or her, made no attempt to embrace her, though his voice was husky when it finally came. "Good-night, Myriah, and . . . thank you."

"Good-night, my lord," she said softly, turning quickly lest he see the need in her eyes. She closed the door behind her, almost wishing he would storm it down . . . to demand her kisses . . . and her hand. She sighed and began to undress, telling herself to be patient.

Kit Wimborne stood transfixed before her door as though she were still with him. He wanted her and his want made him forget his suspicions . . . and if they did still pinch at him, he quickly brushed them aside. Hadn't she helped him tonight . . . hadn't she cared for Billy as though he were her own brother? His body burned as he drew himself up and walked down the hall to his own room.

The eyes of love and youth—what can they not see or accomplish? Myriah awoke to a new day, and life roused joyously within her! She felt her heart tremble with the memories of the night's dreams . . . and it was good! However, 'tis exceedingly difficult for one to be restful or peaceful when one needs to fulfill love's initial yearnings. Myriah found herself behaving in a manner most strange. She sped across the room and flung open the doors to her terrace, stood out in the morning's crisp air, and shouted her greetings to Mother Nature's living art. She laughed aloud without any observable cause. She sang most joyously, humming when the words eluded her, and as she went about her toilette, she skipped as though she were once again a child of ten!

To crown this peculiar behavior, as she tied her hair back with a ribbon, she found her reflection in the looking glass enough to trigger a series of schoolgirl giggles. Furthermore, be it remembered that Myriah had not eaten her dinner the previous evening, and yet no thought of food entered her mind. Even stranger yet, Myriah felt good all over in spite of the fluttery anticipation that tantalized her entire being.

She swooshed across the hall to Billy's room, clucking her tongue against the darkness and pulling open the drapes with a lively vigor. She turned and proceeded to remove herself from his room, calling out gaily, "Good-morning, puppy," as she left!

"Aggh . . ." groaned Billy, blinking at her sudden appearance and departure, shouting after her, "Hold there! Where the deuce do you think you're going?"

"For a walk, love! 'Tis a glorious day!" she answered, not bothering to stop.

Lady Myriah stood on the front portico and breathed deeply. Indeed, it was a lovely day. The light breeze brought the aroma of flowers growing wild in unkempt garden beds. The sun played saucily with its misty mates in the rich blue sky, and Myriah stretched her arms heavenward. 'Twas a new day . . . with fresh hopes!

Myriah rounded the house and crossed the rear lawns past a rich meadow with grazing sheep. They looked like puffs of dirty rags sitting upon black footstools, and Myriah laughed! She came across a small wooden bridge that arched prettily over a steep dyke and crossed it feeling as though she had entered some fairytale land. She walked beside the dike looking down into its dark waters, marveling at the glistening gems it seemed to hold, when all at once the sound of a lamb bleating piteously, halted her!

"Oh, gracious, however did you get there, you silly?" asked Myriah as she spied the poor thing entangled in a mesh of grapevines and just barely out of water. She looked round for a means to get to the animal, but the walls of the dike appeared to be almost straight up and down. However, there was a point at which the slope could be taken, but not without some effort.

"Oh, my! Very well, little one, it looks as if I am going to ruin a perfectly good gown and one my papa paid quite a tidy sum for, I do assure you," said Myriah picking up her skirts and tucking the lace hem into her brown velvet waistband. Off came her walking boots and stockings. As she braced herself with her hands against the grassy walls, holding onto exposed roots and digging the sides of her feet into the dirt for support, Myriah complained bitterly. "You realize, of course, I have but one other gown . . . and I do hope you appreciate what I am doing for you."

"Baaa!" said the lamb.

"Very well . . . there, there . . ." said Myriah, reaching the animal and patting its head. However, the poor thing's neck was being strangled by the vines, so she began to free the creature. A series of tugs set her off balance, and she slid the remainder of the slope and landed up to her knees in the deep water.

"Good lord!" ejaculated Myriah, " 'Tis but low tide and just look how deep it is. I shall probably catch my death of cold, you horrid animal. I do wish you hadn't tried to strangle yourself this morning!" said Myriah, wading out of the water and climbing back to the lamb. 'Twas no easy task freeing him. The vines were made of sturdy stuff, and pull as she might, many of them still held fast; however, a long grunt and a solid pull did at last free the lamb. The fact that it also sent Myriah simultaneously flying backwards (not without the sound of her scream reverberating through the Marshes) seemed to spur the lamb up and over the walls of the dike. Myriah's scream ended with a splash, and it was a moment before her head surfaced.

She gasped for breath, noted that the lamb had escaped to freedom and, thinking him an ungrateful brute, proceeded to swim to safety. Reasonably, most individuals finding themselves fully clothed and in a similar situation, would not stop along the way to sightsee. However, as the reader may have observed, Myriah was a breed of a different beat! A formation caught her eye and, as she was already quite wet, she could see no harm in sidetracking and satisfying her curiosity!

Perhaps it was the charm of finding lush, thick grapevines hanging screenlike over a mesh of driftwood, that for some inexplicable reason seemed to have gathered in this spot . . . and only this one spot. Perhaps it seemed intriguing that this *formation* appeared to be some seven or eight feet in width and could not be reached except by water since a kind of stone platform overhung the place. At any rate, Myriah knew a strange palpitation of the heart as she approached and peered through. Spreading the vines, she was not surprised to find a galleyboat, some forty feet in length and about seven feet in width.

"Myriah!" shouted Lord Wimborne. "Myriah!" He had heard her scream and the splash . . . but when he reached the dike he did not see her, and he was beginning to feel a sick, painful ache in the center of his belly.

She swam to the water's edge and called out thankfully, "Kit! Over here, Kit!"

He ran the distance and came to stand looming above her, "O my God, Myriah!" exclaimed he at first. However, the sight of her completely drenched and struggling to emerge, hindered by her sopping gown, sent him into a convulsion of wicked mirth! He doubled over with laughter, pointed at her, attempted to say something but went off again unable to contain his glee.

As one could imagine, the lady found nothing in her present predicament worth such uproarious and unholy mirth and proceeded to advise him of this. "Fie on you, my lord! You wretch . . . how can you when I am wet and cold and . . . confound it! I cannot climb out of this wet hole!" she declared.

Still chuckling, he made his way down the slope to her and gripped her arm, pulling hard in order to overcome the weight of wet clothing. At length they reached the grassy top and collapsed on the ground. However, they made the mistake of finding each other's eyes, and this sent them both off into a fit of mirth which lasted long enough to wind them for some time!

At last Lord Wimborne collected himself, rose, and pulled Myriah to her feet. He shrugged off his riding jacket and put it round her wet shoulders saying lightly, "Come on girl . . . we'd better get you to the house and into some dry clothes before you catch your death!" She pulled on her boots, and they set off hastily for the warmth of a hearthfire.

She stopped him suddenly and looked intently up into his blue eyes, almost afraid of what he might say when he heard her out. "I . . . I wasn't spying, my lord. Honestly . . . I was not. I was trying to save one of those horrid little lambs who did not even have the decency to thank me for my effort. But then, I fell in, you see . . ."

"I see very well," chuckled his lordship.

"Dreadful man! But . . . then, I saw!"

Lord Wimborne frowned, "You saw what, Myriah?"

"I did not mean to . . . but the driftwood . . . the vines . . . clustered just so. It caught my curiosity . . . and I thought as long as I was already wet . . . I'd have a look. There is a galley, my lord. But you know that already, don't you?" said Myriah, quite serious.

"A galley?"

"Yes, 'tis hidden in what appears to be a man-made tunnel!"

"There is nothing in that . . . many of the fishermen keep their galleys stored in underground caverns . . . 'tis done in the Marsh often. And 'tis nothing for *you* to think . . . or *talk* about!" said Kit, his blue eyes veiled. "Now do come, Myriah . . . I must insist," said he, putting his arm about her shoulders and gently urging her into a run.

She had no time for more as he hurried her along to the house, and her present happiness banished all dreary concerns.

Having changed her ivory silk (which was damaged beyond repair) for her blue gown, Myriah spent the next hour on the hearthrug in Master William's bedchamber. The three young people enjoyed a hearty breakfast, though it was done with much rallying, bantering, and laughter at Myriah's expense. The tale of her morning adventure was the principal topic and one that gave both gentlemen an enormous amount of fun.

Myriah sat with her long red hair towards the fire, drying sections still wet. She pulled a comic face and sniffed amiably, " 'Tis all very well for you two to go on and on, but I am now minus a gown. I think you and your sheep are quite horrid!"

"Listen to the girl . . . as though she didn't enjoy her dipping!" mocked young Wimborne . . . "and it wasn't our sheep you were saving . . . but farmer Todd's."

"Same thing . . . was on your land . . . he is a tenant of yours, isn't he?"

"She has a prodigious way of connecting the two . . .

but she does have a point there, Billy. Very well, we shall concede . . . we most certainly owe you one gown!"

"Ha!" added Billy, "I wouldn't give her one groat . . . didn't ask her to fall into the water. If she wanted to free the poor creature, should have done so without falling into the canal!"

"Billy Wimborne, you just wait till you are well enough to take a beating. It shall give me immense pleasure to administer one," cried Myriah, slamming her towel onto the floor.

"Er . . . er . . . excuse me, m'lord . . ." said a faltering voice from the open doorway.

Myriah looked up to see one of the cook's sons standing uncomfortably before them.

"Yes, boy?" said his lordship, rising from the bed and smiling reassuringly at the young lad.

"There be someone 'ere from Rye . . . he has a note for Miss 'ere . . . and he be wishful of giving it to 'er direct."

"Who is this someone?" inquired Myriah frowning, fear clutching at her heart.

"Aw . . . he be jest some village boy. I tried telling him I'd bring the letter up to ye . . . but he won't have it."

"I see . . . very well, then, I'm coming." She turned and excused herself, and her companions were well able to read the concern on her face.

She made her way down the stairs and crossed the hall to where a beragged young boy of no more than ten years stood waiting.

"Be ye Lady Myriah?" said the boy suspiciously.

Myriah glanced about quickly and hastened to quiet the boy, "Ssh . . . yes, I am. Now may I have the note please?"

He handed it over and sniffed, "I'm to wait fer yer answer . . . won't get my half-crown lest I do."

"Very well," said Myriah breaking open the seal and moving away to read the epistle.

Myriah:

I don't know what game you are playing with the Wimbornes . . . and at the moment I don't care! You have done me an injustice which we must discuss. Meet me . . . at a place of your choosing . . . but do not deny me this one boon . . . 'tis the very least you owe me!

Roland

Myriah sighed. So . . . he already knows where you are . . . soon papa will know as well . . . and then . . . and then?

She returned to the young boy, "Tell me . . . when you asked for me . . . did you ask for Lady Myriah?"

"No . . . the flashcove, he said . . . just ask for a red-haired woman . . . staying with the Wimbornes. Then he told me to give that lady the note if she admitted to be Lady Myriah! That's what I did . . . jest like he told me . . . now I needs an answer so I can get the blunt!"

"You will have to wait a moment," said Myriah crossing the hall to the library. She found paper and quill and jotted down a quick reply, sealed it, and returned to place the letter in the boy's dirty hand.

Myriah watched him leave and stood alone in the hallway a moment before she turned and started taking the stairs slowly up to the second floor, but when she reached the landing, she found she could not return to Billy's room and went to her own instead.

She dropped on her bed and sighed, putting her chin into her hands. Well . . . it was probably all over. She would now have to admit to her identity . . . and if Kit declared himself after he knew her name . . . she would always have a doubt. O God! She wanted him to want her now . . . now when he thought her a nobody . . . when he thought her without luxurious means . . . .

A knock sounded lightly at her door and she moved on her bed to find Lord Wimborne filling the open doorway. "May I come in for a moment, Myriah?" he asked gently.

"Of course, my lord . . . do," said Myriah hopefully.

He came towards her, stopped short just a few feet away from the bed, and clasped his hands together behind his back. "Myriah . . . is there something . . . wrong?"

Yes, you big fool, she thought ruefully, yes, there is something wrong . . . I want you to love me. She said instead, "Wrong? Why, no."

"Look, Myriah. I believe you are in some sort of trouble . . . you may need help . . . and I wish to give it."

"I am afraid there is nothing you can do," said Myriah with a heavy sigh.

He moved forward and took up her chin, "Tell me, sweetings . . . what is it . . . just confide in me . . . and let me be the judge of whether or not I can help."

How can I, she thought. How can I tell you that I want you to declare your love . . . ask for my hand . . . you big oaf! But she said, "I am unable to do that. We all have our secrets . . . don't we . . . my lord?" at once angry with herself for her sarcasm.

"Yes," he said, stiffening, "I had quite forgotten that." Kit Wimborne turned on his heel and left her to her solitude.

Sixteen

The pain of watching Kit leave ripped through Myriah like a whip that hits and snaps back in one motion against its helpless victim. His name lodged itself in her throat, though she was unable to call him back. How could she? What would she say? Her hand went out towards the sound of his retreating footsteps and her mind called out his name . . . but he was gone! She heard him take the stairs and listened for the front door to slam—which inevitably it did!

Myriah wanted to cry. Never before had she had the very thing she wanted and needed more than anything else in the world . . . there just before her grasp and yet totally unable to clutch it. However, she had no time to speculate on this or to allow herself the comfort of tears for a bellowing voice called her to order. —

"Myriah! I say, Myriah!" shouted Billy from his room.

She got to her feet and crossed the room calling in response, "Just a moment Billy . . . I'm coming!" She arrived at his room, put her hands on her hips, and inquired impatiently, "Well, now that I'm here—what was all the shouting about?"

"Don't be a shrew!" admonished Billy. "How else was

I to get you here? Damnation, woman, you must learn to curb that nasty habit you have of unleashing your tongue. 'Tis too sharp . . . you are liable to scare off every buck in sight!"

She pulled a face, and her mood was frosty, "You did not call me here simply to impart that wondrous piece of advice."

"Don't cut at *me* with your tongue," chided her tormentor. "A veritable vixen, ain't you? Well . . . as it happens I called you in here to ask you what's amiss." He saw she was about to give some noncommittal answer and crooked a finger of his right hand. " 'Tis no use trying to fob me off, for I don't take to round tales. I've got all m'marbles so don't try pitching the gammon at me, Myriah! Now, out with it."

She plucked at her blue skirt and then stared at him intently, "Oh, Billy . . . I do want to tell you . . . but I can't . . . at least not everything . . ."

"Well . . . try telling me something . . . and we shall take it from there. Trusted you with m'life . . . I rather think you could do a bit of the same."

"Oh, and I would . . . but . . . I don't want your brother to know . . . you must promise me that anything I tell you . . . will go no further."

"As it happens, Myriah . . . think you're out there. Knowing fellow Kit . . . he could be a help to you . . . but if that is how you want it . . . it isn't for me to say nay! So be it, you have my word of honor on it."

"Very well. I shall tell you this much only. The note I received today . . . it was from . . . from the gentleman my papa wishes me to marry."

"Egad!" ejaculated young Wimborne, much struck with this piece of news. "However did the fellow find you?"

"I . . . well . . . oh, you might as well know . . . I sent Tabby with a note to my grandfather . . . whom I thought might be worried about me . . . and Ro . . . the gentleman in question saw Tabby and followed him.

Tabby discovered he was being followed and detoured him to Rye Village where he is now staying. I suppose he must have seen me with your brother last night . . . though how he could have recognized me is more than I can say."

"Sounds a devilish brute! What does he want . . . why does he hound you? I mean . . . if he loves you . . . ought not to hurt you. Seems to me that a fellow shouldn't force himself on a chit!"

"Yes . . . and ordinarily he would not but I fear . . . well, there are reasons. At any rate, he has asked me to meet him, and I have agreed to do so today!"

"Devil you say!" exclaimed Billy. "Hang me if I let you, girl! Damn . . . but I've come to think of you as a sister, and I tell you frankly, it ain't the thing! I may not be up to all the do's and don'ts of society . . . but I do know a girl of your stamp don't go about arranging clandestine assignations!"

"Oh, but Billy, I must. There is no telling what he may do if I don't meet with him . . . though in truth . . . it probably no longer matters for it now appears as if I will have to return to papa and the consequences of my stupidity very soon!"

"You can't, Myriah . . . I shan't let you. Why—who would tend to me?" bantered Billy, attempting to revive her dwindling spirits.

He received half a smile, "That's why I have agreed to meet him. I am stalling for time . . . but we shall see."

"Myriah, the fellow sounds a rum-touch to me. Don't like him. I won't have any sister of mine meeting such a fellow alone. I'll come with you!"

"No, you will not! Silly puppy, do you want your wound opening up again?"

"Then take your groom with you, for God's sake," said Billy impatiently.

"Yes . . . yes. Perhaps that would be wise . . ." said

Myriah, suddenly thoughtful, for it occurred to her that Roland might at this point be desperate enough to try almost anything. She was no fool and she knew that *he was in need of her money*. She took a turn about the room, looked up at the mantelshelf clock and exclaimed, "Oh, gracious! There is just enough time to change into my riding habit."

"Where do you meet the dog?" asked Billy darkly.

"Land Gate in Rye . . . 'tis public enough to be safe," said Myriah, vanishing from his room and leaving him to his thoughts.

She hurried with her clothes, donning the dark blue velvet habit she had worn on her arrival at Wimborne! Up went her long red hair and she scanned her profile in the looking glass. Not very neat . . . but it would have to do, she thought, as she rushed about looking for her kid gloves. She scooped them up and popped her head into Billy's room. "There now . . . don't fret it, love . . . I shall be back within the hour!"

"See that you do . . . for if you are more than ten minutes overdue, my girl . . . I shall come for you myself!" threatened Billy Wimborne grimly.

She laughed, well pleased with his concern and rushed down the front stairs, out of the house, and made her way to the stables. She would have to maintain all her wits if she were to control Sir Roland.

Sir Roland Keyes gave his neckcloth a final pinch and surveyed himself in the long mirror. He was well satisfied with his appearance. He was, he thought, quite a well-formed buck, and one that certainly had style. His auburn curls were styled *à Brutus* around features that were undeniably attractive. His height and the cut of his clothes did him credit, though his lifestyle and his present plans did *not*. In truth, he was rather surprised at Myriah's lack of proper appreciation for his proposal! How came she to ignore all his exceptional qualities? How came she to run from him?

He had hoped he would win her over with his easy charm. He wanted her to submit to his will and, if she would not be seduced to it . . . then she would be forced to it! It was an irritating thought, for Roland was usually not the sort that had to resort to force and had no liking for it. He enjoyed a challenge, and Myriah had certainly been that! She kept his mind active and though his heart had refused to beat any faster at the sight of her exquisite face and well shaped body . . . he meant to have her.

He left the Inn and called for his horse to be saddled. It struck him that he had never been in love . . . or if he had . . . it had never gone as deep as the heart! Love— 'twas something he would continue to get whenever he chanced to want it . . . marriage would not in anyway interfere with his amatory pursuits. He walked his horse over the cobbles down High Street to East Cliff, rounded the corner, and the Land Gate Arch loomed up before him.

Abduction had entered his mind. He could perhaps entice her onto the road . . . but no, Myriah was a fighter. If he were to abduct her, he would need a coach. At any rate, he could see her coming, and at her back was her groom. There would be no abduction with *that* fellow hanging about.

He pulled out his hand-painted enamel snuff box and flipped the lid open. With a deft movement he had a pinch up to his nostril and inhaled, hoping that its soothing quality would control his temper, for he was much annoyed with Myriah for all the trouble she had put him to.

He watched her approach, and his eye was not blind to her fresh loveliness. He rarely thought of money when she was this close, only of possessing her. Money was but a comfortable end result to the marriage he planned. The snuff box was replaced in his inner pocket, and a smile hovered about his sensitive lips.

Myriah's eyes glittered challengingly as she rode up to meet him, and she looked as wild as the stallion beneath her.

"Dash it, love . . . but you quite take the breath away," said Roland, slipping off his horse agilely and putting up his hands for her.

She allowed him to help her dismount and stood with her back to the horse a moment while Tabby hovered in the background and Roland attempted his usual play with her. He touched her nose, "Naughty Myriah, you have sent a shaft through me. Promising to marry me one minute and vanishing the next. Heartless creature . . . kiss me!"

She pushed his chest away and laughed, for he had always the way to make her smile. "Out with it, Roland. I have come as you *demanded* . . . where do we go from here?"

"To the altar, my love! *I* wish it . . . your *papa* wishes it . . . and deep in your hard little heart . . . *you* wish it!" he said glibly.

"But I do *not* wish it, my friend . . . and if papa wishes it . . . 'tis because he was angry, confused, and at that moment probably *thought* I wished it. Do but listen to me, Roland . . . you don't love me . . ."

"Ah, but I do . . . . from your fiery ringlets . . ." he traced a line from her forehead over her nose and stopped at her lips, "to . . . your dainty little toes . . . ."

"That, sir, is not love . . . that is something quite different."

"My lovely girl, you simply are not up to snuff yet . . . though you think you are. Yes, I love you . . . want you . . . whatever you will call it . . ." he said, reaching for her neat little waist and bending down for her lips.

She pushed him away and stepped back. "What you want and need is my inheritance. Be a man, Roland, admit

it! You are dished, you need to marry to stave off your
creditors. I can name a dozen young women with nearly
as much money as I that would do very nicely for your
game. *They* are willing prey—*I am not!*"

He put a gloved finger to her chin. "They have not your
eyes, Myriah . . . they have not your body . . . and, my
dearest child . . . they have not your name! I do not
intend to marry beneath me. Those whose family names
are acceptable . . . are devilishly unhandsome. You would
not match me with such as that, now would you, Myriah?"

"Oh, Roland . . . you are horrid! You are cold and
calculating, and . . ."

". . . and in need!" he said, taking her by the arms and
pulling her to him. "What do you know of that . . .
pretty chit . . . with a papa . . . a home and a fortune
. . . what do *you* know of need?"

"If you had not gamed what you had left to you . . .
you would not be here now begging for my hand," stung
Myriah.

"I am not begging, Myriah. I have been telling you,
love, you and I will be man and wife. But do not fret
. . . we shall also be lovers," he said complacently.

"Roland, papa did *not* make the announcement. Therefore, I cannot be held to it," said Myriah, no longer
finding him amusing.

"No, he did not . . . *nor* did he give you permission to
remain under the same roof with *two bachelors*."

"That is none of your affair!"

"I am afraid that it is. The Wimbornes are not only
bachelors . . . they are also in the business of smuggling.
That, my dear, is a thing I have very strong feelings about!
After all, Myriah . . . I can not have my future bride
involved with such riff-raff!"

"Smuggling?" ejaculated Myriah, admirably surprised.
"Roland, if you brandish such statements about, you will
be open for a slander suit. The Wimborne house is an
old one."

"Ah, Myriah . . . you are not thinking. I am no fool . . . when I give you warning, take it. Don't attempt to frighten me off the path . . . it won't fadge. I am no schoolboy . . . and I am *not* playing a game. I am in earnest. Now let us understand . . . at present my meaning is this . . . if you persist in your decision to remain in the Wimborne household, I will have no alternative but to report your whereabouts to your father."

"Do what you like, Roland. I shall leave when . . . and *if my father* insists on it—not at *your* command!"

"Do you know? You have put a notion into my head," said Roland, smiling without warmth. "Yes, indeed, Myriah . . . you are hot to protect these smugglers of yours."

A chill shot through her. She put out her gloved hand and held his arm, "Roland, Roland, what are you planning . . . what do you mean?"

His arm went round her immediately encircling her small waist and drawing her to him, and this time, because she had to know, she waited to hear what was on his mind, and did not pull away. "Sweet Myriah . . . wild love . . . what a pleasure 'twill be to tame you. We understand one another. Don't fight me . . . and no one shall get hurt!"

She looked up into his hazel eyes, and they were bright with his meaning. "Pray, Roland, who other than ourselves could be hurt by . . . by my opposing our marriage?"

"You know very well what I mean darling. Your friends . . . the moonshiners. All that is needed to put them to the gallows is a bit of evidence . . . just a thread of tangible evidence. Remain in their house, my love, and I shall find that evidence. Leave with me tomorrow . . . and I shall forget their existence."

Roland frightened her. He was too confident of himself . . . and he was able—well able—to carry out his threat. How did he know this much? She herself had been unsure just what the Wimbornes were up to . . . unsure until . . . oh, faith! How did *he know?* She looked up at his face. "I . . . I will think about it, Roland."

"Tomorrow afternoon, Myriah. I want you ready to leave tomorrow afternoon, and then we shall discuss our marriage plans."

"I will give you my answer regarding my departure from Wimborne Towers tomorrow when we meet . . . but I will never discuss marriage with you, Roland! Understand that!" she withdrew from his hold and turned to Silkie who was being held by her groom. She mounted quickly and motioning to Tabby, who was eying Sir Roland with an expression of severe loathing, they departed.

Sir Roland threw Myriah a kiss for she made the mistake of turning to look at him, and she snapped her head back to watch the road, put out with herself and him.

Lord Wimborne watched them and a sharp discomfort lodged itself in his belly. He had come round High Street just moments ago and stood dumbfounded at its peak, watching Myriah converse with Sir Roland. He watched her, for he had arrived in time to see Roland taking her in his arms at the time she did *not* demur!

He was quick to recognize Sir Roland Keyes, the man who had been sharing a table and conversation with Corporal Stone, the same one who had been asking questions about him. And now . . . Roland was the man whose charms had brought Myriah away from Wimborne and into his arms.

Kit had seen her expression, and it was one of deep intensity as she turned her head toward Roland's. Bubbles seemed to form in Kit's veins as he watched her, and they popped, leaving him agitated and confused. He watched her ride away . . . watched Roland blow her a kiss . . . and every fiber in his body ached. He saw Roland turn his horse about, and Kit led his own into an alley where he sat upon his steed's back waiting for Sir Roland

Keyes to pass. And as he did, Kit noted with a stab of green jealousy that the man was not unattractive. He knew an urge to fly home and confront Myriah . . . he wanted to face her, to demand her explanation. He wanted to know why she had been in that man's arms?

Instead, he turned his horse down the street and made his way to the George's Arms. This, another of Rye's inns, was a comfortable tavern where a man could drown his sorrows in a tankard of ale . . . and in the eyes of a buxom wench.

The George's Arms loomed before him, its brick was mellow and inviting, but his heart ached, his mouth was dry, and he felt that everything was at war with his mind.

Seventeen

The harbor town of Rye was large enough to house the two prosperous inns and though the George's Arms was the smaller of the two, it boasted a bright tavern and a jolly clientele. Its oak rafters, dark against its mellowed ceiling, were solid though aged. Its thick beams striped the walls and served to display nettings, pewter tankards, and a miscellaneous collection of oddities. This afternoon found the Arms bubbling with men, young and old, many singing in the late afternoon revelry. Pewter bumpers full of foaming ale swayed rhythmically, and Lord Christopher Wimborne was determined to join in the frolic!

He took a robust young woman with short yellow curls, a pretty face, and calloused hands into his lap and nibbled upon her ear. The lady, finding Kit's person most admirable, displayed her charms quite amiably in an effort to intrigue his lordship further. Yet when Kit planted a hearty kiss upon her pursed lips, an irritable sensation tingled through his veins, and he had the perverse urge to allow the ardent female to slide from his lap!

His depredations on the tavern's excellent ale and its serving wench had not served to detach his mind from its frenzy. It was with him still, spoiling his thoughts, divorcing his needs from his ability to supply them. Suddenly Kit Wimborne put the surprised pretty on her feet, bidding her adieu, and taking his leave while she watched, hands on hips and face in a pucker.

The devil was in it! He had to see Myriah! He only knew he had to talk with her . . . confront her . . . question her . . . make her his. Her wild, wondrous magic had enchanted his soul and held his heart captive. He rode his horse hard and arrived at his stables only minutes later. Without bothering to call Fletcher to attend his horse, he left it standing and stalked off purposefully toward the house.

His front door flew open and the stairs were taken two at a time. The door to Myriah's room received no questioning knock, but was sent inwards with a masterful show of force. Her room was empty. This in no way assuaged his lordship's strange fever, and he stormed across the hall, exploding into his brother's room, his blue eyes mirrors of his intent.

Young Wimborne scanned his brother's face with a frown. "Eh . . . what's amiss Kit? What has happened?"

"Myriah . . . where is she?" demanded Kit and his tone hinted at his uncompromising mood.

"Myriah? Why, she said something about taking a walk. Said she had to think . . . does it best outdoors . . . I myself like to . . . *Kit* . . . KIT . . .?" he called, for his brother had already departed.

Billy Wimborne sat wondering, for his brother had never before been prone to such whimsical behavior. He listened to Kit's determined steps take him out of the house. He would find her . . . and then . . . then . . . he would demand an answer to the questions that plagued his mind. What was she to the man called Sir Roland Keyes . . . the man from London . . . who sat chatting comfortably with the exciseman. Why had she met him in secret . . . why had she been in his arms? He would have his answer!

Myriah leaned against the tall white elm and gazed down at the dark sea water below. Whatever was she to do? Then she was looking into the blazing blue eyes of Christopher Wimborne and her heart beating against her chest, demanding . . . demanding . . . His hands were burning through her sleeves as he gripped her arms and the fury of his expression shook her with new wonder.

"I want the truth, Myriah! The time for coyness is past. What is Sir Roland Keyes to you . . . and why, my dear, did you meet him in secret today at Land Gate?"

"Secret?" said Myriah, and her voice was pitched an octave too high. Her lips trembled as she responded, "My lord . . . I made *no secret* of it! Why . . . one could hardly call the Land Gate entrance to Rye . . . a secluded spot!"

"Damnation, woman . . . don't play games with me! I want to know why you met him . . . and why you chose to do it *away* from Wimborne Towers!"

She bit her lower lip, and her lashes veiled the expression in her eyes. "Why . . . why must you know?"

"Lord . . . but you try a man's patience," he spluttered, shaking her. "I will know . . . and I will know *now*, my girl!"

She yanked herself out of his grip. "Do you mean to shake it out of me?"

He took one of her arms and brought her up against him. Her face was beneath his own, and a chance observer might have deemed the sight a glorious one. However, each of the antagonists were beyond such thoughts. "By God, Myriah . . . do not tempt me! Your . . . *friend* . . . Sir Roland . . . only last night . . . sat chatting amiably with *our* friend Corporal Stone . . . and *I will know* what *your* connection with him is," seethed Kit.

"Oh . . . is that . . ." began Myriah, as understanding flashed through her mind. So he felt betrayed . . . and she thought . . . she hoped . . . he was jealous. Anger, frustration, and a host of similar sensations swept her body.

'Tis understandable that when one undergoes such uncomfortable emotions, one does not always act rationally. Such was the case with Myriah. Her eyes snapped up at his handsome face. "Well, my lord, I have no notion what all your heat is about . . . ."

"Damnation, woman! You have the audacity . . . did you not hear me before? *I saw you* . . . fiend seize the day . . . the first moment ever I did . . . but I did, God help me and . . . I kissed you, my beauty . . . yet just two hours ago . . . *I found you in another man's arms!*"

She slapped him across the face, stinging her hand as well as his cheek. "*You,* my lord . . . flatter yourself! You kissed me . . . damn your lips . . . yes, you did . . . though I can't think how I happened to allow it . . . and if you think you saw what you did . . . what of it?"

"You witch!" breathed Lord Wimborne taking her into his arms ferociously. His kiss was like a sudden, merciless wind and it left her breathless. . . hungry for more. His hand went to her hair, taking hold of her long red curls and pulling her head back, enabling him to discover the sweetness of her throat. His kisses were wild, unrestrained, and infinitely deft in their enticing skill. She had never before been loved in such a way and, as he pulled her downwards onto the soft turf, she felt her body tremble in his hands . . . frightened by his passion . . . terrified by her own. She pushed gently at his broad chest, fighting the needs of her heart.

"No, please . . . no, Kit," she whispered. "*This* . . . this is *wrong!*"

"Hush, sweetings . . . don't talk . . . don't spoil this moment with words," he replied, kissing her again.

His lips were on hers again, demanding, urging her with the force of his desire and the skill of his experience, but she was tense, unwilling to yield. He was going too far . . . he was taking more than she was willing to give. She shouted at him, "*Stop it.* Please stop it, Kit!"

He laughed in her ear and mounted her, his weight

negating her effort at rising. "Oh, no, sweetings . . . 'tis a devil driving me . . . 'tis you, love . . . and not God himself could stop me now, Myriah! Hush, my beauty . . . hush, and I shall please you as much . . . and more than any of your lovers ever have done."

That, of course, was all that was needed to undo the passion he had aroused within her. With a strength born of fury, her hand once again left its mark across his cheek, and Kit Wimborne found himself off the lady of his desires and stretched solidly on the grass. Myriah was up and off in one movement, and her legs carried her faster than they had ever done before. Her palm, red and burning, served to remind her that she had had at least some satisfaction before she discarded the odious brute she had had the stupidity to fall in love with! A sob tore through her body and stuck deep in her throat. She would leave Wimborne Towers! She would leave . . . tomorrow she would go and never look at his . . . face again. Never would she listen to his merry masculine voice . . . never. . . . The tears that streamed down her cheeks were taken by the wind and slapped into her face again and again until at last she reached the house, found her room and her pillow, and buried her heart within its cool softness.

Kit Wimborne, his face smarting from the blow of Myriah's hand, his head whirling and his heart in the heavings of unsure waters, watched helplessly as Myriah receded behind the sway of the land! Plague take the girl . . . she behaved like a sainted mystery . . . one moment an innocent with childlike eyes . . . and then the next a woman with a siren's magic! Devil take it! When his lips had found her own . . . 'twas all he could to keep from taking her all in a moment. He felt his hands had a will of their own . . . he had wanted her so . . . but what was more to the point was the fact that he wanted Myriah to be his and his *alone*. There now was the crux of the matter. Thinking of Sir Roland Keyes . . . of Myriah in his arms . . . had driven him into a bold rage. He knew the only way to banish the misery of his aching heart was to possess her . . . possess her and strike away all others.

He lay back against the turf and felt the cool blades tickle his cheek. His hand went to his forehead, creating a shield for his troubled eyes. He had to think . . . he had to clear his head—but most of all he would have to get Myriah out of his mind. He knew he must do that if he was ever to be at peace again . . . if he was ever to— oh, God! he thought, feeling the pain sweep through him. He was in hell and on fire . . . and damnation! He wanted her!

Sir Roland rounded the corner and entered the long narrow alley that led to the Mermaid Inn's rear stable-yard entrance. He had visited his gay, buxom potmaid and thereby dispelled some of his frustration. However, that time was past, and his thoughts were again with him, and Sir Roland had a problem. Myriah! Now—what was he tó do? Abduction it seemed, was out of the question, for she was too well guarded by her groom. No, he would not be able to abduct her whilst they had their meeting tomorrow. What of Wimborne Towers? thought he, one brow low over his eye, the other going up for suddenly he had a notion. Yes . . . a possibility. Could he not linger about Wimborne unbeknownst? Certainly he could . . . he could wait for the right moment . . . for the special license he had procured was safely tucked in his pocket. It was a thought and needed serious consideration. He entered the Inn, feeling suddenly ravenous, and proceeded to the tavern room.

"Hallo!" called Stone from the counter. "I was just about to have my dinner . . . why not join me?"

Sir Roland nodded amiably enough and thought, 'why not?' The fellow might have more to tell. Pointing to young Stone's pewter dish, he ordered a plate of the same and a bumper of ale before following the preventive officer to a near-by table.

The young man sighed heavily as he drew up his chair and watched Sir Roland discard his greatcoat, hat, and gloves. "Been about town, have you?" asked Stone putting his own hat on an empty table at his back.

"You might say that."

"Eh?" The exciseman scanned Roland's face for his meaning and caught a look in the gentleman's eye that spoke clearly enough. "Oh . . . aye . . ." he grinned knowledgeably.

"And you . . . have you anything new?" asked Roland idly.

"Aye, that we have. One of our men discovered a bit of information in Winchelsea."

"Oh? Anything interesting?"

Stone opened his mouth and then shut it quickly for the innkeeper had sidled over with Sir Roland's dinner. They waited for the man to depart, then Stone inclined his head and lowered his voice. "I think we got 'em . . . yes, sir. Tonight I do believe we got 'em."

A lad, thin, small, and not more than nine years of age, pressed himself against the narrow opening of the tavern counter and sighed. His mother had placed the brown package in his hands and bade him deliver it to the innkeeper's wife. He had tried to hand the thing into Thomas's hands but found the busy tavern keeper almost impossible to halt. Then the sound of Stone's voice filtered through his boredom, and his head moved sharply at the words. Stone was well known to him. The preventive officer was known to all the men who worked Lord Wimborne's galley, and his father had pointed the exciseman out to him more than once. Cautiously, he painted himself against a recess in the tavern wall and was just barely hidden from view.

Stone continued, feeling safe by the emptiness of the

room. "Know they plan on a crossing just about seven
or so tonight . . . and mean to be there. Tide is in, and
we have it on good authority that their galley be leaving
from Wimborne Dike. Our Winchelsea informer tells us
they plan their drop at Knockholt Beach, and our Revenue
Cutter will be waiting on 'em. Lord, but I've been waiting
for this night!"

"You do talk as if they were the Hawkhurst Gang
themselves," smiled Roland mockingly.

"Aye . . . maybe I do . . . and maybe they ain't . . .
for in truth the Hawkhurst were a bloody bunch, and
these gentlemen be but a speck of dust in comparison.
All the same . . . they be traitors to the Crown for they
are giving the French our gold."

Sir Roland's sharp eyes caught the movement at the
bar entrance, and he motioned Stone to silence. The
preventive officer turned round at once, and his dark
brows met over his hawk nose. "Eh . . . what are you
doing there, boy?" he demanded of the lad.

"Me? Nuthin' . . . I be waiting on Thomas . . . got
a gown m'mum done up for his wife, I do."

"John Bilkes!" bellowed Thomas the innkeeper appearing from nowhere and taking the lad by the arm,
"The missus be upstairs waiting on that dress . . . you
best take it to her quick!"

"Aye," said the lad scurrying out of the tavern room
and rushing down the corridor. He turned to find the
heavy Thomas laboring after him and shoved the package
into his hands. "Take this, sir . . . got to go after m'pa,
I do . . . got to tell him."

"Tell him . . . tell him what, lad?" asked the innkeeper
frowning.

"No time . . . no time . . ." said the boy, disappearing
from sight.

It was some three miles to Wimborne lands, where he,
his parents, and his three younger brothers lived in a
small two-room cottage. The time was fast approaching

seven, and soon Stone would be on his way to the Dike with his military minion. John Bilkes had to reach his father and stop him from going to the galley to meet Lord Wimborne and the others. *He had to protect his pa!*

He reached the small cottage with its dark thatched roofing and screamed for his father, but only his mother appeared, wiping her hands on her apron. "Bless ye, child . . . what be all the hollering about?"

"Pa . . . where be pa?" shouted the little man, beside himself.

"Why, you know very well, John Bilkes, that your pa goes tonight!"

"No . . . no . . . he has left?"

"Well, now, and sure he 'as . . . but . . ." She stopped and watched wide-eyed as her son took off down the dirt path once again. "Hey, John . . . John Bilkes . . . you come back 'ere this instant . . . ."

Her son couldn't answer . . . the only chance left to him was to get to Lord Wimborne, for the child had no idea where the galley boat was docked. He was windless, his legs felt numb, but he ran all the way, crossing the wide meadow and taking the drive that led to the front doors of Wimborne Towers. He was sure it was nearing the hour, and he pounded wildly at the front doors. He felt as though his heart, small as it was, had the might of force to break through the chest confining it. He knocked hard with both fists until he felt his hands burn, and there suddenly stood the loveliest lady he had ever seen. Myriah stood before him, one delicate brow up inquiringly. "Oh, you poor boy . . . whatever is wrong, child?" asked Myriah, observing his condition.

The boy blinked, opened his mouth to speak, and found no breath left with which to form the words. He sucked in air and held himself steady against the oak frame of the door. At last he heaved out the words, "Lord . . . Wimborne."

"Lord Wimborne . . . oh, dear . . . he is not here. He has been gone this hour and more."

"Oh, no! No! Then my pa . . . all of 'em is done up! I knows it . . . I knows it," cried the boy, beside himself.

Myriah put an arm about him and soothed him with her voice, "If you tell me what has occurred to upset you, perhaps we can set things to right."

"Lookee, I don't know if I should be telling ye this . . . but now I ain't got no choice . . . besides it don't make no ha'porth o'difference, do it? So . . . I'll tell ye all I know. I was in the tavern and I heard Stone. He was saying to some flashcove how's they got 'em tonight. Oh, lordy, lordy, my poor pa . . . they mean to catch 'em and hang 'em, they do!"

"What?" shrieked Myriah. "Explain yourself."

"They know the galley be going down the dike . . . plan on cornering 'em there. But if they don't manage the thing . . . then they aim to 'ave at 'em at the Knockholt Beach where they be landing the stuff."

"I see. Allright, son . . . you don't know where the boat is, but I do. Go upstairs, lad, and tell Master William what has occurred. Don't let him get up . . . mind now. If he tries, you get my groom and bolt him to the ground if you have to. Tell him I know where his brother is and mean to warn him. Hurry!" said Myriah as she rushed out of the house and felt the night air on her cheeks.

Sir Roland watched young Bilkes as the boy scrambled away from the tavern room and it struck him oddly. The lad had heard them speaking—of that he was certain—and more to the point, he had the fancy that the boy was about to go off and give warning. Within a short space, he had decided to leave the remainder of his meal, bid his excise acquaintance adieu, and leave the inn. He made his way to the stableyard and had his horse brought to him. A few minutes later, he was tethering his horse to a tree and watching Myriah flash out of the house. He was on her trail in a trice, keeping her in his sight and himself well out of hers!

Eighteen

Thank God, she had fallen into the dike this morning, thought Myriah, as she sped across the little arched bridge on her way to the spot where the galley boat was housed. Faith! This morning! How long ago it seemed . . . and how much had passed since. Nothing meant anything to her at this moment. Not all the pain, not the tears that loving Kit Wimborne had caused her to shed! She only knew that she would not, could not, allow him to be uncovered in his game. His game . . . it was wrong. She knew that and did not care. What had she to do with right and wrong? What had she to do with proprieties? She only knew she loved and for that love would give her all.

They would hang the smugglers . . . but they would not hang Kit . . . no, there was a far more subtle way to destroy a nobleman. They would take his name and drag it through the slime, destroy all trace of his heart . . . of his pride . . . and that she would never let them do. She had to get to him . . . warn him . . . stop him from going out.

She held up her skirts as she ran through the tall swaying grass, her eyes peering into the darkness, and she stopped. Two men across the dike moved a huge rock back into its original spot and then ran along the dike. They did not see her as they came to a point directly across from her and began their scramble down the sloped bank toward the water. She looked down and saw the galley boat. It was filled with some eight men at the oars and Kit Wimborne at its helm. He looked up at that moment, saw her, and cursed aloud, though his eyes opened wide with amazement as she half-slid down the slope to the water's edge.

"Kit, oh, Kit . . . Stone . . . he will be here soon . . ." she called desperately. His arm went out and scooped Myriah into its fold, lifting her without any seeming effort over the water and into the depths of the galley boat. "Now what is all this about, Myriah?" he asked sternly, his eyes searching her face.

"Oh, Kit, a boy . . . John Bilkes he called himself . . ."

"John . . . my lad John . . .?" asked a young man beneath a woolen cap turning round to her worriedly.

"Hush man, and allow Miss White to continue," ordered Kit, frowning at him.

"Aye, sorry, m'lord," said the man.

"Go on, Myriah," whispered Kit.

"Yes . . . well, the boy said he had overheard Stone telling someone that he and a band of preventive officers are coming here to this dike tonight to search you out . . . and that if he didn't get you in the Dike . . . a cutter would have at you when you landed your cargo at Knockholt Beach."

"Saints preserve us! 'Tis that stalled I am to know whet divil spoke agin us, m'lord," said Fletcher coming up behind Kit and scratching his head.

"That doesn't matter at the present, Fletcher. We will have to act quickly to get out of this." He turned and eyed one of the boys from the Winchelsea group, a group of professional smugglers that had been working the tide with Lord Wimborne. "You, Ben . . . you'll ride to

Winchelsea and have our landing crew meet us at Beachy Head instead of Knockholt. Off with you . . . make it blue lanterns! Ride sharp now, mate."

"Aye," said the heavy-set boy as he scrambled out of the boat and up the slope, disappearing from their view.

"No Kit . . . no . . . you don't mean to go still . . . you can't. It's too dangerous. I . . . I won't let you . . . think of Billy . . . think of your name . . ." cried Myriah, taking his lapels into her hand and attempting to bring him to his senses.

"Hush, sweetings. Lord knows I want to set your mind at ease. I've got to go tonight. There is no help for it . . . don't ask me questions, only believe me . . . it will be allright. Now you've done us a good turn . . . out with you . . . and go home, Myriah . . . we will talk later," said he, putting her firmly from him and taking her arm so as to aid her out of the galley.

"NO!" shouted Myriah, "I won't go . . . Kit Wimborne . . . I won't . . ."

"You will go and now . . . I've got no time to waste convincing you, love. If I have to pick you up and dump you into the sea in order to get you to go home, I shall . . ." His tone indicated that he would not spend any time arguing the point, yet Myriah felt she had to stay with him, couldn't leave him now.

"Please, Kit . . . I . . . I could help . . . I could be a lookout . . ."

He laughed and chucked her chin, but at that moment they heard horses rumbling in the distance. The sound sent a shaft of silence through them all, and Myriah found herself face down against the wood planking of the boat.

Sir Roland watched Myriah and stopped suddenly behind a clump of evergreen bushes nestled against the edge of the dike. He was forced to soil his buff-colored knee breeches, for the height of the bushes made it expedient for him to crouch on his knees. He watched Myriah's form become eclipsed by the steep walls of the causeway and himself dropped to his silk waistcoated front that he might continue to observe her movements. The voices of the moonshiners below were carried to him by the accommodating breeze, and as he listened to Myriah and Kit Wimborne, a slow satanic smile took command of his features. So Myriah, 'tis the dashing potential gallows dangler you want?

Then came the rumble of the King's men, and as their horses beat the earth, Sir Roland retreated quickly. He had learned quite enough, and what he had learned was not for the preventive men. No . . . he had a far better use for his knowledge.

The smell of seaweed, salt encrustations, and fish threatened to overcome Myriah. Her eyes were shut tight, and her nose was pressed against the bottom of the seaworthy galley. She was vaguely aware of tremendous quiet above her, and she barely heard Kit's command: "Steady, lads . . . keep the beat steady!"

The open boat was moving through the still water at an incredible rate. She had never known what force men could apply to the oars. She heard the swish of water against wood, listened to the quick even beat, and a tingle of excitement swept through her. Then the sound of the dragoons slashed through the night. She heard Corporal Stone's staccato orders and knew him to be close, too close. Still Kit urged his men on. He was like a god, wholly at ease, confident . . . instilling his men with the spirit to go on. Again came the Corporal's command, followed by a series of gunshots, and Myriah prayed. She had often heard that smugglers would turn on the dragoons, engaging in gunfire that usually left the preventive officers outnumbered. She couldn't bear it if Kit were to kill anyone. She put the fear away. She re-

fused to think of it. She loved him . . . and at the moment
that was all that mattered . . . loving him and being with
him.

Suddenly the boat pitched to the left, and Myriah put
her hands round the firm strong leg beside her. Hoisting
herself up to Lord Wimborne's knees she could see that
the causeway had split. Faith! It had forked and left the
Riding Officers standing foolishly at bay. The dragoons
were on the wrong embankment with no immediate way
to the dike they had taken. They stood like a pack of
foolish boys, waving their blunderbusses and shouting
threats and curses at the tidesmen's heads.

Kit looked back at them and without slowing his pace
at the oars, began to laugh. It was a merry sound and
infected his crew until they were all giving way to mirth,
well pleased with themselves and each other. Myriah
shifted her position so that she sat, legs tucked under
herself between the span of Lord Wimborne's knees. She
felt the salt-water breeze rush at her for they were at
the head of open water and she heard Kit's merry voice,
"Allright, lads . . . keep a sharp eye out . . . it's to
Boulogne!"

He was answered by their grins and the steady splash
of water against the boat's side and Myriah gazed up at
his rugged face with wonder. He was everything she had
ever dreamed of . . . everything and just a bit more . . .
for she could have done without his moonshining. Myriah
eyed the pistol in Kit's belt, touching it lightly, and her
fine dark brows drew together. "You . . . you never
thought to use it . . . did you, Kit?"

He chuckled. "What's this, sweetings? What sort of
fiend do you take me for? Use it?" His grin was wide
and yet caressing. "If I did . . . 'twould be to lay a
few poor devils low, and I'm not the sort that kills a
man for doing his job . . . it wouldn't be sporting!"

She smiled, but the seawind was strong, and the cold
shot through her thin silk, causing her to tremble. Kit

frowned and pulled in his oars, balancing them as he shrugged off his cloak. She found herself being wrapped gently, felt a kiss planted on her forehead. "Here, sweetings, keep low between my legs, and you should be warm enough. I wouldn't have had you on such a journey, but there was nothing for it . . . couldn't leave you to the dragoons."

"Oh, Kit, here . . . with you is precisely where I want to be," said Myriah. He looked deep into her eyes—another mistake, he told himself . . . for those eyes—they bewitched. He shook himself, and his eyes once again found the sea as did his oars, and the boat moved on towards its destination.

She scanned the men . . . his men . . . smugglers all, and yet . . . they had the look of men born to the land, not the sea. To be sure, they were dressed as seamen with woolly caps covering their heads, kerchiefs round their necks . . . and the oars moved solidly in their gloved hands. They all had leather straps slung round their bodies, from which hung empty leather purses. She sighed and supposed those purses would be filled tonight.

The sea was kind to her voyagers this night, and the wind was light and in their favor. There was no tossing to slow their pace, and Myriah's eyes looked at the calm water and sighed. It was too beautiful . . . and far too deceiving, she thought. The moon-light made a narrow white path from the sea to Heaven, and the stars twinkled brightly in the black velvet sky.

"It's a full moon tonight . . . 'tis what we've been waiting for," said Kit to her lightly.

"I . . . I don't want to hear it . . ." answered Myriah, suddenly sad. This way of life . . . his smuggling had set a barrier between them. She could see it . . . and this barrier might keep them apart.

"You don't? You are a mystery, Myriah . . . a veritable mystery," smiled Kit, nudging her gently with his leg.

She placed her cheek against his knee, and the action brought his eyes upon her.

"Myriah . . ." said he, needing to say her name, but not really having anything he could say here in front of all the men.

"Yes, Kit?"

"Are you warm enough, love?"

"Yes, Kit," she said. She didn't want to talk, and she didn't want to think. What was she doing here? Good God! She had finally plunged herself into a scrape from which there would be no escape. Here she sat between the legs of a man that captained a smuggling galley! And where was their destination . . . why . . . Boulogne, France, of course . . . where else but to the port of the enemy?

The bay was now well behind them and their galley was but a dark strip on a vast sea. Her map at home outlined the English Channel, and there on paper it looked so very narrow . . . but that was paper, and this . . . this was reality, and no land could be seen.

Kit eyed Myriah and, finding her mouth dour, rallied her. "Well, sweetings, something has you by the tail . . . out with it!"

She pulled a face at him. "That, my lord, is a most odious thing to say to a lady!"

He grinned. "Lady? My dear girl, tonight you are nought but a female smuggler!"

"Thanks to you, you brute!" snapped Myriah.

"I thought you wanted to tag along with us?" returned his lordship amiably.

"I did. What does that signify?"

He laughed and began reciting,

"With her pistols loaded she went on board,
 By her side hung a glittering sword,
 In her belt two daggers—well arm'd for war,
 Was the Female Smuggler, who ne'er feared a scar!"

She giggled. "You are jolly, aren't you? For I do assure you I have no weapons about me, and I am very fearful of being scarred."

"Then why are you here, Myriah . . . if not for the adventure?" asked Kit, his eyes serious, his mouth suddenly grave.

"I . . . I don't know . . . certainly *not* for the adventure!" returned she. "Oh, dear . . . how long will it take, Kit?"

"Can you not see Boulogne, love . . . 'tis there," said Kit, maintaining his grave expression.

She stretched her neck and peered through the darkness, finding only water swaying about, making gentle peaks as though kissing the air. "No, no, I don't see land at all."

"Don't you? Must see about your eyes, love, when we return. 'Tis there . . . some ten miles or so ahead of us," he grinned.

She slapped his leg and then once again cuddled against it for warmth . . . and something else!

"Ten miles, Kit? Why . . . how far have we traveled . . . it feels as though we've been on the water for hours," she said thoughtfully.

"We have, sweetings. We've gone more than fifteen miles . . . and without checking my timepiece I'd say we've done it in less than three hours. Damn good time! The same trip took us in what was a gentle breeze—of some eight miles an hour—a good five hours last time. Lord, but our arms ached that night, and we didn't make it back until light was upon us."

"Oh, Kit . . . must you smuggle?" she asked in a hushed whisper.

He laughed. "Must I . . . no, there are many that would say I definitely *must not!*"

"Do not poke fun at me, Kit . . . I am serious," said Myriah appealingly.

He looked at her and opened his mouth, wanting to

tell her, and not yet able to. It would be so easy to set her mind at ease, tell her what he was really doing when he crossed the channel on these excursions . . . he should trust her . . . for hadn't she come to warn him tonight? Later . . . later he would explain everything to her . . . perhaps. Then Sir Roland's features flashed across his mind, and the image of her leaning into Roland's arms that very afternoon admonished him, and he stiffened. "Hush now, I don't want to lose my stroke."

She sighed sadly and looked again at the endless stretch of dark water and wondered why he had suddenly turned his 'wintry look' upon her.

Nineteen

The next thirty minutes passed swiftly, and suddenly Myriah heard one of the men call 'land.' She peeped up, excited in spite of herself, for she had never seen France. She had heard so much about it from her father who had made the Grand Tour and who had seen Napoleon during the brief peace in 1802. Here she was actually setting foot on French soil . . . and how she wished it was Paris and during peacetime!

She saw two wagons and a crew of French seaworthies flapping their arms about in greeting and suddenly she felt the galley scrape against the shore. Kit's men were jumping nimbly out of the open boat, and then Kit himself was taking her hand and leading her away from the stern of the boat, down its center. He jumped down onto the pebbly beach and took her waist in his strong gloved hands and with a quick movement she stood beside him gazing up into the face of a small dark stranger. The man was dressed like a French gentleman, and his many-tiered gray greatcoat came from the hands of a skillful tailor. He inclined his head towards Kit and said in French, "Bon soir, mon ami . . . it was a good journey, oui?"

"Oui, it was a good journey," replied Kit, moving away

with the man on his one side, Myriah on the other. She marveled at his French, for she herself spoke the language only passably.

The French crew and English alike began loading the galley, and they worked in unison, totally unmindful that their two countries were at war. War—it was a fearful thing. It emptied a man's veins and bore hungrily through his gut. What had they to do with such as that? This work . . . though noblemen deemed it dishonest, put food on their table and clothes on their back! It was hard, back-breaking work, but it served, and thus, there were no complaints as they did their jobs. The galley's belly was loaded with the tubs of French brandy and Frenchman and Englishman smiled peacefully at their work!

"Who is the pretty with you?" inquired the stranger, still speaking in French to Kit.

"My . . . my woman," answered Kit quickly. "Don't fret it."

She understood Kit's last remark and, blushing, gave his sleeve a twist. He grinned at her, found a log, and placing her forcefully upon it, commanded, "Stay here, sweetings . . . I have some business to transact."

She pouted, but made herself as comfortable as possible and waited, watching Kit as he walked a short distance away from her with the Frenchman.

His eyes were constantly darting in her direction, keeping her in sight, for they were on foreign soil, and Myriah was a beautiful woman. He would take no chances of her being hurt.

"Have you the money?" asked the Frenchman.

"Thirty-five shillings a tub. It's a high price, Louis. Others pay you but twenty shillings," complained Kit.

The Frenchman smiled affably. "Yes . . . and they take off my hands eighty tubs . . . one hundred tubs . . . and they come regularly my lord. You come . . .

once every two weeks . . . and what do you take . . . but thirty tubs!"

"Still . . . my landing crew has complained about it . . . say that there is not enough in it for them," argued Kit.

"Your landing crew . . . what are they but nodcocks who slink, carry, hide, and run. . . ."

"They also break heads," said Kit dryly.

The Frenchman laughed. "Ah, yes . . . but not yours, Kit, never yours. You're far too clever."

Myriah's eyes opened wide with amazement. She could not believe what she had heard. She had been straining, trying to pick up bits and pieces of their French conversation when suddenly she heard the Frenchman say in perfect English: "not yours, Kit . . . you're far too clever."

She had heard it and yet could not believe it. Why, the man sounded as much an Englishman as did Kit! She was so curious she stood up and inched her way towards them. However, Kit took the Frenchman by the arm and moved him out of hearing distance.

She saw him take out a fat leather bag and place it in the man's grasp. She also saw that oddly enough, the bag was followed by something white and gold, something that looked like an envelope.

Then it was over and, as if she had never heard the man speak in English, he was once again speaking French. They returned to her and the Frenchman was speaking, "What are you complaining of, my lord? You pay me thirty-five shillings, yes. But you sell each keg for five pounds . . . do you not?"

Kit laughed and gave the fellow a robust slap on the back. "That we do, Frenchy . . . that we do!"

"Very well, hein . . . we are pleased . . . for you have made your profit . . . I have made mine."

"I have not done so yet. I still have the Revenue Cutters to pass through."

"May they be damned! Bon voyage to you, mon ami . . . until we meet again," said the Frenchman and then once again something peculiar hit Myriah. Kit and the Frenchman took each other's hands and clasped them . . . for all the world as though they were brothers. "Soon, Louis . . . soon you'll be on *the* soil . . . the soil that makes you what you are."

"Oui, mon ami," said the Frenchman hopefully.

They parted, and Myriah watched wide-eyed as Kit stood standing looking after the Frenchman, and she heard him sigh. She looked into his eyes. "You like him, don't you?"

"Louis? Why yes, yes I do," said Kit, smiling warmly at her. "Now . . . if I don't mistake, my lads have loaded the galley and 'tis time I paid them their wage. He went amongst them and distributed their pay. There would be more after they had made their sale on the other side of the channel.

Myriah was lifted into the boat and pulled along to the stern, and once again Captain Wimborne and his men were rowing into deep water.

One of the men grumbled that his arms and back were a thing of pain. Young Bilkes laughed, "Ye old goat, stop looking like a dead crow, and maybe ye'll feel a might better."

"Wot sort of talk be that, young'n?" grumbled Fry, "and if I'm not mistaken looks like the durned wind is about to start on wobblin' us," he said, staring up at the sky with his one eye.

"You ney like an old woman, Fry," bellowed one of the Winchelsea lads, a spry fellow ready for a bit of sport.

"Old woman? Why ye wait, ye daft child . . . ye'll lose ye sweet face for that priggly remark!"

They all laughed and continued their firm steady strokes, but Kit was frowning and gazing up at the clouds.

Myriah noticed and pulled at his coat. "What is it, Kit, what's wrong?"

"I don't like the scudding clouds." He stood up and began shouting affably. "All right, my fine able buckos, let's move, on the count! Just look at the tail of that maid . . . she's swimming just a touch away . . . after her, boys."

The boat, loaded down with its weight of brandy, slashed through the water, the men grinning and moving their oars with great strength of heart. Kit took up his oars and shouted the count, keeping them in line. There was a storm brewing . . . and he wanted to land his cargo before it came upon them!

"If a gale comes on us . . . then wot?" asked a young man of Fry.

"Hold yer fiendish tongue, boy. Gale . . . yer fool, ain't no gales in May!" with which all around the young man broke into mirth and a renewed strength. They pushed on, putting the miles behind them. They made long tracks through the water, slicing their way home. They prided themselves on their ability . . . the ability of arriving at their prescribed destination at the time they had stipulated. The land smugglers, a group of professional headbeaters, armed with bats, lest any landsguard had the foolish intent to deter them, would be waiting with their lanterns and their horses to carry the cargo away . . . and the Wimborne crew would be there on time!

"I do like the sea I do . . ." said Bilkes suddenly breaking the quiet, "but, in truth . . . will be good to be grounded a bit."

" 'Tis a lot o' trouble for jest a wee bit of pleasurin'," said another. "Lordy, but it do put bread on the table better than any other way I know."

The tubs of brandy rolled in their confines, and the men picked up a tune to its beat. The wind seemed to join them and it wasn't long before they were stroking, all in harmony. The salt spray splashed at their faces, and they laughed at each other and themselves when suddenly Fletcher pointed silently and Fry hissed, "Wot's that?"

Myriah pressed herself against Kit's leg, a sudden fear clutching at her heart, for she knew. *Without seeing* she knew!

"Look lively, lads . . . we're in for a run now!" shouted Kit, oaring with determination.

"Dinna they see us, m'lord?" asked Fletcher.

"No, they haven't spotted us yet but it's a cutter all right, and a swift sea vessel she is, for she is the *Swallow*!"

A sea mist hung about in foaming clusters and the men idled their oars quietly, their hearts in their throats, watching as the cutter passed. Her lanterns, red glowing in the night, looked like the eyes of terror, and no man made a sound as they waited for the ghostly vision to continue on its way. The cutter was but thirty yards away, and they saw the tall sails white against the black sky, and each man prayed to himself they would not be spotted.

She passed, and it was like the breath of new life. They waited still, for none would move without Kit's command, and it came softly, firmly, "Swiftly now, m'fine buckos . . . swiftly. There's no time to lose, for she'll soon turn and head inland!"

They were heading for a short sandy beach, off the village where they would be met by a band of land smugglers who would relieve them of their burden, pay them for their trouble, and allow them to continue home.

Myriah raised her head, and Kit laughed at her wide-open look. "You look like a veritable kitten—all wonder! Now put your head down low . . . one never knows when one might be shot at."

"Oh, oh, but Kit! You are right up there . . ." said Myriah.

He laughed and flicked her nose, "There it is . . . there boys!"

Myriah saw the flash of a blue light and heard Fletcher mumble, "Aye, the flinks be steady. Safe enough, m'lord!"

She saw the stretch of narrow flat shore, and Kit was ordering a man to light their answering lantern. The lights answered each other, and then they were approaching the pebbles of the beach.

Two dozen men came running from behind rocks and trees, appearing suddenly from nowhere. Another six leading horses and wagons and carrying wooden bats followed, and Kit and his men were jumping out of the galley. Kit sidled over to a grizzly looking man, and Myriah could see that money was exchanged. Then all at once men seemed to surround the galley. Kit returned to her and picked her up in his arms and without speaking, set her on a near-by rock before returning to supervise the unloading. Myriah watched, fascinated with the speed of their work, so engrossed that she didn't see the glittering eyes of a boy bending towards her. She felt her hair touched and turned suddenly and with a scream she cringed backwards, scaring the addle-brained fellow who had dared to touch her.

Kit was there and between her and the frightened youth in a moment, but pity rather than anger swept through him. The lad, no more than fifteen, dirty, be-ragged, with large terrified eyes, jumped about moving his hands agitatedly in one another and crying, "I meant no 'arm . . . no . . . 'arm . . . jest wanted to tech 'er, I did . . ."

A tall wiry man appeared out of the darkness and put his arm about the boy's shoulders, his own head high in the air. " 'Ere now, m'lord . . . the lad meant nothing. He be but a half-wit . . . can't 'elp 'imself . . . he be always teching wot he shouldn't. 'Tis m'fault if fault is to be laid . . . I should've been watching 'im."

"Oh, please," said Myriah at once, "I am not angry

. . . I was merely startled." She smiled warmly at the frightened boy, and he peeped at her shyly.

" 'Tis time we moved," said Kit, once again picking her up.

"I do have legs and they are well able to carry me," said Myriah objecting to his handling.

"I am sure . . . but we want no more incidents to-night," said he curtly.

"Oh, and I suppose that was *my fault?*"

He laughed amiably. "In truth, yes, for you are far too beautiful to be left amongst a pack of devils. Now in with you, love," said he depositing her in her place and hopping in after her.

Lord Wimborne's crew shoved their galley into deeper water, jumping nimbly into the boat, and picking up their oars without so much as a backward look. Myriah looked though; she watched until the last landsman was out of sight, and it occurred to her that those men were far different than the men who rowed Kit's galley.

"Kit?" said she.

"Yes, sweetings?"

"Those men . . . the ones that took the brandy . . . they were a bad lot."

"Yes, love . . . but what makes you say so?"

"There was a cruelty in their eyes . . . and they looked ready to bludgeon anyone in their way . . . just in the manner they held those dreadful bats."

He said nothing to this, and Myriah quieted into thought. It was really amazing how quickly the galley was emptied. Just a short while ago it had held some thirty tubs of brandy and now . . . it was almost as if she had dreamed it. She was tired and she snuggled against Kit's firm leg and closed her eyes. They had been out now some eight hours, and there was still another thirty minutes to travel the shore line to Rye harbor. A moment later she was asleep, and Kit found that when he glanced down into her sweet face, he was overcome with what he felt within. He loved her . . . how he loved her!

Then the peace and the beauty of the moment was shattered by the blast of fire in the air. A shot had sounded reminding all that they were still not home safe, that the money in their pockets had still to be earned.

Myriah awoke with a start and felt herself squeezed between Kit's legs, for he did not wish for her to get up. "Heads low, lads . . . it's to the Marshes . . . we will lose the Cutter in the Marshes! 'Twill be a whale chasing an eel. Heave, lads!"

She was a swift vessel, the *Swallow*, and she was upon them in a moment. Her guns hissed out into the night air and warned them of death. It loomed at them, cold, unforgiving, and Lord Wimborne's crew forgot their aches as they rowed harder than they had all night. A stranger's voice slashed through the blackness of the night, commanding them to halt, but their little galley sliced its way to safety and then the vessel at their backs could go no farther, for the water had drained into the Marshes and 'twas but a small galley that could tread what was left.

They turned into the waterway and it was narrow as well as shallow. Myriah felt the sides of the boat brush against the grassy walls of the dike, and she looked up into Kit's face, alive in the moonlight and lined with concern. They had escaped the cutter but he was still worried, thought Myriah . . . why? Her own heart was beating at a wild pace and she was exhausted from its thumping. She had to catch her breath and steady it before it exploded in her chest. The boat moved solidly through the causeway, forking, circling with the winding movements of the dike, and then she saw the little arched bridge that marked Wimborne lands and her joy reached her eyes and her lips. "Oh, Kit, we are home . . . home!"

"Not yet, my sweet . . . I have the unshakable feeling that it is not over just yet!"

There it was again! The terrifying break in the air! It had an unmistakable sound, and Myriah cried within herself, for the dragoons had spotted them and their horses were carrying them closer. Corporal Stone was, it seemed, a determined man. He had waited all night for their return. He had planted himself at the head of the dike and was suddenly rewarded when he looked wearily onto the water to find a galley plodding its way down the canal.

He ordered his men to horse, and they were riding in a moment. Myriah could see Stone's face in the moonlight and wondered if he could see theirs. "Can, can he see us?" she asked.

"Hurry, lads . . . a few more feet, and it looks as though we will be taking a swim tonight. No, we're in the thick of darkness down here in the dike . . . though he can just barely see the galley."

Just as Kit was saying this, she felt the vines and driftwood parting and found herself in total darkness. They were in the cavern and the silence as they waited blasted through her ears. She heard herself breathe and put a hand to her heart, sure that all could hear its pounding. They waited, no one looking at the other, for all eyes were turned to the cavern ceiling above them. Myriah heard the water lap at the boat and wondered if the dragoons would be able to hear and recognize the sound.

"Fiend seize you stupid brutes!" shouted Stone at his men. "They couldn't have disappeared . . . they were there. Find them!"

They heard the trampling of horses above their heads, they heard the shouting and the retreating as the dragoons scurried up and down along the dike, searching for the galley, and the Gentlemen waited.

Twenty minutes might be thought to be a short space of time, when one needs more, but to the crew in the cavern, 'twas interminably and damnably long. However, at length it passed and with it all sounds from above.

Kit lit a candle which was set into the cavern wall, and Myriah observed a wooden ladder hung against the moss-covered wall leading to the ceiling above.

"Very well, lads . . ." said Kit quietly and he grinned, "we have come through . . . but we will have to swim home. No sense risking coming up through here . . . so boots off, and into the water with you. My promises still hold . . . so wait for my word early next week!"

He watched his men as they grumbled quietly to themselves and slumped over into the water, making brackish wetness spray all about. Kit turned to Myriah, "Now you, sweetings. I am afraid you are in for another swim today."

"Oh, do not let that bother you, my lord," said Myriah sweetly. "After all, it was *yesterday* morning I had my swim . . . 'tis a new day now." She slipped off his cloak and her boots and tied the laces carefully together before slinging them round her neck. He picked her up and eased her into the cold water, and she screeched quietly to herself. His lordship, not wishing to spoil his boots that were without the benefit of laces, decided to leave them in the galley for future retrieving. He doused the light and was in the water beside her a moment later.

They swam side by side, making slow even breast-strokes until they were out of the cavern. They could no longer see all the men who had swum swiftly downstream. "Come on, sweetings, or you shall have it I am out to give you a cold," said Kit, smiling and urging her on.

" 'Tis not so very bad in the water . . . it's when we shall get out . . . and oh . . . I left your cloak in the galley . . . does it matter?"

"My cloak? Dash it, girl . . . how could you . . . it needed a washing!" teased Kit.

She giggled, and they continued to swim downstream until she could see the arched bridge above them. Then she was swimming towards the enbankment, and he was pulling her out of the water. The breeze was no longer comfortable as it hit their wet bodies, and they ran the distance across the meadow until Myriah pulled back on her hand. He stopped as she bent over her knees, sucking in wind. "Are you all right?" he asked, worried.

She nodded and gave her hand into his outstretched one, and they ran again, cutting through the pastures, along the dirt pathway that led toward the Wimborne Drive. They passed the stables, and Fletcher met them in the doorway and waved before returning to his fireplace and Tabby's unending questions.

Finally they were standing dripping in the center hallway of Wimborne Towers, and they turned and saw each other and laughed.

"Eh!" shouted Billy from above stairs. "Kit, Myriah . . . are you there . . . Kit . . . Kit!"

"Yes, Billy . . . hold a moment," said Kit taking Myriah's hand and leading her up the stairs to Billy's room. They arrived in young Wimborne's room and stood there sopping wet, looking ridiculous while Billy took one long look at them and burst out laughing. He attempted to speak, pointed instead, and went off into another peal.

"Go take a damper!" snapped Myriah good-naturedly. "I'm going to get out of these wet clothes."

Kit outmaneuvered her and rushed to her room before her. "Where do you think *you* are going, my lord?" asked Myriah.

"To your room, my love," said he whimsically.

"What?" she fairly shrieked.

"To light your fire, my dear," said he.

"What?" repeated Myriah.

He laughed, entered the room, and put a kindling log in the hearthgrate. "I want you to be warm, my sweetings . . . 'tis the least I can do for you."

She watched him work at the logs, and when he had it blazing and was about to leave, she reached out her hand and clutched his jacket, heavy with water. "Kit . . . I am so glad you are safe."

He touched her cheek and planted a soft kiss on her forehead before turning resolutely away and making for his own room. Myriah sighed, closed her door, and dropped off her wet garments. Well . . . she now had but one thing to wear . . . her riding habit!

Five minutes later she was in bed and fast asleep, and her dreams, as well as the fire, kept her warm.

Twenty

"So there you have it, Billy," said Kit, leaning back against the hard wood chair and sipping his coffee in leisurely fashion.

"Yes, indeed . . . there I have it . . . of all the paltry things to say, Kit!" said Billy wagging a finger.

Kit laughed, "Now what? Lord, but you're pesky lad."

"You had the most splendid adventure of them all . . . chased by the *Swallow* herself . . . dragoons all over the place . . . Lord, but I'd have given almost anything to have been in it," said Billy sincerely.

Kit shook his head. "Young scamp!" He looked at the mantel-clock. The hour was well past ten, and the morning had still not given him Myriah. "I wonder what she is about still sleeping," said he thoughtfully.

"Devil a bit . . . she will sleep till noon. Didn't I tell you, Kit. Said from the start . . . the girl is pluck to the backbone, she is! What a great gun . . . going off and giving you word like that! That rascally Bilkes boy wouldn't let me budge from the bed. Said it was her orders, and he was more afraid of *her* than *me* . . . imagine, Kit!" said Billy chuckling.

Lord Wimborne imagined all too well, and he stood

up impatiently. He wanted to see her. He wanted to be near her and feel the strength of her being beside him . . . he had to tell her how he felt!

"Lord, you are in a fidget," grinned Billy. "Why don't you go wake the chit. Tell her she's had enough beauty sleep . . . tell her *I* said 'twon't do her any good at any rate!" He laughed at his own jest and continued to watch his brother with keen eyes.

"Confound it!" ejaculated Kit, suddenly breaking into a determined stride. "I think I *will* go and wake her . . . the sweet slug-a-bed!" He passed the doorway and banged affably at Myriah's door. "Wake up, wench! The sun is smiling, and there are things to be done!" bellowed Kit.

Billy in his room smiled to himself and thought, '*Sweet slug-a-bed?* M'brother is besotted!'

Kit received no answer from Myriah but was not about to be put off. "Myriah!" he called loudly. "Up, girl! The coffee is brewing . . . and I'll wager your belly needs filling after last night's run . . . MYRIAH!"

A sudden wave of anxiety swept through his veins, cooling his blood, and a sickly sensation crept into his vitals. What if she were gone? She had appeared from nowhere . . . what if she had decided a smuggler's haunt was nowhere to stay. He couldn't bear the thought. He opened her door sending it flying against the wall, and the sight of her empty ruffled bed left his heart in a frenzy. He stormed her closet, and found two rumpled, damaged gowns. Her riding habit was gone . . . and her portmanteau was not in sight.

He turned and made for the stairs. She couldn't have fled him . . . not now! Please, not now . . . when he knew he couldn't live without her! Oh God! Why hadn't he told her last night how he felt, told her the truth about . . . about the smuggling! He had known—deep in his heart—he had seen the innocence and honesty in her eyes. He knew she belonged to no other man . . . never had. What he had seen . . . had an explanation

. . . her connection with Sir Roland . . . must have an explanation, and he had banished it from his thoughts for Myriah was to be his bride.

Lord Wimborne's honey-colored hair flew about his rugged face and his bright blue eyes were lit with fear as he reached the stables. "Myriah!" he shouted, "Myriah . . ." and there . . . he saw her stallion, and air refilled his lungs. The unutterable had not come to pass . . . she had not disappeared!

Tabby came up from behind him and coughed deprecatingly for attention, "If ye be wanting m'mistress, she took the west fields." Lord Wimborne gave the wiry old man a smile, and left the old groom grinning to himself. "So, that be the way of it," said Tabby to Myriah's horse, "thought it before . . . and it be a blessing."

The sun seemed pleased with the earth and glistened huge and majestic in its own rich blue field. What little clouds there were formed dainty pinafores and cotton balls as they skipped on their way to the sea! Mother Nature tittered merrily for she was in her glory. It was Spring and she had waved her wand well. Wild blooms of purple and yellow tripped and flirted with their special magic amongst the tall, sweet-smelling grass. Oaks spread their arms and their years told a story to the passing breeze, enticing the gentle wind to stay awhile and chat. Budding leaves poked the air with their new life and asked demurely to be admired.

Myriah stood on the peak of this scene and was herself a part of Nature's wonders. She was absorbed with the radiance of Spring, the strong feelings within her, and the call of her heart. She wore the dark blue velvet riding habit she had worn when she first arrived at Wimborne, but today the sun was too warm, and she slipped off the velvet jacket. The breeze dallied with the soft white muslin blouse, whipping the sleeves away from her delicate arms. It found her long red curls and sent them dancing away from her face. Her eyes sparkled in their almond contours, alive in a face as fresh, as impish, as the spirit that moved its body. The sight of a badger playing with its mate tickled her, and she laughed, and the sound was music to Kit's ears.

As he came upon her, his heart in his eyes, she turned and she smiled full upon him. She adored him and went into his arms as easily, as naturally as love allows. It was the best of all that is tender, the sweetest of all that is good. Her lips surrendered to his, and they pressed against each other there in the beam of the morning light.

"Oh, God, Myriah . . . how I love you!" said Kit into her ear, and the magic of his words caressed her soul. "I must have loved you from the very start . . . my Myriah."

There is something to be said about keeping one's eyes closed at such a moment, for had Myriah done so, she would not have seen Sir Roland steady on his path in their direction. The sight of him coming upon them sent Myriah backwards out of Kit's arms and swept her face with a worried frown. Kit gathered his shoulders and drew up straight, a sternness flickering into his countenance.

"What is it, Myriah?" he said, turning his head to find the source of her discomfort. The sight of Sir Roland brought a derisive sneer to Lord Wimborne's mouth, and his brow went up as he waited for the gentleman to arrive.

Sir Roland, wearing his dark brown velvet cutaway, his cream-colored silk waistcoat, and buff-colored breeches, looked the epitome of London fashion. His top hat was rakishly set on his head, his kid gloves and cane held in one hand, while his Hessian boots caught the gleam of the sun's rays. He had witnessed the tender scene, and it had left him irritated and . . . ruthless!

"Ah, Lady Myriah . . . how well you are looking!"

exclaimed Sir Roland, reaching them and tipping his hat in her direction.

Lord Wimborne's head snapped round and he gazed in disbelief at Myriah. She blushed, and her voice trembled. "Good-morning, Sir Roland . . . I did not expect you so soon."

"No . . . but then, I thought I had better come fetch you early if we were to arrive at your grandfather's before luncheon. We shouldn't let Lord Whitney . . . concern himself any longer . . . now should we!"

Kit Wimborne felt the knife of betrayal stab through his back and pink his heart! So . . . she had lied after all . . . only she was no shopkeeper's daughter . . . she was no adventuress as he had once suspected. Not she . . . she was *merely* Lady Myriah Whitney . . . and who had not heard of *Lady Myriah*? Why . . . how many times this year had he heard her name bandied about at the clubs on St. James. It was Lady Myriah the incomparable . . . doing this . . . flaunting convention here . . . there . . . turning up her nose at a duke . . . and then just recently . . . hadn't he heard that Lady Myriah was displaying more than mild affection for Sir Roland Keyes . . . yes, that was where he had heard Roland's name before . . . he had heard it coupled with Myriah's! Something snapped in Kit Wimborne, and his eyes and mouth hardened. His teeth gritted and he turned to Myriah, rage filling his veins.

"I . . . I haven't decided to go with you, Roland . . ." she was saying uncertainly, her eyes darting in Kit's direction.

"Myriah . . . come . . . I am sure Lord Wimborne . . . will excuse us while we discuss the matter."

Lord Wimborne's lip curled and he felt the need to strike. Sir Roland's face presented itself as a particularly desirable target for such an action. However, he contained himself and instead glared down at Myriah. "I am sure *Lady Myriah* . . ." he said, putting deadly emphasis on her name, "will be quite ready to go with you shortly. Her . . . adventures here at Wimborne are at an end."

With that he turned, and his rapid strides took him away from the being who had given him life and had taken it away. She had lied . . . and having lied . . . she had betrayed him. Not once had she tried to give him the truth. Why? The answer presented itself all too painfully, because she was Lady Myriah, and she was all her reputation said she was . . . a willful lady whose sole pursuit was excitement! Well . . . she had found it at Wimborne . . . and now she would go, but she would never know all . . . he only wished he had not opened his heart to her.

Myriah turned on Roland and her eyes filled with angry tears. "You wretch! You conniving . . . hateful beast! Well, it shall not work, for he will listen to me in the end. It may take a bit of shouting and pain . . . but in the end . . . *he will listen!*"

"I am afraid not, Myriah . . . for you will not try to speak with him again. You will fetch your horse and your groom, and we will return now to your father and be married at once!"

She laughed scoffingly. "You are no fool, Roland, so don't make foolish statements!"

"I do not! Myriah, you have been playing a dangerous game here with your smuggler. He is very close to having his neck in a noose. Last night I followed you when you went to warn him. I know where his galley is hidden and what is more . . . I am witness to the fact that it was he, Lord Christopher Wimborne, that captained the vessel ordered to halt by Corporal Stone."

"Oh, God!" breathed Myriah, "what are you saying?"

"I am saying, dear girl, that unless you return with me now and become my bride, I shall be all too happy to turn evidence for the crown and testify against his lordship!"

"You wouldn't . . . you don't have enough proof!"

"I have enough to ruin him, my girl . . . I have enough to bring him to trial."

She began to cry and the tears streamed down her lovely cheeks. "Roland . . . please do not do this . . . I beg of you. I will pay you anything . . . anything . . ."

"I need more than that, my darling. You could not sign over your inheritance . . . 'tis in the hands of the trustees . . . but it will become mine on our wedding day." He caressed her cheek. "Myriah, love . . . I shall not be so very difficult to live with. In truth . . . I shall be a most comfortable husband. I have no intentions of curbing your pleasures . . . and ask only that you be discreet!"

She groaned, "Oh, God . . . therein lies the difference, Roland, Don't you see? You wouldn't mind where I was . . . whom I was with—but *he* would!"

He growled, "What is that suppose to imply! Do you fear you shall never see him, my love? I have already told you . . . I would allow you your pleasures . . ."

"Yes, *you* would . . . but he would not take me! Do you think him anything like yourself? He wouldn't take another man's wife."

"Come Myriah, enough talk! Do you marry me? Or *do I ruin him?*" he said without pity.

"*I hate you*, Roland . . . I never thought that one day . . . I would hate you . . . but I do. And God help me . . . yes . . . I will marry you and then . . . I will destroy you. I swear it!"

"Very well, then, Myriah. We have made a pact. Let us go." He took her arm and guided her towards the stables. She left her riding jacket behind her and it lay sadly on the ground. Tabby looked to his mistress after receiving Sir Roland's orders and she inclined her head. Grumbling he saddled the horses and led them out. "I . . . I just have to say good-bye to Billy . . ." she said, turning from Roland, her face a masque of pain.

Roland took her arm and restrained her. "No, Myriah

. . . no good-byes. Their groom will advise them of your departure."

A tear formed and rolled silently down her cheek, and she tasted the salt and promised herself that one day she would repay Roland. God . . . if he ever tried to touch her . . . she would kill him!

Tabby shook hands with Fletcher, giving him an answering frown.

"I don't know whet this be about, Fletch, but I means to find out, I does. 'Tis more than half smoky."

"Aye!" agreed Fletcher.

Sir Roland, Lady Myriah, and Tabby following behind, moved down the Wimborne drive and met the river road, taking it northwest to Northiam. Myriah sat stoically on her saddle, her stomach grumbling for she had not eaten, yet the thought of food made her ill. Everything she wanted was at Wimborne Towers . . . and it was lost to her forever. She knew Roland, and she knew he would not hesitate to ruin Kit and Billy if she did not give in. She would marry Roland, she would allow her money to go into his hands . . . and then somehow she would leave him . . . she would go to Kit and explain. Oh, faith! Why . . . why was this happening? These thoughts tumbled about in her cudgeled brain, and her heart felt numb, no longer able to contend with the troubles that possessed it. An hour passed slowly and there, welcoming, warm, and mellow in the sunlight, stood Guildford House. Her father and grandfather would be there . . . but they would be helpless to untangle her web, for she would be unable to lead them to it!

Twenty-One

Kit slammed the front doors closed with a resonance that shook the floors above. He crossed the hall, found the library doors, gave them a powerful blow, entered the room and brought out a decanter of cognac! A glass was poured, consumed, and another followed, and then he was looking up into his young brother's startled face.

"Deuce take you, lad! What are you doing about?" thundered Kit, downing his third glass in a swoop.

"Whoo . . . that is one devilish breakfast, Kit. What has she said this time?" asked Billy, grinning widely.

"*She?* Your—what did you call her? Greatgun? *She* did not say a thing. She never did . . . it seems . . . except to lie! And . . . by the way . . . we have had the good fortune to be entertaining Lady Myriah Whitney in our home!"

"Lady Myriah?" said Billy who had been to London only on rare occasions and whose romps had not taken him into the more exclusive clubs.

"*You*, my buck, are too young and inexperienced . . . but Lady Myriah . . . enjoys larks of a sort. It seems *she* has been having one—at *our* expense," said Kit slumping into a cushioned chair and straddling its arm with his leg.

"Our expense . . . lark . . .?" asked Billy, all at sea. "I don't know what you are about. If you mean that Myriah didn't give us her correct name . . . what of it? Told you she was running away from her father . . . probably didn't think at the time we could be trusted."

"Naive child!" said Kit. "Knew if she gave her name we wouldn't believe the story. Why would Lady Myriah's father force her to marry anyone? Spoils her rotten!"

"Well, what does it all signify anyway?" asked Billy, unconcerned with such details.

"Damn . . . but she really had you taken in!" said Kit, swallowing hard, "but then . . . she finally took me in as well. Then Sir Roland flashed upon the scene and opened my eyes . . . and oh, God! I wish they were closed still!" he said, shutting them and putting his head back against the cushioned chair.

A knock sounded at the open library door, and Fletcher loomed in its entrance. "Thought ye ought to know . . . shoo'll nut be coming back . . . shoo went off wit that cove."

Kit sat up and his eyes stared hard at the groom. Even in his bitter misery . . . he had not expected this. He had still thought there would be another meeting . . . perhaps an explanation to banish his pain . . . but she had left . . . with Roland.

"What?" ejaculated Billy, ". . . and her groom . . .?"

"Aye . . . 'im, too . . . though he spake of it being smoky . . . and *I* dunnot like it none!"

"Nor do I! Saddle my brother's horse, Fletch . . . he shall be riding . . ."

"You will do nothing of the sort!" snapped Kit interrupting. He turned to Billy. "She left of her own free will . . . she'll not come back any other way."

"You are my brother, Kit and I have admired . . . looked up to you . . . egad, man! You've always known just what to do . . . and I never thought I'd see you come to such a pass . . . you are in the wrong of it, Kit!" said Billy turning sadly away and taking up another chair. Fletcher sighed and moved towards the kitchen, for before long his master was sure to need some coffee and cook would have to be prepared. They were in for it, of that he was sure, for he had never before seen Lord Wimborne in such a fury as he was now.

Myriah stood playing idly with the yellow daffodils in the crystal vase resting on the round stainwood table of the central hall in Guildford House. The aroma of the flowers drifted round her head as she waited with Sir Roland beside her for her father and grandfather to appear. The house exploded with their presence as the butler stood aside from the parlor door to allow them to enter.

"My child . . . Myriah!" said Lord Whitney, taking Myriah into his arms and then allowing her to be embraced by her grandfather. He turned and took up Roland's hand, shaking it vigorously. "You found her, you sly fellow! Why, you are just the man for her!" beamed her father, missing the wince in Myriah's blue-green eyes.

Her grandfather, however, did not miss it, and he glanced at Sir Roland and decided he definitely did not like the fellow! "Come along," he urged gently, "we were about to have tea . . . and a light lunch . . . come along." He led them back into the parlor and seated Myriah on the elegant, gold-cushioned sofa.

"There is something . . . an urgent matter we must discuss immediately," said Roland to the younger of his hosts.

Myriah stood up and moved away. She went to the window seat and gazed out onto the long drive and plush grounds. She wanted to hear nothing . . . she wanted to divorce herself from their words.

"As it happens . . ." continued Roland, "we were not able to escape notice. It is with tremendous regret that I advise you that Myriah and I were seen *together* in Rye by some chance acquaintances. There was nothing for it but to advise those involved that we were married and spending our honeymoon in the area."

Myriah's head went round and her mouth dropped. Lord, she thought, *that was good*, Roland . . . what an excellent prevaricator you *do* make! Her father's reaction was to sigh heavily and put a thumb to his lip and a knuckle to his chin. His father-in-law's sharp eyes went to Myriah. She was listless and pale, but what was worse . . . she was apathetic, and he had never seen her so before. A strong revulsion for Sir Roland swept him and he turned on the man. "Hang me, lad . . . any number of lies could have done as well."

"Perhaps . . . but it occurred to me that as Myriah's name and mine have been . . . linked more often than not . . . all other lies would not be believed. I had no wish . . . to have your granddaughter's reputation put to the dust, my lord," said Roland glibly.

Lord Guildford wanted to slap him, instead he paced about the room a moment, and then returned to confront him again. "Then, sir . . . you should not have gone in search of her, thus putting her in such a position."

Myriah's eye met those of her grandfather, and they smiled with warmth. Dear grandpapa . . . so intuitive, and yet this time, he was without the power to save her.

Her father too was hit with the impropriety of the situation. He didn't care for Roland's highhandedness. "Very well, Roland. However, the trouble is that Myriah will not marry you, so I don't see how such a tale will serve."

"Ah, but you mistake, my lord . . . Myriah *will* marry me . . . and with your consent, she will do so today!"

"What?" ejaculated both her father and grandfather in one voice.

Sir Roland produced an official-looking form from his pocket and waved it before their eyes. "I have gone to some lengths to procure this. It is a Special License. Suffice it to say, that the position I discovered Myriah to be embroiled in when I discovered her in Rye makes it expedient that we get married without further delay."

Both father and grandfather took exception to his insinuation and advised him of his lapse in etiquette. He promptly apologized but turned to Myriah. "Nevertheless, Lady Myriah and I wish to be married immediately, is that not correct, love?"

"I . . . I have agreed to marry Sir Roland; it matters not when."

"No!" snapped Lord Guildford. He did not like this— he did not like any of this. "Myriah, what say you to such things?"

"I have already said, grandpapa . . . I will marry him."

"Good Lord!" ejaculated her father. "You ran away because you would not marry him . . . what has altered your mind?"

"It is of no consequence why, only that I have altered my decision . . . and I will marry him," said Myriah firmly. "Now, if you will allow, I would like to go to my room, wash, and change."

"The last time she did that," said her bewildered father, "she disappeared."

"She will not do so now, however," said Sir Roland confidently, commanding her response.

"No, she will not do so now," agreed Myriah finally beaten.

Myriah made her way to the hall to find Tabby fidgeting in its center. "M'lady . . . I been waiting on ye . . . might be I'm out of the way on this, but, I got to speak m'mind!"

"Of course, Tabby . . . you must always do so to me," said Myriah.

"It would be best . . . if we walk a bit outdoors," said he.

She inclined her head and allowed him to amble before her, as the door was opened by the butler and they strolled outside. She sighed heavily and looked away from him into the distance. There would be no great knight charging up to rescue her. That happened only in fairy tales and silly girl's dreams. After today she would be Lady Myriah Keyes . . .

" 'Tis this . . . we left Wimborne quicker than a bee could buzz . . . and . . . we left without word . . . I be wondering why?"

"I . . . I can't tell you, Tabby."

"Oh, so now it's I can't tell you, Tabby! How you do use me, it fairly sets me sore, it does!"

"Tabby, there is nothing for it. Roland has a gun, and it is pointing at Lord Wimborne's head. If I don't marry him, the gun will go off. 'Tis that simple."

"Eh? A gun, is it? What ye mean is that the scoundrel knows what they be up to at Wimborne . . . means to give 'em away if he don't hear wedding bells?"

"Precisely," said Myriah, sighing again.

"And you . . . you don't think *him* at Wimborne should have a choice in the matter."

"Choice . . . what choice could there be?"

"Ain't that for him at Wimborne to say? He be a *man,* Lady Myriah. He be a right proper one at that . . . I don't hold with what he been doing . . . but sure as I be standing here talking . . . he knows what he be doing . . . and he do it well . . . could be he'd 'ave the answer to sew things up right and tight!"

"No, Tabby, he would not . . . he would only be all the more miserable knowing. Oh, God . . . he would give himself up if he knew . . . and he must not. Tabby, you will not tell him."

"Aye, m'lady . . . happen . . . I always obey ye . . . right or wrong!"

"Yes, Tabby, as it happens you do . . . and you will do so now. I'm going to my room, Tab . . . don't worry . . . we shall make out!" She turned and, no longer able to contain herself, a sob shook her small body, and she fled to the safety of her room where the memories of little-girl pleasures and children's hopes would help her escape the terrors of today!

Tabby watched her go, and her sob spun round his heart and squeezed out his blood. "Happen I always obey her . . . but now, old man, do ye obey 'er 'ead or 'er 'eart?"

His decision was made in an instant and his roan saddled. Moments later he was on the road to Rye. This time . . . just this one time, he would disobey her orders . . . and God! he thought, let an old fool be right—jest this onct!

"I suggest that a clergyman be sent for at once, my lord. There is no need for unnecessary scandal, and it can be avoided if we time our movements," said Roland blandly.

Lord Whitney had no liking for this turnabout, neither did he care for Roland's attitude; however, it would appear that the man was correct. Myriah had agreed, and having agreed . . . what more was to be said. "Very well," said the Viscount pulling at the bellrope. A lackey appeared and was sent on the errand to fetch the local vicar whose living was received at the hands of Lord Guildford.

Lord Guildford grumbled and moved agitatedly, he did not like this . . . any of it. He was not blind, and he had seen clearly that Myriah had no heart for the suave rake sitting and giving out orders to them. Furthermore, there was something neither Myriah nor Roland were divulging. He was sure of it. There was more to all this, and for some reason they were both quiet. Could Roland be blackmailing his granddaughter? Could he have found her . . . perhaps in a compromising position. Well, he would have his answer. He suddenly stormed out of the room and made his way to the room Myriah had always occupied when at Guildford House.

"Myriah, dearest . . . do allow me to come in," said her grandfather gravely at her closed door.

"Of course, love," she called from her bed and sat up waiting for him to admit himself.

He moved in and placed his hands behind his back, clasping them and pursing his thin lips. His eyes were light and watery with emotion, and Myriah wanted to comfort him, but was herself too lost to do so. "Darling . . . you . . . you are not in love with that man downstairs?"

"No, grandpapa . . . I am not," she said quietly, not wanting to lie to him.

"That is what I was sure of. Then why, my angel, why do you agree to become his wife?"

"I must, grandpapa, there is nothing for it. And you must not ask me why . . . I cannot tell you."

"I am older than you . . . and have more answers. Trust me . . . perhaps if there is one . . ."

"There is not! I am in love with a man who is a smuggler by trade . . . a nobleman by birth, and Sir Roland will expose him if I do not go through with our marriage," said Myriah, suddenly sobbing and throwing herself onto his chest. The tears flowed over his dark coat and he patted her head, "Oh, my child, my poor child, but you cannot sacrifice yourself for . . ."

"For the man I love . . . I can and I will, and, grandpapa . . . you cannot stop me!"

"Nor can I allow you to do such a thing," said he.

"If you do not, I will run off and marry Roland. It is the only way . . . if I do not . . . he has the evidence to ruin . . . please, grandpapa . . . do not make it any more difficult than it is already."

They clung to one another, sorrow for each other engulfing them, and Myriah heard the sound of her grandfather's grief. She kissed his cheek and smiled tremulously. " 'Tis not so very bad . . . really, grandpapa. Roland was wont to amuse me in the past . . . perhaps he can do so in the future. You will see . . . it will be all right!"

Twenty-Two

~⌒~

Tabby rounded the corner and headed his roan up the drive of Wimborne Towers. Fletcher heard him coming and sauntered out, hand in the air, but Tabby did not stop at the stables. He waved and continued up the drive to the house. The vicar had been sent for and there was little time left.

Grumbling and mumbling as he was wont to do when deeply disturbed, he clanked at the knocker and waited. No one answered the door, and he tried the latch. The door opened wide in his hand, and grumbling all the more, he entered the house. He heard the sound of men's voices, and the sound came from the library, and then he went to stand at its open doors, sour face making up his countenance as he surveyed the occupants.

Billy spotted him and cried out thankfully, "Tabson, why, Tabson, old friend . . . you are back . . . what word have you for us from Myriah?"

"What I 'ave fer ye . . . lord bless the day m'lady was born . . . for all her wild ways, they be none finer! I do beg yer pardon, lad . . . but curst be the day m'lady laid eyes on 'im there!" he motioned with his chin in Lord Wimborne's direction.

Kit put up a brow but refrained from responding. A good half-bottle of cognac had left him a trifle foxed and he hummed unconcernedly to himself. However, his brother took umbrage on his behalf. "You go too far, Tabson," admonished Billy, " 'tis no way for you to speak to us!"

"Why not?" put in Kit, displaying that he had heard the proceedings. " 'Tis no better than his lady's way!"

"Aye . . . my lady . . . and her name be above your tongue!" slashed Tabby, anger making him forget his position. "What do ye know of her way? Begging yer pardon . . . ye be of noble blood, but still yer blood be red and flesh be no more than flesh . . . and there's things that got to be said! 'Tis on yer account she left 'ere with that villain wot calls 'imself a gentleman!"

"Go tell her to try her tricks on another . . . they won't work in this house any longer!" snapped Kit, his eyes blazing.

"Hold, Kit," said his brother. "What do you mean, Tabson? Stop jabbering at us and get to the meat of the matter!"

"M'lady, she do him that sits there a favor . . . and ye . . . if it comes to that! She does ye both a favor, up she goes with the very man she ran from that night she found you, Master William, lying bleeding in the road! Aye . . . she be running from the villian then, but she goes with 'em now, she does, her poor fine heart breaking all the while . . ."

"Do stop, man!" shouted Kit standing up and throwing his glass into the fire. "Your sorrowful tale means nothing here!"

Tabson pulled his rounded shoulders up, and he looked Kit straight in the eye. "You be a lord . . . and I thought . . . you be one . . . in yer 'eart as well as yer blood . . . but maybe it happens I be wrong! Aye . . . maybe it happens I be wrong . . . and she be right. Said I shouldn't come 'ere . . . ordered me agin it, and

I disobeyed her, I did . . . first time I went agin her word . . . and fer whet? My lady needs saving . . . and ye . . . can do nought but eye the bottle! Good-day to ye!"

Kit was across the room in a moment, the alcohol in his veins played havoc with his brain, but he still had some coordination left. He held Tabby roughly by the collar. "Explain yourself, man! What the devil do you mean your lady needs saving?"

"From him that forces 'er to the altar!" replied Tabby shrugging out of Kit's fearful hold.

"How can he force her, man? There is no way . . . she is not without protection. She has her father!" snapped Kit. "You don't make sense."

"He is right there," agreed Billy frowning.

"He be a fiend, that one! He knows about your business 'ere at Wimborne . . . plans to open his mummer to the court agin ye if she don't give over!"

"Never say she has agreed to marry the devil . . . in order to save us?" asked Billy startled. He turned to Kit to find his brother's eyes suddenly alight. "Oh, God! Kit, she does not know . . . we never told her!"

Kit was still in command of his faculties. What was needed now was haste. He turned to Tabby, "All right there, my friend . . . hurry now . . . get my horse saddled . . . I'll be at the stables directly." He shrugged on his riding jacket and donned his gloves and turned to find Tabby still in the doorway. "What the deuce are you waiting for?"

" 'Tis m'duty to tell you that the gent . . . Sir Roland . . . he be a covey one . . . he does mean you 'arm if you get in his way."

"No doubt, Tabby, but I am also a fearful enemy to those who point the sword at me. Now hurry with you."

Tabby disappeared, and Kit turned to Billy. "Let us hope the ride will clear my head . . . for I've got to admit its a bit tipsy."

Billy strode to a pot of hot coffee, resting beside the fire, which Fletcher had produced a short time ago. With his good arm he poured, brought the cup, and shoved it at his brother. Kit laughed and drank the hot liquid down. Billy eyed him. "What are you planning to do, Kit?"

"Why, you heard the man . . . there is a lady that needs saving. What else should I do . . . but save her?"

"Kit . . . bring her back!" said Billy quietly, his eyes grave.

"That I will, brother . . . that I will!" said Kit Wimborne, striding hard out the library door and leaving his brother smiling behind him.

Vicar Holmes pulled at his long nose and eyed Sir Roland from the top of his spectacles before returning his gaze to the Special License he held before him. None of this met with his approval. He had been fetched from his house just before he was about to sit to his mid-day dinner, he was hungry, and out of temper.

"Hmmm . . . well . . . this document is in order at any rate. Now . . . would you mind telling me what all the rush is about?"

"I do mind. You have the license, Lady Myriah is of age, and here are her immediate relatives as witnesses . . . that is all you need know," said Roland smiling calmly.

The vicar, much affronted, attempted to stare Sir Roland down, but finding this hopeless, returned his attention to the father of the bride. "Most irregular . . . most irregular, my lord," said he.

Lord Whitney could not have agreed more, but he was not going to have some outsider bathing them with his unwanted opinion. "Is it? I can't imagine why you would say such a thing. I find everything Sir Roland has just expressed . . . most relevant to the matter at hand."

The vicar stood up and paced the room. "Very well, then. Bring on the bride . . . where is she, where is she?"

Myriah appeared, resting her arm on her grandfather's. She had changed into a day gown of pale cream muslin, dotted with yellow velvet. The bodice was scooped and banded with the same velvet and her long red hair was piled in curls upon her head. Her eyes did not sparkle, and her cheeks had no glow, and as she approached Sir Roland, her body trembled. It would soon be over . . . all the hopes of the past few days . . . they would soon be at an end, and Kit would be a dream . . . a memory to live on in the mind!

"Ah . . . this, I take it, is the bride?" said the vicar, taking up his prayerbook. "Very well . . . come, child . . . stand here . . . just so . . ."

She found herself beside Sir Roland and the thought of him disgusted her . . . the sight of him made her close her eyes. Oh, God! Why weren't there charging knights?

Tabby tried to keep pace with Lord Wimborne as they spanked along the road at a wild rate. Northiam would be reached in no time, thought the groom, torn between his dislike for such dangerous speed and his urging to return in time to save his mistress. He wondered how the deuce his lord was able to keep such an excellent seat, for he had drunk enough to put a lesser man under the table!

As they approached Guildford House, Tabby attempted to point out that they would have to halt temporarily to allow the gatekeeper to open the gate, however, no sooner were the words out of his mouth than he heard Lord Wimborne laugh and take the fence as though he and his horse were one with the wind. He reined in his weary roan and watched, left in the background but sure this was a man that would take on the forces of Hell to protect the woman he loved.

Kit Wimborne had one thing on his mind . . . Myriah! There was no one who could keep him from her now.

She was his Earth, his life's blood. She was the air he breathed, she was the stars that brought him light. She was Myriah, and she was magic to his being and without her—he would survive, for he was a man and knew the way—but such a survival was something he could not bear to think upon!

The house was reached and a lackey hurried out to take his horse and cast startled eyes at the man who jumped nimbly off and ran up the wide slated steps to the front door. A butler appeared and Lord Wimborne demanded to be taken to Lady Myriah.

"I am sorry . . . but Lady Myriah is in the process of her wedding ceremony."

"Damnation, man! Take me there at once!" shouted Kit looking half-crazed. The butler, unsure but somewhat terrified, decided to do just that and led him across the hall. Here he was pushed roughly aside, and the white door of the parlor was flung open with a force that nearly removed it from its hinges. Christopher Wimborne, sixth Viscount of Wimborne Towers, blazed on the threshold. His honey-colored hair massed about his handsome face, and his blue eyes surveyed the scene. Myriah looked up into his countenance and once again believed in fairy tales . . . for here was her charging knight!

Kit saw the prayerbook in the vicar's hand, he saw Sir Roland and the two strangers at Myriah's side, but they were all meaningless. It was Myriah who captured his senses. It was Myriah who moved him and he took that room like a demon possessed. She would stand by no other man! She was his . . . and he meant to make it known!

He crossed the dark Oriental rug and took her hands in his. They said not a word, for at that moment, words would not do. Hearts do interlock . . . and the moment is priceless—yet when such a miracle happens and the minds are one as well, ah . . . there is nothing in the world worth more!

* * *

He was here—was all she could think . . . Kit was really here! She gazed up at him and looked long into his eyes, for they were alight with all she could have hoped for. Then suddenly he had her by the arm and she was rushing to keep up with him as they moved away from Sir Roland.

Vicar Holmes set his spectacles in place and closed his open mouth. "Really . . . wait . . . *hold there, you scoundrel* . . . what the deuce do you think you are doing?" His eyes discovered that the villain in question had put Myriah behind him and he shook an admonishing finger. "See here . . . let go of that woman . . . she is bride to Sir Roland here."

Kit turned on Sir Roland who had stood his ground, brow raised in the air and waiting. Kit Wimborne's voice was low and underlined, "No, my friend . . . she is not *bride* . . . she is *widow!*" Kit crossed the few steps that brought him to Sir Roland's side, and his kid glove slashed across Roland's face.

Roland's hazel eyes glittered wickedly. "You mistake, my lord, however, it will give me infinite pleasure to accommodate you . . . another time! At this moment you will excuse me for I am about to complete the wedding ceremony with Lady Myriah!"

Myriah came up behind Kit and pulled at his sleeve, "Kit, Kit, I don't know how to tell you . . . I *am* marrying Sir Roland . . . I must. I don't know how you came to know I was here . . . but you don't understand . . . ."

For answer Kit stooped down and took her to his breast. His lips found hers, and there was but the two of them. He had burned in these last hours . . . burned with love and pain, and his kiss told his story.

The vicar brought up his spectacles again and began pounding on the stainwood table with his book. "Dear me . . . I say . . . I say . . . my lady . . . you, you there, young scoundrel . . . are you listening?" He turned to Sir Roland. "This is most irregular . . . most irregular . . . I do think, Sir, that you ought to put a stop to it!"

"Why?" asked Roland. " 'Twill be their last—for the time being."

The vicar's amazement was evident, apparently this particular bridegroom was a chap with marvelously broad notions. He turned to the lady's father instead. Now, Lord Whitney had observed the previous proceedings with a look of profound confusion. His mind was in a jumble and he was attempting, without explanation being offered, to clear his head. The vicar interrupted his thoughts. "My lord . . ." tried Holmes, "I do think as the lady's parent . . . you should . . ."

"Do be quiet . . . can't you see I am trying to listen!" snapped the other.

As neither Kit, nor Lady Myriah were doing any talking at the moment, the vicar did not feel this to be an adequate response. He cleared his throat and attempted to bring the father of the bride to a proper sense of what was right. "*Really*, my lord . . . I object to these entire proceedings. In fact . . . I find the behavior of your daughter . . . most . . . irregular!"

"Shut up, Holmes," beamed the grandfather of the lady in question. He was quite pleased with the dashing methods of Lord Wimborne and, as Myriah had had the good sense to inform him exactly where she stood when they had spoken earlier, he found none of the goings on to be the least bit confusing. Myriah's love had indeed come charging in . . . defying all to stop him, and Lord Guildford liked such a man and such bold action. He was enjoying himself thoroughly, for this man was exactly what Myriah needed!

Kit hugged her to him fiercely and for him, she was the only being that existed. He kissed her curls and she heard his voice breathe in her ears, "Oh, God, Myriah . . . I was so hurt . . . I thought . . ."

She put her finger to his lip, "Hush, my love . . . it doesn't matter! You *must* go now . . . you must . . . you see you still don't understand. I *must* marry Roland . . . there is nothing that can stop me!"

He laughed and held her shoulders, gazing down into her eyes and his own were once again merry. "Then you know nothing of me . . . for I tell you that you will marry this afternoon . . . but the groom will be no man other than myself!"

"Please Kit . . . you will ruin yourself . . . you don't yet know . . ."

"No, you do not!" agreed Roland, deciding the time had come for deliberate action. "She will marry me now . . . or, my dear Lord Wimborne . . . you will find yourself involved most uncomfortably with . . . the law! Do I make myself clear?"

"Very. You swine!" said Kit taking a step forward and landing Roland a flush hit that sent him flying backwards over the furniture and putting him down.

Myriah pulled at Kit's sleeve and cried desperately, "Stop it, Kit! Stop it . . . he can ruin you . . . Kit, Kit, he knows . . ."

Lord Wimborne laughed and scooped her once again into the folds of his embrace. "No child . . . no . . . he only thinks he knows . . . and *you*—does your *heart* believe me a *smuggler?*"

The vicar held his chest and sat down, "My lord . . . he *says* he is a *smuggler!* I think it your duty to call for the magistrate at once."

"Can't you shut the dratted fellow up?" inquired Myriah's father of her grandfather.

"Shut up, Holmes," said Lord Guildford most amiably.

"But, but Kit . . . what do you mean?" inquired Myriah, wide-eyed. "I . . . was with you . . ." she dropped her voice. "I know Kit . . . why do you pretend?"

"Yes, beloved, you were with me," said Kit aloud,

heedless of the starting eyes of her guardians. "But what you think you saw was very different from what really occurred! The trip you took with me—though it was my last—was one of many . . . and they were all on King's business!"

"What?" shrieked Myriah. "What are you saying?"

Roland came upon them, rubbing his chin, his eyes narrowing. "He is bluffing!"

"It no longer matters as I will no longer be making the run, so you might as well know . . . and *you* . . ." he pointed with his chin at Roland, "you may be a swine . . . but I don't think you are a traitor to your country . . . and if you should prove to be that as well . . . what I am about to tell you will bring you no profit. 'Tis ended."

"What . . . what is ended?" urged Myriah.

He chuckled. "I was about to tell you, my impatient love. When I sold out and decided to remain home to handle my estates . . . they were in a state of mismanagement. The funds were there . . . intact . . . but payments had not gone out . . . things were not properly handled. At any rate . . . it set Wimborne Towers up perfectly for the Marshes were at our back . . . and smuggling would be an excellent disguise whilst we got our messages to and from France!"

"You are a spy?" shrieked Myriah.

"He is lying!" roared Sir Roland, losing control.

"Am I? Then lay your evidence, my man . . . and see how far it will take you!" said Kit contemptuously.

"But . . . but . . . *they shot Billy!*" said Myriah in hushed awe.

"Precisely why I made up my mind that it was time to pull out. The war is near its end, and seven years of my life and a year of Billy's is quite enough for the Wimbornes."

"But, but if you were working for the Crown, why did they shoot Billy?" persisted Myriah.

"The problem was this. The Regent could only promise that if we were caught . . . our names would be cleared . . . eventually. However, he had no way of keeping us from being shot during the process. We couldn't take the excisemen and Riding Officers into our confidence because leaks do happen, my girl . . . and too much depended on the secrecy of the mission. It had to appear as though we were merely smugglers and nothing more. The men were in fact paid from the profits we derived!"

"But then, who was Dibbs?" asked Myriah, still amazed.

"He worked in the capacity of go-between. I had gone to London as usual and received the papers they wanted delivered to our agent in France who by the way is a personal friend . . . we fought together in Spain. However, they had one last-minute thing they wished to have delivered . . . Dibbs brought it and received the news from me that I would make no more trips. By now, I have been replaced."

"Replaced?" expostulated the vicar. "You should be hanged . . . confessed smuggler . . . doing it up brown with your tales! I don't understand this . . . not any of it! I came to perform a wedding and I am not in the habit of . . . of doing them without a bride and groom. Since the lady seems to have some doubts with regards to the choice of her groom, I believe I should go home and have my dinner," complained the vicar, putting down his prayerbook.

"Hold there . . ." ordered Kit before turning to Lord Whitney, never doubting the authority of his command, and indeed Vicar Holmes stood in his tracks, though he made some blustering remarks about the ill manners of young noblemen who go about the country smuggling, spying, and stealing other men's brides!

"Contrary to popular opinion, the Wimborne estates are intact and as Viscount of Wimborne Towers, I will be able to support your daughter in the manner to which she is accustomed. In addition to that, I love her and intend to spend as much time convincing her of that fact as I am able. I ask, Sir . . . for your consent and blessing on our marriage."

"And . . . if I were to withhold them both?" said the Viscount putting up a brow.

"I regret to advise you that I would marry her anyway. I mean to wive your daughter, my lord . . . but it would please her if she had your blessing."

"Then take her! You certainly deserve one another . . . for a wilder pair . . . I never have seen! Besides . . . 'tis the first time ever I beheld such a light in her eyes . . . and it seems to me 'tis you that has put it there!" smiled her father warmly.

"Indeed . . . indeed! Allow the ceremony to begin!" added the grandfather of the bride, most pleased with the outcome.

Sir Roland had managed to slip away unnoticed. There was nothing further to be gained, and every possibility that if he lingered, the hotheaded Lord Wimborne would follow up his challenge, and Roland had no wish to fight a duel.

He was not by nature an easy loser. He disliked having to give up, but he had no choice. To remain and seek his revenge would not serve his immediate needs . . . and *they* were pressing! The battle was lost and he sighed heavily, for now there was but one thing left to save him. She was the daughter of a rich merchant, a *cit*, he thought with disgust. However, she had cast out her lures . . . and her parents were skirters . . . trying to get into society through her marriage. He supposed he would enable them to do so.

Twenty-Three

Myriah turned to find Kit watching her from across the room. She glowed standing there at the window in her nightdress of white organza. The moonlight made a shaft of brightness enveloping her in its mysterious glory. Kit gazed at his wife, and found her wondrous to behold. He crossed the room quickly, taking her in his arms, and neither one spoke. His mouth took hers sweetly, tenderly urging her to surrender. She put her head against his shoulder at length and gazed out the window seeing little, for the night had settled its dark beauty over Wimborne lands. She was finally Lady Myriah Wimborne now. She was Kit's wife, lover, his friend . . . and totally at peace.

"Myriah . . ." said he, suddenly breaking the stillness, "There is but one thing haunting me."

"Then tell me at once. We will have no ghosts wisping at us, Kit Wimborne."

"Why did you not tell me who you were sooner? You had ample opportunity . . . and you knew so much of me."

"Because, my darling . . . I have been Lady Myriah, rich Lady Myriah for so long . . . accepted only because of my name . . . my wealth, and then suddenly here I was, Miss White, having to *make you* like me. I wanted you to love me before you knew my name."

"But . . . did you not trust me . . . did you think *I* would woo you for *money?*" asked Kit, just a bit hurt.

"Kit . . . Kit, how can I make you see. You led me to think you were in need of money. You led me to believe you were a smuggler . . . that in itself shook me . . . for it was not the sort of thing I believed a man of your stamp could be! It was so hard, Kit . . . so hard to decide . . . so hard to know what to do! But that is not the question that should concern you now . . . ask *me* whether *I* would have married you . . . still thinking you were a smuggler."

"Would you have?"

"Oh, yes, Kit . . . though I would have done all I could to stop your evil work." She smiled tremulously. "I would have married you . . . were you the King of Smugglers himself!"

He grinned suddenly and picked her up in his bold strong arms, allowing the whiteness of the sheer material to flow away from her body. "And now . . . my sweetings . . . shall we take up where we left off, that first night we met . . . in my bed?"